THE
MONEY
MAN

ALSO BY NANCY HERKNESS

Second Glances series

Second to None: A Novella
Second Time Around
Second Act

Wager of Hearts series

The CEO Buys In
The All-Star Antes Up
The VIP Doubles Down
The Irishman's Christmas Gamble: A Novella

Whisper Horse novels

Take Me Home
Country Roads
The Place I Belong
A Down-Home Country Christmas: A Novella

Stand-Alone novels

A Bridge to Love
Shower of Stars
Music of the Night

THE MONEY MAN

—NANCY— HERKNESS

Montlake

Text copyright © 2020 by Nancy Herkness
All rights reserved.

Published by Montlake, Seattle

www.apub.com

Amazon, the Amazon logo, and Montlake are trademarks of Amazon.com, Inc., or its affiliates.

ISBN-13: 9781542000161
ISBN-10: 1542000165

Cover design by Eileen Carey

Cover photography by Regina Wamba of MaeIDesign.com

Printed in the United States of America

*To Maria, Anh, and my whole amazing
Montlake team:
Thank you for making my books soar.*

Chapter 1

Alice Thurber was losing her mind—or at least the part of her mind that she used to add and subtract. She stared at the computer screen, willing the $3.37 discrepancy to resolve itself into perfect balance. But no matter how often she ran the numbers, her client, the Mane Attraction, still had a shortfall of $3.37 for the month of February.

She felt a tremor of panic ripple through her, making her suck in a breath to calm herself. Never before in all the years she'd been a bookkeeper had she been unable to find the problem in a client's books. Yet in the past six months, *four* of her clients had tiny errors that she could not account for.

"Gosh darn it!" She shoved her rolling chair back from the desk in her newly redecorated home office. One of her two cats, Sylvester, the Duke of Salford, gave her a regal glare from his bed on the multi-level cat tree that stood beside her desk. As she started to pace between the matching cream-painted desk and credenza, his golden eyes closed again.

A few months ago, the first discrepancy had shown up in the books of Sparkle, a special-occasion dress boutique. She'd combed through all the debits and credits but found no explanation. However, the owner had dismissed her concerns, assuring Alice that she didn't care about a few dollars of shortfall. Alice had reluctantly let it go because she simply didn't have time to go through every piece of paperwork.

But it nagged at her pride. And at her need for control.

The second discrepancy appeared the next month at Work It Out, the gym where her friend Dawn was a personal trainer. The gym owner dismissed the problem as someone forgetting to fill out the proper paperwork when they took money out of petty cash, but Alice couldn't let it go so easily. Because now it wasn't just her pride taking a hit. Her worldview was beginning to tilt.

She'd chosen her career in bookkeeping for a reason: numbers were objective and reliable, unlike her parents. She could count on two and two always adding up to four. Until now . . . with her own clients.

However, it wasn't until Nowak Plumbing Supply showed a $4.12 shortfall that Alice began to freak out. Especially because the owner complained loudly. Of course, that was because Alice had talked his son into switching from paper ledgers to a computerized system and the older man didn't trust computers.

The panic swelled into her throat as she wondered if he was right.

She tugged at the collar of her white cotton blouse as she felt the unpleasant sensation of being dragged back into the crazy unpredictability of her childhood, a life she had hated and that she had carefully constructed her adult career to avoid. Her stepfather's fortunes had fluctuated so wildly that Alice never knew when she'd get pulled out of summer camp or ballet class for nonpayment of the bill. Her mother's moods changed right along with their monetary status, so Alice also never knew what kind of parent she'd be dealing with at school pickup time. Alice had sought and found comfort in the predictable outcomes of algebra and geometry as a barrier to the constant zigzagging of her life.

And now her beloved reliable numbers were becoming as untrustworthy as her parents.

She bent over the long work surface and scanned through the pages of debits and credits, unable to believe her own calculations. Which made the panic rise up again, this time twisting her stomach into a knot.

"Nothing! Nothing! Nothing!" she muttered, flipping back the long brown ponytail that had fallen over her shoulder.

Of course, she'd double-checked with the banks to see if their records agreed with the monthly balances. They did. The same with the credit card companies. No obvious issues.

She paced back to the computer and stared at it. Was it possible that the software was the problem? It was a relatively new package that several businesses had bought in the last six months or so. The program's creator, Myron Barsky, had held a sales seminar at the local hotel, which Alice had attended as a service to her clients. She had been impressed with the software so when seven of her clients decided to purchase BalanceTrakR, she had no problem with that. In fact, she'd gone through the training webinars and set up the system for those clients.

But the numbers were telling their own story once again. *Seven* clients were using the software. Only *four* had an accounting issue.

That meant Alice was the problem.

Now the panic began to close up her throat as she felt the foundation of her world crack under her feet. If she could no longer count on her skill with numbers, what could she count on?

She pushed past the knot in her throat and tried to consider the situation with some calm. If there was a software problem, it should have a thread on the help forum for BalanceTrakR. Yesterday she had searched through all the questions and answers posted online. None touched on her problem.

So, swallowing her shame, she had posted her problem on the support forum. No one had responded yet.

Dropping down into her ergonomic desk chair, she typed in a more general search query, looking for bookkeeping advice. Maybe someone with a fresh perspective might find her problem.

She clicked through several sponsored ads that offered nothing useful. The next entry was affiliated with the KRG Consulting Group, a powerhouse firm based in New York City but with a worldwide reputation. She couldn't imagine what sort of help such an elite group had to offer a local bookkeeper. But her sanity was on the line.

She slipped off her wire-rim glasses to rub her tired eyes before seating them back on her nose and clicking on the link. The tagline read: *Are you a small business owner with a problem? We want to help—free of charge.* The introduction went on to say that KRG Consulting Group had started small too so they remembered the struggle. They had met with success and now offered to lend their fellow entrepreneurs a hand through their Small Business Initiative. All she had to do was fill out the online form and KRG would be in touch.

"If it sounds too good to be true, it probably is," Alice said to Sylvester, who had leaped off the cat tree to walk across her keyboard. She stroked his sleek black head as she stared at the website.

It wasn't a marketing ploy to draw in new customers, since no small business owner would be able to afford KRG's services. So either it was genuine—in which case she might end up looking like an incompetent idiot when one of their genius consultants took three minutes to figure out what she was doing wrong—or they would just ignore her request because it was so far beneath their high-level abilities.

She weighed the two possibilities for a moment before gently setting Sylvester on the floor and starting to type.

Derek Killion sat down at the conference table and braced himself as his partner Tully Gibson strolled over, his big, athletic frame encased in a charcoal suit.

"Good job on bringing in the Argon International assignment, partner," Tully said, giving Derek a hard congratulatory thump on the shoulder before heading for his usual chair at the end of the table.

Derek rolled his abused shoulder under his suit jacket, while Tully sat down and pulled off his handstitched Lucchese boots before propping his sock-covered feet on the table. He'd once put his boots on the expensive zebrawood surface, but Derek had put a stop to that by threatening to deface them with a permanent black marker.

Tully tilted the chrome-and-leather chair back, making it creak under his solid muscles. "That's quite a coup for KRG, beating out two of the biggest accounting firms in the world, but you have your work cut out for you."

"It's going to entail a lot of travel too. I'm heading for Asia in two weeks to hit their Tokyo and Singapore offices," Derek said. Not because the project required his physical presence in those places but because top Argon management wanted to see the face of the founding partner who'd promised them his special attention in order to win their business.

He'd gone after the Argon International project with every resource at his command because it was a huge feather in the cap of KRG Consulting. A lot of major corporate players had set their sights on the Argon business so it was a triumph when he'd won it, capturing a revenue stream that would make this a banner year for the firm. However, the sense of accomplishment was fading under the weight of the short deadlines and the complexity of the task.

The third KRG partner, Leland Rockwell, strolled in, wearing his usual uniform of jeans and a T-shirt, and slid his laptop onto the table. "I hear we are taking on the foreign-currency hedging issues of Argon International, thanks to Derek's brilliant financial plotting. Nice work. We should have a celebratory dinner since that's going to bring in a ton of money."

"I wish I had the time," Derek said. "I'll take a rain check for when we complete the project." The truth was that he didn't feel like celebrating. Neither the money nor the prestige seemed all that meaningful in the face of the tedious work and travel that came with it. What the hell was wrong with him? He'd never shied away from a big job before.

"Too bad," Leland said, flipping open his laptop and adjusting his tortoiseshell glasses. "I guess that means you won't be able to enjoy the first hit on another project of yours."

Leland swiped across his screen a couple of times and the wall display lit up. Derek recognized the KRG Small Business Initiative header and all the gratification he should have felt about Argon surged through him.

The SBI had been his idea, born of his dissatisfaction with the constant emphasis on bringing in the big corporate accounts like Argon International. Of course, KRG Consulting needed those—he couldn't ignore that because a lot of people's livelihoods depended on their profitability—but Derek remembered the company's roots, the years of struggling to get traction in a highly competitive market. Without the kindness of a few mentors who had believed in three young MBAs with degrees on which the ink had barely dried, KRG would have failed. Derek wanted to pay it forward.

"It only took four days for someone to find us," he said, leaning toward the screen as anticipation focused his interest. "Who is it?"

"It's from a bookkeeper in New Jersey," Leland said, scrolling down the screen with his long, nimble fingers. "She handles seven clients on the same accounting software. She recently noticed that four of them have small shortfalls that she can't account for. Seems pretty straightforward, so I'll handle it while you focus on Argon."

Frustration made Derek drum his fingers on the tabletop. "How long could it take me? Fifteen minutes?"

"You could probably do it in your sleep, Killion," Tully said. "But you're going to need all your shut-eye to stay sharp for Argon. Let Leland handle it."

"The SBI was my idea and accounting is my area of expertise," Derek said. "I want first crack at it."

His partners weren't opposed to the SBI, but they weren't committed to it in the same way that he was.

"You just turned down a celebration dinner," Tully pointed out. "Why do you have time for this?"

Derek shrugged. "Consider it a burnt offering to the business gods who brought us Argon. We should never forget to be grateful for our good luck."

Tully snorted. "You and your team worked your asses off to develop the best possible proposal for Argon. There was no luck involved."

Derek shot a wry glance at his partner. "There's always luck involved. Honestly, though, I look forward to dealing with a problem that I can solve with just my wits and a calculator."

At that, Leland looked up from his screen, his thin, intelligent face lit with wry amusement. "Alice Thurber seems pretty sharp from her summary of the problem. The answer might be harder to find than you think."

⌒

Just as Alice was pouring hot water through the loose-leaf tea in her bone china teapot, her cell phone tinkled its minuet ringtone. She glanced at the caller ID and groaned.

She was very particular about how long her tea steeped, four and a half minutes being optimum, but this was a call she needed to take. "Thurber Bookkeeping."

"I'm calling for Derek Killion of the KRG Consulting Group," a woman's smooth voice said. "Is this Ms. Alice Thurber?"

"Yes, it is." Alice tried to sound confident and professional.

"Hold for Mr. Killion, please."

A prickle of surprise and anxiety ran through Alice. Derek Killion was the *K* in KRG. She hadn't expected the big guns to handle her little problem.

"Ms. Thurber, this is Derek Killion." A mellifluous baritone flowed into her ear. "We received your request for assistance through our Small Business Initiative, so I'm getting in touch to see how I may help you."

"That's great . . . I mean, I appreciate it," she stuttered. His voice was so perfectly modulated that little tingles danced through her ear.

"I've read your description of the problem and believe I can help you. Excellent presentation, by the way. If I sign a confidentiality agreement, would you be willing to share your clients' books with me via computer?" he said. "I assure you that our cybersecurity is excellent. Also, I will, of course, help you confirm that I am really who I say I am before you send such sensitive information."

"I can imagine that your security is top notch," Alice said. One of the KRG partners, Leland Rockwell, was famous for his expertise in defending against hackers. He was rumored to have helped the US government more than a few times. "I'm glad you understand my need to protect my clients by checking on your identity." Of course, Derek Killion handled corporate information that was infinitely more valuable than her clients' so he would expect her to check up on him. However, his offer still impressed her.

"Once you've verified my identity, I'll email you the instructions on how to give us access."

He seemed to be about to end the call, which surprised Alice. She hurried to speak. "I think you should know that every month I do one client's books by hand and then compare it to the software's balances. Once I caught the second discrepancy, I began checking *all* the balances by hand. That's how I discovered the next two."

"I'm impressed by your diligence on your clients' behalf." His tone held a touch of impatience.

"My clients may be small but I owe them perfectly balanced books." Alice wanted him to know that she took pride in her work, even if she was a small-town bookkeeper. "Anything less is unacceptable to me."

"An admirable attitude," Derek said.

Alice was incredulous when he didn't ask any questions. "Would you like to know where I found the discrepancies?"

"No, I prefer to come at the issue with fresh eyes," he said, his tone downright brusque now. "I'll be in touch when I've found the problem. Goodbye, Ms. Thurber."

"Goodbye, Mr. Killion." But he had already disconnected.

Irritated by his abrupt behavior, Alice glanced at the time. The conversation had taken under two minutes because he assumed he could find the solution without any input from her. Either he believed she was incompetent or he had a high opinion of his own abilities.

However, her annoyance abated slightly when she realized that Derek Killion's dismissive attitude meant that her tea would still be drinkable.

After she'd poured milk into her mug and added the tea and sugar, she carried it to her desk. Moving her gray tabby cat, Audley, the Earl of Worth, off her keyboard, she ran a search on Derek Killion. When an array of photos—mostly from feature articles in business magazines—came up on her screen, she gasped.

The consultant looked like one of her fantasy Regency dukes from her favorite romance novels, only in a business suit. It wasn't just his cleft chin or razor-sharp cheekbones. He projected that bone-deep confidence that only spectacular success—or generations of aristocracy—could imbue a man with. The tilt of his head stated that he had conquered the world, and his blond-streaked brown hair waved away from his forehead with a gloss and thickness that spoke of generations of good DNA.

In one photo, his head was turned so she could see the haughty slash of his nose as well. She peered at it more closely. Yup, a small bump marred its straight line, as though it had once been broken. That made her feel better somehow.

His bio said he was in his early thirties. Far younger than she had expected of a founding partner in such an elite firm. Although she'd never aspired to the heights Derek Killion had attained, she'd once hoped to join a major accounting firm and work her way up through the ranks with talent and hard work. Those dreams had been derailed when her stepfather lost her college fund in one of his many unsound investments. Derek's achievements were a sharp contrast to what felt like her failure.

She pushed the depressing thought away and scrolled to another photo that showed him in a tuxedo at some charity event. A wave of longing swamped her. She would never be swept off her feet by a handsome duke, but Derek Killion would make an excellent stand-in. She imagined those long legs of his encased in close-fitting buckskin breeches, his broad shoulders stretching the wool of a tailcoat, and a perfectly tied neckcloth emphasizing his strong jawline. Her eyelids fluttered closed for a moment as she pictured waltzing with him in a crowded ballroom. A languorous curl of desire licked through her, shocking her into opening her eyes and sitting up straight.

Shaking her head to clear the image out, she took a sip of her tea and gave her cat a pet. "Let's face it, Audley; he'll pass my case off to some underling and I'll never hear from him again."

Which should be fine with her. Her mother, a former model, had taught her valuable lessons about the pain of loving someone beautiful. Gabrielle had been disappointed in Alice practically from the moment she was born because her daughter's looks were nothing more than ordinary. A teenage Alice had once made the mistake of asking her stunning mother whether she thought Alice was pretty. Gabrielle had considered her daughter for a long moment before saying, "You look intelligent."

The memory still hurt.

She shoved it away and looked back at the web page of photos. Derek Killion might be a founding partner of KRG but she bet that his main job was to be the face of the company, making his clients feel special when he bestowed that dazzling smile on them or tilted that handsome head to listen to their concerns.

Then he would hand over the job to some subordinate, who would do the real work while Derek Killion took all the credit and waltzed off to the next sales call.

"Nope, I don't need someone like you, even in my fantasies," she said, closing the web page with a decisive stab on her mouse.

But she wished she'd thought to ask the impatient Mr. Killion how long he expected the project to take. March was flying past, and her stomach clenched at the thought of finding another mistake in her clients' books.

Chapter 2

Alice was settling into the chair at the Mane Attraction, her just-shampooed hair twisted up in a clip, when her minuet ringtone wafted up from her handbag where it sat in a basket on the floor. "I'm sorry," she said to Natalie, the salon's elegant blonde owner, who held a lavender cape in her hand, ready to drape it over Alice. "It's a business call."

Alice plucked the phone from her purse and answered. "Thurber Bookkeeping."

"Ms. Thurber, I'm Barbara Ryan, Derek Killion's assistant." Alice recognized her voice. "Mr. Killion apologizes for inconveniencing you on a weekend, but he wonders if you might be available to meet with him on Saturday."

Shock held Alice silent for long enough to notice the blow-dryers buzzing around her. "Where?"

"Wherever you would prefer to meet. Your office, perhaps?" Barbara said.

"I . . . Why?" Alice stammered, walking into the restroom and closing the door to get away from the salon noise. She leaned her hip against the lavender sink.

"I believe he would like to review the hard copies of the transactions with you."

Alice straightened away from the sink abruptly. Now Derek Killion wanted to look at all the paperwork? "I, well, I suppose he could come to my home office. I have all the paperwork there."

She rubbed her forehead, trying to imagine the lofty and gorgeous Mr. Killion parked at her Ikea desk with Sylvester and Audley looking on. She loved her new office furniture but it wouldn't stack up to the kind of luxury a founding partner was accustomed to. Unfortunately, parts of her body that had nothing to do with her brain were tingling with anticipation at the thought of actually meeting with him face-to-face. It was insane to react so strongly to a bunch of photographs. And a deep baritone resonating through the phone.

"Would ten o'clock work for you?" Barbara nudged.

"Sure. Ten o'clock." She was thinking of all the housecleaning she'd have to do before his arrival. Her clients did not come to her office; she went to theirs and picked up their paperwork.

"Is the address the one on the input form from the website?"

"Yes, that's right." She would have to borrow another card table from Natalie to have extra space to spread out the papers for Mr. Killion.

"Excellent. Mr. Killion will see you then. Thank you again for taking time out of your weekend." And Barbara was gone.

Would Mr. Killion expect her to serve him lunch? Was he allergic to cats? Did she have extra vacuum bags so she could go over everything twice in her town house? She'd have to clean two floors since her office was located upstairs in what was intended to be a bedroom for a child or guests. That's why she'd bought the two-bedroom model in the new development on the outskirts of Cofferwood.

She flung open the door of the restroom and marched back to the chair, determined not to let Killion's looks or position intimidate her. "I apologize for making you wait, Natalie."

The salon's owner waved off the apology with a graceful gesture before she flipped the cape around Alice. "Your mouth was hanging open for a second there at the beginning of the call. Who was it? Or is it confidential?"

Alice squared her shoulders under the cape and glared at herself in the mirror as Natalie combed her long brown hair, carefully working out the tangles. "It was Derek Killion's assistant."

"How about another clue?" Natalie said, her huge blue eyes gleaming with amusement. The salon owner was a walking advertisement for her business with her short, layered hairdo that danced just this side of edgy. Natalie had sported hair down to her waist until a year ago. The day of her fortieth birthday, she had announced that she was too old for long hair and cut it all off, much to Alice's shock. Although, honestly, Natalie looked amazing in the new style.

Alice sighed. "Remember the problem I had with your books?"

"The piddling little three-dollar thing that I don't give a toot about?"

"Well, I give a toot because it's not right."

"I know, sweetie, and that's why you're such a great bookkeeper." Natalie spread Alice's hair over her shoulders. "Are you sure I can't take a little more off and give it some layers? With your natural waves it would look stunning."

"No, just neaten up the ends, please." Alice had a strange relationship with her hair. It was almost like her mother's: thick and glossy with a perfect ripple of waves that Alice did nothing to create. However, her mother's hair was honey blonde with streaks of gold, while Alice's was mousey brown. Of course.

Alice kept it long because she could braid it or pull it back in a ponytail to look professional. But at night, she slept with it loose and spread over her pillow, despite the tangles she had to unravel in the morning. That's how the heroes in her beloved Regency romance novels arranged their heroines' hair before they made love to them. Somehow having the hair of a Regency heroine made it seem easier to fantasize that something like that would happen to Alice.

Her dreams made up for her lack of luck in the real world of dating. Or maybe they contributed to it.

"Earth to Alice," Natalie said, trimming just the tips of Alice's long locks with an air of frustrated resignation. "Are you going to tell me who Derek Killion is? That's a strong name, by the way. Sort of like one of your dukes."

Alice threw the hair stylist an astonished glance. Natalie knew about Alice's secret reading addiction, but it still seemed like she was peering into Alice's mind. Of course, she did that a lot.

Their friendship began the day Natalie intervened in a particularly unpleasant encounter between Alice and her mother, Gabrielle, who also patronized the Mane Attraction. Gabrielle didn't approve of Alice's lack of interest in being fashionable, so her mother was pressuring her to cut her long hair into a more contemporary style. Natalie told Gabrielle in no uncertain terms that Alice's hair was beautiful, the style suited her perfectly, and that Gabrielle should shut up and mind her own business.

Amazingly, Gabrielle had shut up.

When Alice had thanked the salon owner after her mother left, Natalie looked her in the eye. "You have to set firm boundaries with a person like Gabrielle. Otherwise they will destroy you."

It turned out that Natalie spoke from hard-won experience and Alice had valued her advice ever since.

"Derek is far from a duke," Alice said. "He's a partner in a big-time consulting firm who's going to help me figure out what's wrong with your books. For free."

Natalie's well-groomed eyebrows rose in two graceful arches. "For free?"

Alice explained her impulsive submission to KRG's Small Business Initiative. "He was in a big rush to get off the phone and I was sure he'd pawn me off on some staff member. Which would have been fine because they do all the actual work. But now he wants to come to my office at ten a.m. on Saturday."

Natalie frowned. "You're going to be alone in your house with a man you've never met before? I'm not sure I like that."

"Too bad you're so busy on Saturdays or I'd ask you to stop by to chaperone me," Alice said with a grin. She would love to see Natalie's face when she met the gorgeous Derek Killion. But she didn't want to worry her friend. "Trust me, there's nothing to be concerned about. Derek Killion wouldn't give me the time of day if I hadn't filled out that form."

"I'm going to call you between clients on Saturday, though. If you don't answer, I'll send over Gino." Gino was only male hairdresser at Natalie's salon. He was also a gym rat with muscles that turned his black T-shirt and jeans into works of art. The ladies at the salon had nearly risen up in protest when he got engaged two months before.

"Not a problem. It will make me sound important to get a phone call on the weekend," Alice said. "My side of the conversation is going to sound like your business will fall to pieces without my immediate intervention."

Natalie laughed and turned on the blow-dryer.

⸺

At ten o'clock sharp, Derek walked up three steps to the small porch of Alice Thurber's town house, which evidently doubled as her office. Two pots filled with red geraniums splashed color against the gray brick facade. An ornate brass door knocker gleamed against glossy forest-green paint. Ms. Thurber kept her place nicely maintained.

Guilt sent a pulse of pain through his already aching temples. Even though he'd spent the entire limo ride out to Cofferwood working on the Argon project, he didn't have time to spare for a minor bookkeeping problem, no matter how much he wanted to solve it. He should have let Leland and Tully handle this, as they'd wanted to.

But neither he nor an associate he'd enlisted to give the numbers a first look had been able to find any errors in Ms. Thurber's work. Except for the inexplicable discrepancy between what she had added up and what the bank statement showed. Now not only was he hooked on the intriguing puzzle but his pride was involved. If KRG couldn't solve a small-town bookkeeper's problem, he shouldn't be handling foreign-currency hedging for Argon International.

So he was going old school by looking at the hard copy—possibly down to the level of reams of receipts—where he was sure the issue would become obvious. Then he could return to his office with a clear conscience and a sense of satisfaction.

As he rang the doorbell, he was considering another possible strategy for Argon. When the door swung open a few seconds later, he was startled to find a striking young woman eyeing him with a wary expression.

"I'm Derek Killion," he managed to say as he took in a luxuriant mass of hair spilling over one of her shoulders and huge velvet-brown eyes behind fashionable wire-rim glasses. He'd been too rushed to look at the background information Barbara had gathered on the bookkeeper, so he'd been envisioning an older woman with a bun and bifocals, probably based on her rather prim, old-fashioned first name.

"I'm Alice Thurber," she said as she extended her hand. "I appreciate your interest in my little problem. I'll admit that I wasn't expecting an in-person visit from a founding partner."

Derek refocused, taking her hand and finding her grip firm and warm. "I wasn't expecting to come either. I thought the problem would be easier to solve." He realized how that sounded and offered a rueful smile to go with it. "My pride is smarting."

However, it was too late. Alice's elegantly full lips pressed together in a stern line.

"Come in," she said, her tone somewhat frosty. She stepped back to invite him into her foyer, a small space containing a half-round table of varnished walnut and a portrait of a woman in elaborate Victorian attire whom he felt he should recognize.

"That's Ada Lovelace," she said.

"Ah, the pioneering computer programmer," he said. "I knew I'd seen her before."

"You know about her?" Alice sounded astonished.

"Just that she's credited with creating the first computer program and was one of the very few well-known female mathematicians of her time."

Alice unbent enough to give a little nod. "She was the daughter of Lord Byron. Her mother had Ada educated in math to counteract what she saw as Byron's poetic madness."

"She thought numbers would cure insanity?"

"She believed math encouraged rational, orderly thinking. Don't you agree with her?"

Alice stood with her hands on her hips. She wore black trousers and a white blouse, but the bland clothing could not hide the rather sumptuous curves of her figure. Another surprise.

She continued to look at him with one eyebrow raised and a challenge in her eyes.

"Of course I agree with her," Derek said, irritated by his wandering mind. "I work with numbers all the time." Numbers were how he'd justified his career choice to his father. Numbers were what he had immersed himself in when his fiancée broke off their engagement. Numbers defined his life. He pushed aside the odd introspection her question had evoked. "In fact, let's take a look at the ones we're having an issue with."

"Would you like some tea or coffee before we start?" Alice asked.

"No, thanks. I polished off a large coffee in the car." While he wrestled with Argon's vastly larger numbers.

She headed up the polished oak stairs and he followed, enjoying the way the wool of her trousers pulled taut over her nicely rounded bottom as she climbed.

He frowned. It was not professional to picture black lace bikini panties under the fabric. He needed to get to those numbers to keep his mind orderly and rational, like Ada Lovelace's.

When they reached the top of the flight of stairs, Alice led him into a light-filled room fitted with sleek cream-colored office furniture as well as two high-end ergonomic chairs. He'd expected something much less modern and sophisticated because he'd made more incorrect assumptions based on her name, her location, and the fact that she worked for small businesses. This was why he and his partners needed the SBI: to keep them grounded.

He glanced around the room, thinking he wouldn't mind working there himself. Neat stacks of papers were spread out on the work surfaces. Those included a couple of card tables, the only jarring notes in the well-laid-out space. She swept her hand around the office. "Each one of these is a different client's paperwork from the month when the discrepancy occurred. Where do you want to begin? First or last in?"

"First."

She shifted a laptop from her desk to a card table and then rolled one of the chairs up as well. "Here you go. Sparkle, a special-occasion clothing boutique. A discrepancy of $2.59 six months ago."

"Are your clients concerned about these shortfalls?"

A guilty look crossed her face. "Not really, no. In fact, most of them couldn't care less." Her voice became passionate. "Look, I know it isn't a lot of money, but the deficits shouldn't be there. Numbers don't lie. At least, they never have before."

"I was just curious." The crazy thing was that he understood her obsession with making the numbers add up all too well. "Will you walk me through it?" he asked, wheeling the other chair over and holding it for her.

Rather than sitting down, she looked surprised. "Sure, but that's just going over the same erroneous path I took. Don't you want to come at it fresh? I thought that was your preference." There was a slight edge to her last words.

"I'm hoping the problem will manifest itself as you go through the records," he said. "Remember, I've already looked at the computer files without your input and found nothing. So did a colleague of mine." Both of them had been baffled and shocked by their inability to pinpoint the issue. He winced inwardly at his unconscious arrogance.

A fleeting look of approval crossed her face before she perched on the chair. "Okay, here we go," she said, pushing a stack of papers in front of him.

Her movement sent a waft of scent to tickle his nostrils. It was something floral and old-fashioned, like her name, but he couldn't place it. Asking her wouldn't be any more professional than admiring her behind, so he inhaled deeply to draw it into his lungs and imprint it on his sensory memory.

"My first reaction was that someone had forgotten to record a withdrawal from petty cash," she said. "However, the petty cash in the drawer matched the balance on the accounting system so that couldn't be it."

Derek pulled his attention away from the graceful movements of her ringless hands with their short, neat nails and focused on the numbers as she talked through her methodology. Her explanation was clear and logical. He could find no fault with anything she had done, which was unfortunate since she had to have made an error somewhere.

After twenty minutes of working beside Alice, he forgot that she was a small-town bookkeeper. Instead he treated her just like he would one of the senior associates at KRG Consulting, listening to her suggestions with respect and offering his own ideas without dumbing them down. He found himself exhilarated by the give-and-take with a mind that could keep up with his own.

That exhilaration did not explain why when she flicked her ponytail over her shoulder so the mass of chocolate-colored waves flowed down her back, he had an almost overwhelming urge to comb his fingers through it. That would be even less appropriate than asking her what kind of perfume she was wearing. Or speculating about the color of her panties.

⌒

As she and Derek worked through the numbers for Sparkle, Alice could almost forget how good-looking he was. But the yearning hollowed out her chest when he turned his head to ask her a question and she could see how his dark lashes contrasted with the silver gray of his eyes. A slash of sunlight glinted off the slight scruff of blond whiskers on his chin and cheeks. She imagined that soft roughness pressed against her skin.

She needed to fight down her reaction to his beauty and focus on the work. But even that didn't help because his mind was as sexy as the rest of him. He didn't treat her like a second-class citizen as they analyzed the books. His questions were incisively phrased and his ideas were complex. She had the heady feeling that he thought she was his equal, which was clearly ridiculous.

But the worst was when she handed him a pile of papers and their fingers brushed, the tiny friction sending sparks racing over her skin. From then on she was careful not to make contact, even though she longed to feel that delicious response again.

"That's it for Sparkle," Derek said, flipping the last page of the report over. "No explanation for the discrepancy." He rubbed his forehead, bringing her attention back to the glorious thickness of his golden-brown hair.

"Ready for Work It Out?" She madly shifted papers to yank her unruly thoughts away from the shining waves that tempted her to touch.

As Derek opened the first report for the gym, Alice's phone played its old-fashioned tinkling tune.

"Interesting ringtone," Derek said as Alice rolled her chair over to the credenza where she'd left her phone. The caller ID was Natalie's and Alice remembered her friend's determination to make sure Derek wasn't going to attack her in her home office. The irony was that she was more likely to attack him.

"Excuse me, I have to answer this," Alice said. "Thurber Bookkeeping."

"Oh, good, you're not bound and gagged," Natalie said. "How's it going?"

"I'm making good progress on the issue." Not really true. "Actually, I'm in a meeting. Maybe I could call you back later?"

"Now that I have proof of life, sure. Although if I don't hear from you by four o'clock, I'm calling again. He could just be lulling you into a false sense of security before he pounces."

"That might be the best outcome. I'll talk with you after I'm done here."

"You *want* to be pounced on?" Natalie asked in a teasing tone. "Now I'm really intrigued. Off to do a search for a picture of Derek Killion right now." She disconnected.

That would get Alice into some hot water. All of her friends thought she dated the wrong kind of men, just because she chose safe, stable, and yes, slightly boring ones. But she didn't trust the charming, handsome ones because growing up with her mother and her stepfather, she'd learned how destructive they could be. Of course, she hadn't seen a lot of charm from Derek yet. He wouldn't waste that on her. Nor should he. They were just trying to solve a business riddle together.

"You didn't have to put off a client on my account," Derek said, looking up from the papers he was examining with a frown of concern.

"You trekked all the way to New Jersey to help me." She was disarmed by the fact that he didn't expect her to focus entirely on his important presence. "That deserves my attention."

He gave her a look that said he didn't entirely believe her. "So far, I haven't been very useful."

"If nothing else, you've reassured me that I'm not losing my ability to handle numbers."

"No worries about that. These records are flawless."

"Except for—"

"I know, $2.59." His rueful smile brought out a single dimple in his left cheek and softened the flint of his eyes. A sensation like warm honey flowing through her made Alice reach for a random stack of papers and start flicking through them. She wasn't going to fall for a dimple. She knew better.

Halfway through his pile of hard copy, Derek pushed his chair away from the desk and stood up. When he laced his hands behind his neck to stretch, Alice tried very hard not to look, but she couldn't resist watching the way his white cotton button-down shirt pulled across his shoulders and biceps.

He paced around the office once, the gray wool of his trousers outlining the muscles in his thighs with each stride. Raking his fingers through his perfect hair in a gesture of frustration, he came back to where she sat. "I don't see any point to continuing this transaction-by-transaction analysis. Your methodology is impeccable. The records match up every time."

His words lit a glow of pride in Alice, who ducked her head to hide an involuntary smile of gratification.

"We're not going to find the problem here," he continued.

Her smile died. "We're not? Where will we find it?"

"It's got to be a software problem," he said, settling into his chair again. "I'll get our tech expert, Leland Rockwell, to look at it."

So she was being passed along to the next partner. She would never see Derek Killion again. The fizzing exhilaration she'd been fighting all morning got doused by a firehose of disappointment. "But this software is used by hundreds of small businesses. Don't you think someone else would have found the problem by now? I checked all the user forums and there's no mention of the issue."

"You said that none of your clients cared about such small discrepancies, so other users might feel the same way. Also, you're one bookkeeper handling multiple sites using the software. That might be unusual for what's intended to be a single-business system. Not to mention that you are extraordinarily meticulous," he said with a glinting smile that seemed to thin the air in the room so she had to inhale deeply to get enough oxygen.

"Thanks," she managed to gasp.

"It was a statement of fact," he said, but that smile indicated otherwise before it disappeared. "You mentioned that BalanceTrakR is relatively new. How far into the cycle did the first discrepancy appear?"

"Sparkle was the first to get up and running. I converted her boutique to the new software four months before anything went wrong. And there's been nothing since. I've double-checked every month since."

"How long did it take for the Work It Out issue to surface?"

Alice had to consult her calendar for the conversion date. "Five months." She continued to check dates. "Nowak Plumbing was four months and the Mane Attraction was five."

"So it clusters but isn't exactly the same." Derek stood up again, while Alice's heart sank at this sign of his imminent departure. "Leland will run some structured test data through it to see what happens."

"I don't think I can let you use my clients' copies of the software," Alice said, rising as well.

"Not a problem. We can purchase our own copy, so everything is aboveboard."

"But you're not being paid to work on this."

He flashed that arrogant smile she'd seen in his photos, with his even white teeth and upward-tilted chin. "I think we can afford it."

But somehow the arrogance worked now, maybe because he was using it on her behalf.

He glanced at his watch. "Do you have time for a quick lunch?"

"Lunch? In Cofferwood?" she asked in shock. Why would he want to have lunch with her?

"It's noon and I'm hungry. You know the area, so you can choose the restaurant."

She continued to stare at him, while her mind spun in confused circles.

"Let me redeem myself," he said, holding out his hands with fingers spread.

"What do you mean? There's nothing to redeem. You've been great." Alice waved at the papers on the table.

"I couldn't solve your problem." His eyes glinted with dry humor. "Maybe I can impress you with my conversation instead."

So he was just making up for what he saw as his failure. She decided that she didn't care about his reasons. She'd get to admire him from across a table for a little longer before he disappeared back to his corporate office in Manhattan. "I don't need impressing but lunch sounds good."

Satisfaction lit his face. "My driver is waiting outside."

Of course he had a driver. But now she had to figure out where they should eat. He'd said "quick" so that was a factor. Was he a vegan or a carnivore? Did he like Italian or Chinese? As the questions rolled through her brain, she thought of the perfect place: one where he could get almost anything he might want.

"Let's not make your driver wait any longer," she said, grabbing her phone and heading for the door.

Chapter 3

When Alice told the driver to turn left into the parking lot of Nick's Diner, with its neon motto flashing FAST AND FRESH, she glanced sideways to see Derek's reaction as he ducked his head to look out the window.

"This place is straight out of *American Graffiti*," he said, his expression bemused.

"You asked for quick," Alice said with a challenge in her tone as she climbed out of the limo.

He held the diner's door for her, and she stepped into the familiar cacophony of voices, canned music, and clattering china and silverware. The interior sported the classic diner decor of black-and-white floor tiles, red vinyl upholstered booths and counter stools, and gaudy murals of local sites of interest. A glass case displayed towering wedges of lemon meringue pie and cheesecake smothered in bright red cherry topping. The aromas of garlic and cooking grease floated past her nostrils, making her salivate.

When they sat down in a booth, the host handed them multipage plastic menus the size of blueprints. Derek flipped through his.

"You look overwhelmed," Alice said, not without a certain satisfaction.

He lowered the vinyl tome. "Not at all. I'm just enjoying the nearly infinite range of offerings. It's been a while since I've eaten at a diner."

"How long a while?" It was hard to picture him frequenting diners. "A few years ago when I had a project in Philadelphia. How's Nick's Specialty Burger?"

"Huge and messy."

"Sounds like my kind of lunch." He closed the menu.

When the waitress appeared, Alice ordered her usual frittata with ham and peppers while Derek ordered the burger with the works.

After the waitress raced away, Derek folded his arms and leaned back, his shoulders spanning half the vinyl banquette. "When I arrived this morning, you seemed somewhat . . . wary. I'm interested in finding out why."

"Wary?" She swallowed and stared down at the place mat printed with coupons. "Just a little overawed by having a founding partner from KRG in my humble office."

"Overawed?" His tone was skeptical. "*Challenging* would be a better description."

Alice glanced up to find his attention focused on her with the intensity of a laser. She hadn't expected this because she didn't think he'd care how she felt about him.

She cast around for a way to deflect his question, but what difference did it make anyway? He was going to shuffle her and her issue along to the company's resident computer genius so she'd never have to deal with Derek again.

She lifted her chin. "If you want the truth, it was your phone call that made me 'challenging.'" Her stomach twisted into a ball of nervousness. Who was she to criticize a man with his position and success? "You made it clear that you thought I was simply incompetent and you didn't need any input from me."

His frown seemed directed more at himself than at her. "I don't remember saying anything to indicate that."

"Of course not. You're too professional to come right out and state it. But it seemed obvious when you asked me no questions and got off the phone in less than two minutes." She considered adding that she suspected her gender had contributed to his assumptions, but she couldn't honestly say that she'd seen any indication of sexism from him. She'd give him a half a gold star for that.

His frown had deepened with every sentence and she waited for him to explode. Instead he twirled a spoon between his fingers while he stared out the window, affording her an excellent view of the slight bump in his nose, along with his perfectly angled cheekbones. Her fingers itched to touch him in both places.

"But you knew who Ada Lovelace was, so that's a point in your favor," she finally said, trying to make up for her frankness.

He turned back to her. "My apologies. I didn't intend to give that impression."

Alice goggled in disbelief. Had he really apologized? Her mother never felt the need. Gabrielle believed that a mere smile on her beautiful face would take the place of a sincere "I'm sorry." In fact, she couldn't remember Gabrielle ever acknowledging that she had been at fault.

"The truth is that I was *hoping* that you were incompetent," he said with the smile that brought out his dimple. "I have to be in Asia in about ten days to work with a new client and I have a huge amount of preparation to get through before I leave. If you didn't know what you were doing, I could find the problem quickly and go back to my project. Instead, you've hooked me on the mystery of the tiny discrepancies."

"I thought you were going to turn it over to Leland Rockwell." Alice raised the objection to cover how he had knocked her off-balance with his admission.

"Only because he knows far more about software than I do. I expect to be kept in the loop."

"I see." Alice took a sip of her iced tea while she considered the fact that he wasn't foisting her on his partner so he could bail. She was also giving herself time to recover from that darned smile of his. It wasn't the full-on, master-of-the-universe flash of dazzling white teeth that got to her. It was the self-deprecating dimple that sent a wave of longing rippling through her body.

"Not to mention that I failed to find the problem." His lips curved into a rueful slant. God, she wanted to know what they would feel like against hers but she never would. Men like Derek Killion didn't kiss small-town bookkeepers who wore glasses and looked intelligent. "I'm hoping Leland can restore the honor of KRG Consulting."

She could feel her bones melting under his charm. Soon she would become a puddle on the red vinyl cushion. She braced her spine. "Honestly, you've done me a favor."

He raised his eyebrows in surprise. "How so?"

"I thought I was losing my ability to add and subtract. You've restored my faith in my work."

"Never doubt yourself," he said, his expression turning serious. "You are quite brilliant at what you do."

His words flowed into her and sealed up the cracks in her professional confidence. "Thanks. You're not too shabby at financial analysis yourself."

Alice silently blessed the waitress who arrived with their food. The distraction allowed her to absorb Derek's compliment without doing something stupid like bursting into tears or grinning from ear to ear, two equally possible reactions. That's how great her relief was.

Of course, what she did was multiple levels of complexity below what he did, but she would accept the validation with gratitude.

As their server slid the plates onto the table, Derek eyed the mountain of his hamburger with dismay. "Can I get a forklift to eat this with?"

Alice laughed, albeit with a slight quaver, and took a bite of her frittata, watching as the urbane Mr. Killion wrestled with Nick's oversize creation. He finally decided to cut it into quarters and managed to take a bite without splattering anything on his immaculate white shirt.

"Now that's a burger," he said after swallowing.

"I warned you."

"You have to see a hamburger like this to believe it." He maneuvered a second bite into his mouth.

She liked watching him manipulate the food with his big, square hands. She'd expected elegant, tapering fingers. Instead, his seemed made to chop wood or lay bricks. She could also imagine them controlling the reins of a high-spirited team of horses. And that was as far as she would allow her imagination to go about what his hands could control.

Once he'd eaten some french fries, he said, "Tell me about the BalanceTrakR software. How did you hear about it? What made you decide to use it for your clients?"

"Some trainers at Work It Out were talking about an upcoming event at the Lipton Hotel a couple of towns over, where you would get free wine, beer, and munchies if you listened to a presentation." Work It Out was the gym where Alice exercised with her personal trainer and friend, Dawn Galioto. They worked out, practiced martial arts and self-defense moves at Dawn's insistence, and talked a lot. "It's ironic that the trainers there are always looking for free booze and food, since they advocate a healthy lifestyle to their clients."

Derek's eyes narrowed in agreement as he chewed another bite.

"When they said the presentation was about accounting software, I got interested. A couple of my other clients had heard about it too so I figured I'd go check it out."

"And get some free wine?" His tone was teasing. An odd thrill ran through her.

"I can be bought."

"Good to know," he said with a wicked little gleam.

She cleared her throat. "Anyway, the guy who gave the presentation was named Myron Barsky." She thought for a moment. "He was a classic nerd. Black-rimmed glasses that he had to keep pushing back up his nose as he talked. Jeans and a wrinkled button-down shirt and sneakers." When she'd shaken his hand before the demonstration, his grip had been weak and his greeting slightly monotone.

But when he'd gotten up on the stage, Barsky had projected a surprising authority. His pride in his product seemed to energize him so that his voice took on a deeper resonance as he strode back and forth across the raised platform. A couple of women she knew had even speculated about his marital status.

She shrugged. "Barsky gave a good presentation and you've seen the software. It's user-friendly, has some innovative features, and integrates seamlessly with other systems, like payroll, tax prep, credit cards, and bank accounts. And the cost is surprisingly reasonable. After checking some references, I recommended it to three of my clients." She gave him a wry look. "Hard to believe, but one company was still doing their books on paper, so I wanted to bring them into the twenty-first century."

"I've seen worse at large corporations. People don't like change."

"Eventually, seven of my clients bought BalanceTrakR, some entirely on their own. I took several webinars to get up to speed and converted them all to the new system. It looked great until that first issue showed up." She balled up her napkin in her lap. "Now I wonder if I jumped into the new program too quickly."

"Don't beat yourself up." Derek dabbed a french fry in ketchup. "The truth is that we don't know for certain that it's a software bug. I just can't see any other explanation right now."

"I agree, which is why I feel responsible for recommending that my clients buy a bad accounting package."

He held up his hand to stop her self-castigation. "The discrepancies are very small and Leland will figure it out. In the meantime, tell me how you got into being a bookkeeper."

A shiver of shocked delight ran through her at his question about *her*, not the software. On the other hand, the answer to his question wasn't a happy one. She'd planned to be a CPA, saving money to go to college to study accounting. Then her stepfather had begged her to loan him her funds to invest in a "can't miss" scheme. It had been during one of their financially difficult periods and he'd been desperate. Since her biological father had exited the scene before she was born, her stepfather was the only male parent she'd known. So how could she say no? Her college fund had disappeared into the smoke and mirrors of a Ponzi scheme.

"I went to bookkeeping school." She shrugged with a slight smile to hide her discomfort. "How about you?"

He gave her a hard look but let it pass. "I got into it by accident. I was a theater major, but I minored in accounting so I wouldn't starve while I auditioned. I discovered that I liked numbers better than acting."

"That's an unusual path." She could imagine his face on the big screen, the camera loving his bone structure and the sharp intelligence in his eyes. She'd certainly go see any movie he was in. "What kind of acting? Do you sing and dance too?"

"I can carry a tune and tell my right foot from my left, but I guarantee that no one would hire me for Broadway." His expression turned reminiscent. "Although I enjoyed belting out 'Seventy-Six Trombones' while leading the band in *The Music Man*. That was in high school."

She pictured a younger version of him as Harold Hill in a braid-bedecked drum major's uniform. It was easier than she expected because Derek had that smooth confidence and arrogant tilt of the chin.

The nostalgia faded from his face. "Of course, my father never forgave me for not putting the Killion name up in lights on a marquee."

"Seriously? Your father wanted you to be an actor? Most parents push you to do something with a steady income."

Derek shrugged. "He was a pretty decent singer who never quite made it. I was supposed to make up for that." A muscle tightened in his jaw. "When I took my fancy MBA and started my own company instead of joining an established firm, Dad let me know that he considered that just as risky as being an actor. And he was almost right. KRG had some tough times at the beginning."

Sympathy made Alice's heart twist. She knew something about disappointing a parent. "I hear you. My mother is a former model. She wasn't thrilled with my career choice either. Not that I was headed for modeling anyway." She didn't want him to think she had any illusions about her looks.

"You're too smart to be just a pretty face," he said, leaving her to debate whether that meant he thought she was pretty. At least he thought she was smart. "So why did you choose numbers as a career?" he asked. "To combat poetic madness like Ada Lovelace?"

He'd hit closer to home than he knew. "Maybe a little." He'd shared so she owed him something more. "My mother isn't the most reliable parent, and my stepfather's finances were . . . unsettled, so I gravitated toward more dependable things, like numbers. They're orderly and rational—except for the irrational ones." She exchanged a math-nerd smile with him.

"And the BalanceTrakR ones," he tossed back at her.

She grimaced. "Yeah, well, that's human error."

"Where did you study bookkeeping?"

"The local community college." Since she couldn't rely on her parents, she'd had to keep her costs down. Now she was saving her money to get an online degree in accounting, although she couldn't justify it on practical grounds. She just wanted to be able to put "CPA" after her name. "Nothing fancy but it was a good foundation."

"You've demonstrated that very clearly, although I suspect you've gone beyond their curriculum at this point."

She was beginning to believe his compliments were sincere. That made them dangerous because his words soaked deep into her thirsty soul. "Experience is an excellent instructor."

Their waitress appeared beside the table, her pen poised over her order pad. "Can I get you anything else?"

"Just the check, please," Derek said.

Disappointment jabbed at Alice. She'd thought Derek was enjoying their conversation, yet he wasn't going to linger over a cup of coffee. She should have known that he would need to be skilled socially as well as professionally to succeed at high levels in business.

The woman scribbled on her pad, tore off the slip, and slid it across the table to him, saying, "Thanks, hon. Pay up front."

Alice reached for the bill. "The least I can do is pay for your lunch since you're doing me a favor."

He laid his large hand on top of the paper. "I have an expense account."

His hand was just inches away from hers. She wanted to put her hand over it, to feel the texture and warmth of his skin. She whisked her hand off the table and into her lap to grip the crumpled napkin again.

Thank goodness he was handing off her problem to his partner. Otherwise she'd be worried about her state of mind.

After seeing Alice to her door, Derek settled into the back seat of the car. He'd shaken hands with her in an entirely businesslike way but her touch seemed to linger on his palm. He glanced down at his hand where it lay on the leather seat beside him before lifting it to see if any hint of her fragrance had transferred itself to his skin. But only a faint aroma of grease from the french fries remained.

What the hell was the scent she wore? A flower of some sort, he thought. Something sweet, woodsy, and elusive, which seemed at odds with her no-nonsense personality. Something that made him speculate about the color of her panties and what her glossy hair would feel like twined around his fingers.

He snapped his fingers. *Violets.* That's what her perfume was.

Maybe it was a good thing he was handing her off to Leland. He needed to focus all his attention on Argon International. Alice would be a distraction.

The thought reminded him of his last argument with Courtney. Courtney, who was hell-bent on making partner in her big law firm but who couldn't understand Derek's equal commitment to his own work. She had the misconception that being the boss meant he could take time off whenever she needed his presence at her corporate social events or to taste potential wedding cakes. It had taken a broken engagement, but he had learned his lesson about the pitfalls of mixing work with romance. And he wasn't going to forget it.

On the other hand, he wanted to prove to Alice that he wasn't the arrogant ass he'd sounded like in their phone conversation or when he'd first arrived at her home. Even though his brusqueness was caused by the time pressure he was feeling, that didn't excuse his treatment of the first request for assistance that the SBI had received.

The whole reason he'd proposed the Small Business Initiative was to remind them all of how thin the line was between success and failure . . . as his father never missed a chance to point out. He and his partners had been lucky to have supporters in high places who'd given them wise advice—and once even an infusion of cash—to pull them back from disaster when they teetered on the brink. They needed to remember the days when they didn't travel on private jets, or have a tailor come to their offices to measure them for suits, or eat at the finest restaurants in New York, London, and Paris while barely noticing the food. He smiled as he remembered his hamburger at Nick's. *That* he had noticed.

He'd nearly failed at his own project. Thank God Alice had the honesty to call him on it.

He respected that almost as much as he respected her talent for numbers. Working with her—trading ideas about the problem, watching the way her mind operated—had been an unexpected pleasure.

In fact, everything about her had been unexpected, and he considered himself hard to surprise. To discover that she was young, smart, and—he had to admit it—attractive in a sexy-librarian kind of way had knocked him off-balance. At least he had the sense to recalibrate his ideas about her swiftly.

And then his ideas had gone beyond the professional as his attention wandered to the glimpse of cleavage visible when she bent over the desk to gather up papers. He'd wanted to brush his nose against the tantalizing upper curves of her breasts to see if her perfume lingered there.

He definitely needed to let Leland handle this. He pulled his phone out of his pocket. "Rockwell, I've got a special project for you."

"Because I don't already have four special projects going." Leland's Georgia drawl was pronounced.

Derek smiled. Leland's drawl hadn't fooled him in years. His partner could handle twelve special projects without blinking. "Makes you feel needed."

"Aren't you supposed to be in New Jersey, fixing that bookkeeper's problem?"

"I am in New Jersey, but I couldn't fix the problem. I couldn't even *find* the problem. That's where you come in. It's got to be a software glitch."

"That's what all you financial geniuses claim when you screw up. That it's the programmer's fault," Leland said, but Derek could hear the interest in his voice. His partner loved a computer challenge.

"You wouldn't sound so dubious if you'd met Alice Thurber. She's got a mind for numbers and is conscientious as hell. That's the only reason she caught the issue. Most bookkeepers would have just written it off as within the bounds of acceptable human error."

"How many times has the error occurred?"

"Once for each of four clients. That's the other reason she noticed it. She handles multiple small businesses who use the same software.

The developer did a dog and pony show with free booze at a local hotel to entice people to buy it."

"Now you're beginning to interest me. What's the software?"

"BalanceTrakR." He spelled it out and heard the click of keyboard keys from Leland's end of the conversation.

"Nice website. Looks legit, but we know any idiot can make a good-looking website these days." More clicking. "Buying a copy of it now for my personal use. No point in raising red flags with the KRG name."

"I'll send you my notes on the problem. How soon can you take a look at it?" Derek pushed.

"Because you've got me curious, I'll do it now. After all, it's the weekend so I've just been lounging around the pool, drinking margaritas."

"Two hundred dollars says you're at the office." Everyone at KRG was highly motivated, but Leland worked more hours than anyone else in the company.

A slight growl came through the phone. "Your two hundred dollars are safe. And no, I'm not going to a charity ball or a hockey game with a client tonight."

Derek was pretty sure that his partner hadn't lounged around a pool in years. Leland swam, all right, but only in the lap pool on the top floor of their building. He said the repetitiveness freed his mind to unravel problems. So even that wasn't time off for him.

In fact, Derek and Tully worried about their partner's obsessive dedication to work and had tried to lure him away from his computer screens. The first few times they dragged him out to a bar or a shooting range or a car show, Leland was polite and participated because that's what his southern upbringing required. Soon, though, he dropped the pretense of civility and told them where to go in no uncertain terms before returning to the work that absorbed him. Leland had put KRG on the map with his devotion to technological wizardry, but it wasn't healthy for him on a personal level.

"I know you're not going to a hockey game because I'm stuck with that duty tonight." Truth was, Derek liked hockey so he didn't mind escorting the CEO of Argon to KRG's luxury box that evening, especially since she knew the sport well enough to watch it instead of just drinking and talking.

"I'll have the answer for you by the time the hockey game is over," Leland promised.

"Pretty confident, aren't you?" But it wasn't an idle claim. If Alice's brain was a steel trap, Leland's brain was pure titanium.

"Just a statement of fact. I'll keep Ms. Thurber informed so you can focus on Argon and toothless Canadians slamming each other into wooden walls. Why you enjoy that is beyond me."

Derek ignored the gibe at hockey as he felt a pang of regret that Leland would now be the one dealing with Alice. He would miss that tantalizing scent of hers.

⌁

Alice gaped at her computer. A confidentiality agreement signed by Leland Rockwell of KRG had just landed in her in-box. She glanced at the time on her screen. Sixteen minutes had elapsed since Derek dropped her off at her front door.

"Jeez, those guys don't mess around," she muttered, saving the digital agreement to her newly created folder labeled KRG CONSULTING.

At the sound of her voice, Audley jumped onto her desk and inserted himself between Alice and the screen. She ran her hand over his sleek coat, savoring his loud purr.

Until her phone rang. When she saw Natalie's name on the screen, she sighed and answered.

"So Cindy down at the diner says you had lunch with a guy who looks like a young Brad Pitt, only better," Natalie said, the sound of hair dryers humming in the background. "Since I found pictures of Derek

Killion online and he fits that description, I'm thinking it was the same guy. Now I know why you wanted him to pounce on you."

"I never said I wanted him to pounce on me. I was just using a clichéd business phrase to cover up the reason you called," Alice explained. "And how do you know he's not still here?"

"Because Cindy heard him say you all were finished with your business. And, hon, if you didn't want him to pounce on you, then you're crazy. He's a hottie." The other woman whistled in appreciation. "Did you and Derek track down the missing $3.37 and go out to Nick's to celebrate? Personally, I would have expected him to take you someplace a little higher end."

"He asked to eat quickly," Alice said in his defense. "And no, we couldn't find the problem. Derek thinks it's a software glitch, so he's enlisting the help of their resident computer genius."

"So you'll still be working together. That gives you another chance to get him to pounce."

"There will be no pouncing. He's a partner at an international consulting firm." But Alice had a sudden vision of Derek winding his fingers into her hair so he could pull her close and kiss her as they sat side by side in her office. She swallowed hard as yearning slid through her like a warm spring tide.

"What does his job have to do with anything?"

"Our relationship is purely professional," Alice said primly.

"Who said anything about a relationship? He's a very attractive man and you're a very attractive woman. What happens when you add those two together? They equal sex," Natalie said. "Hey, you're the one who's supposed to be good at math."

Alice sighed. They'd had this conversation before. Natalie insisted that Alice was beautiful whereas Alice knew she was not. "Derek Killion isn't my type."

"Honey, he's everybody's type." Natalie's tone softened. "Look, I know you're not one for casual sex, but you have to stop doing a couple of things. The first is selling yourself short because, trust me, Derek Killion was thinking about having sex with you. And the second is assuming that just because someone is good-looking, they're as shallow and self-centered as your mother."

"Derek Killion was thinking only about finding the missing money." He *had* seemed to flirt with her those couple of bone-melting, brain-twisting times, but that had to be wishful thinking on her part. "Anyway, it doesn't matter. He's handed me off to his partner, the tech genius."

"What's the partner's name? Maybe he's a really cute computer nerd."

Alice couldn't help laughing. "Leland Rockwell, but I doubt he'll come out here to meet with me."

"His name sounds kind of snobby, but I'm not going to judge him for that." Another voice was speaking in the background with some urgency. "Gotta go. My next color-and-cut just arrived."

Alice set the phone down and allowed herself to wander into Natalie's fantasy world. What if Derek Killion *had* tried to kiss her? Would she have kissed him back?

She would have wanted to be sophisticated enough to enjoy the touch of his perfectly sculpted lips without wondering how he felt about her. She would have tried to shut up the little voice that said, *Why is this gorgeous man kissing plain, boring you when he's going to be disappointed?*

She shoved her desk chair back and stalked over to where Sylvester sprawled across his favorite platform on the cat tower. Scooping the startled cat up, she cradled him in her arms and rubbed her cheek against his soft fur.

"And that is why I am a crazy cat lady."

Chapter 4

Derek felt rather than heard the phone in his pocket ring because the hockey spectators were on their feet screaming their disapproval after a referee ruled an apparent goal no good.

Paula Erskine, Argon's CEO, shook her head. "The ref is right."

"Right and wrong don't matter when the fans have two periods' worth of beer in them," Derek said, checking his phone to see that it was Leland.

The Rangers' coach called a time-out, so he held up his cell, "Would you mind if I take this call?"

She gestured for him to go ahead and pulled out her own phone. When you ran a multinational company, there was never really any downtime so he wasn't surprised. He got up and walked back into the dining area of the luxury box, where it was marginally quieter.

He called Leland back. "Tell me you have the answer even *before* the hockey game is over."

"No answer. But a lot of questions," Leland said. His Georgia drawl was barely in evidence so Derek knew his partner was deep into tech mode. "Tell me again how your bookkeeper found this software."

Derek repeated Alice's description of the hotel presentation and the software's useful features.

"Interesting. This software has all the fingerprints of either Russian or Eastern European programming."

"That's not unusual these days."

"Except the website goes to great lengths to look all-American. Their headquarters is in Dallas. They claim the development is done there. If you call their help line, you get Texas accents. When I traced the call, it did indeed go to Dallas."

"Which seems consistent. Did you ever consider that they might have simply hired Russian programmers? And since Russian programmers have a reputation for less-than-stellar quality control, maybe they want to keep that fact hidden."

"Still seems hinky to me. Do you mind if I call your Alice and ask her some more questions?"

If Leland thought something related to computers was hinky, it probably was. "Well, you might not call her right now. It's Saturday night, so she's likely to be out or going soon." Odd that the thought gave him a pang.

"Then I'll leave her a voice mail. She doesn't have to answer my call."

It was useless trying to convince Leland that not everyone wanted to be on call 24-7. "It's your project now, so you do what works for you. I'm just an interested bystander."

"Keep the interest to a minimum. You've got Argon to worry about."

Irritation flared at his partner's warning. "I can actually hold two thoughts in my head at the same time," Derek snapped.

"Yeah, but you were pretty impressed with the bookkeeper. I could tell by your notes. You don't usually comment on a client's skill and intelligence."

"I thought it was relevant to the project since you haven't met her. What's your point?" The game was starting again, and Derek didn't want to leave his client alone much longer.

"Just seems that there might be more going on than getting some numbers straightened out." Leland's drawl was back. "And KRG needs your full focus on Argon."

Leland disconnected before Derek could ask him why giving Alice credit for being on the ball meant there was anything other than work going on. He shoved his phone back in his pocket. Having partners who were also old friends could be a royal pain in the ass.

Although uneasiness nagged at him as he remembered his thoughts about Alice's hair and perfume. And panties.

But that wouldn't prevent him from giving Argon one hundred percent of his effort.

⟿

Alice was curled up on the couch with Sylvester ensconced on her lap and Audley stretched out beside her, rereading one of her favorite Georgette Heyer novels. When she had scanned her romance collection after she'd put on her pajamas, *Arabella* had suited her mood for the evening. As she read it, she realized why. When she pictured the hero, Mr. Robert Beaumaris, a very rich, very eligible grandson of a duke, he had the face and body of Derek Killion. However, Arabella wasn't overawed by his riches or his looks, and Mr. Beaumaris fell hard for her. Alice knew that only happened in fiction, but a girl could dream.

An email chimed into her phone, which Audley was using for a pillow. She considered not disturbing the cat, but she thought a dose of reality might be a good thing for her Derek-hazed brain.

The message was from Leland Rockwell. The man was at work at nine thirty on Saturday night? He must have even less of a life than Alice.

She swiped it open.

> I have some questions about the software. May I
> call you?

Did he mean now? Had Derek somehow sensed she was just like his partner and told Leland to go ahead and contact her? The idea sent a jab of hurt through her.

No, that couldn't be true. Leland was just giving it a shot.

She looked down at her pajamas covered with dancing llamas. It wasn't a video call, but she felt weird about doing business while dressed for bed.

She tapped back, Please give me fifteen minutes and then I will be available for your call.

She extricated herself from the couch without causing either cat to do more than blink at her disapprovingly and then dashed up to her bedroom to throw on a pair of jeans and a T-shirt. She even pulled her hair back into a ponytail to get herself into the right frame of mind.

When her phone rang, she was in her office in front of her computer screen.

"Ms. Thurber, this is Leland Rockwell from KRG."

For a moment she couldn't reconcile the honeyed southern drawl with the computer-wizard reputation, but why shouldn't a tech geek be from the South? "Please call me Alice," she said. "Thank you for working on my problem on a weekend."

"Right, Derek did mention something about it being Saturday night." Leland's tone had a little edge of irony that she didn't understand. "I should not have bothered you. I can call back on Monday."

"No, no, it's fine. What questions do you have?"

"Does Myron Barsky have an accent of any kind?"

That wasn't what she expected Leland to ask, so she had to think a minute. "Um, he had kind of a twang, not quite southern and not much of one."

"Could he be from Texas?"

"I suppose so. I'm not great at pinpointing accents." Why would Leland care?

"Did he have anyone else with him?" He might have a drawl but Leland's interrogation was still sharp.

She frowned and thought back to the hotel presentation. "The hotel manager introduced him, but no one else was on the dais with him that I remember."

This was getting weirder and weirder.

"Did the hotel manager mention whether he used the software himself or whether the hotel did?"

"No, he just told us Myron was from BalanceTrakR and handed over the microphone. Then he circulated afterward, asking if the food and beverages were to our liking." She hadn't much liked the manager because his concern seemed all about whether his guests would say anything negative online rather than a genuine wish that they be happy.

"Does the hotel run many events like that one?"

"I don't really know. It's outside of town, near the highway, and caters mostly to business travelers. It's part of a reputable chain, though."

"One more question and then I'll leave you to your weekend plans. Did the manager mention Barsky's title or position with the company?"

Alice tried to rerun the manager's opening speech in her mind. "I don't think so. If you give me a minute, I'll see if I can find my notes to double-check that." She put Leland on mute and opened the drawer where she had filed the software information. Pulling out the file, she found the sheets of lined yellow paper. No title. Flipping through the glossy brochure she'd picked up, she found the same thing. She unmuted the call. "Nothing about his position. Only his name and the toll-free number." Leland was not going to be impressed with her as a resource. "I wish I could help you more with this," she said in frustration. "Can you tell me why you're interested in Barsky and his presentation?"

There was a pause before he said, "I took a look at the software and it has many signs that it was programmed in Russia or Eastern Europe. Some of those guys are really good, but there's a whole underground network where the programmers work cheap and deliver an inferior product. I think it's possible that there may be a bug in the system. I admit that I haven't found it yet, but give me a couple of more hours." His combined frustration and determination came through clearly.

Alice frowned. She hadn't really believed Derek when he proposed that as a possibility. "But there's not a single discussion about this bug on any BalanceTrakR user forum. I even posted about it. I'd expect to see something if there was a systemic bug."

"That is puzzling."

She wanted to ask if Derek knew about Leland's theory but remembered it was Saturday night. Since Derek wasn't a computer geek, she was sure he had a date . . . or two.

"I have an idea," she said, prompted by a powerful need to contribute to the project. "I'll go talk to the hotel manager and see if he has more information on Barsky."

"That could be useful." Leland sounded as though he wasn't convinced. "It's worth a try, at least."

"I'll see if he's on duty tomorrow." The thought of doing a little corporate espionage sent a zing of excitement through her. Accounting was her passion, but it didn't often provide an adrenaline rush.

"Once you talk with him, call me back at this number." There was a brief pause. "I'll be keeping Derek in the loop. He was very impressed with your analysis and expertise and will continue to be involved with the project."

Pleasure spread through her like a warm, tropical tide. "That's good to hear." And Derek wasn't just dumping her in Leland's lap. He'd still be in touch. The pleasure burrowed into her chest.

Of course, it would all be by phone and email, but still . . .

"I look forward to hearing what the manager tells you." Leland disconnected.

Alice stared at the screen and the columns of numbers that she hadn't needed for her conversation with the tech wizard. She didn't understand why he cared where and by whom the software was created. Either it had a bug or it didn't.

Certainly, she had heard about Russian hackers but this wasn't a security breach at some major corporation. This problem was about tiny amounts of money from a bunch of small businesses, some of which barely met payroll every month. Alice snorted. No Russian hacker would get rich off *her* clients.

She was still puzzling over this when her phone rang. This time the caller was Derek. A delicious shiver danced through her and she almost laughed. Her quiet Saturday night reading Georgette Heyer had become surreal with this barrage of phone calls from high-powered consultants.

"Thurber Accounting," she said because she didn't feel comfortable with a casual "Hi, Derek."

"Alice, it's Derek from KRG."

"I know."

There was a pause. "Then why the . . . never mind. Leland said he spoke with you."

She could hear the honk of a horn in the background. He must be in a car, probably in the city. She hoped his date didn't mind him discussing business in the middle of their night out.

"He had a lot of unusual questions."

"He said you were going to talk with the hotel manager. I'm not sure I'm comfortable with you doing that."

"Well, Leland needed information that I didn't have, so I figured out a way to potentially get it." And to keep herself involved with Derek.

"But if this involves the kind of people Leland thinks it might, they could get upset about being accused of making a programming error." Derek's voice held an edge of worry. "They might go after you, try to ruin your professional reputation."

She couldn't decide whether to be touched by his concern or annoyed that he thought she couldn't face down a pissed-off programmer.

"Myron Barsky didn't strike me as the reputation-destroying type." She thought of the thick-framed glasses that kept slipping down his nose and the shaggy hair that curled up at the ends. He had rounded shoulders, probably from too much time at the computer. "In fact, I think he would be grateful to learn about the bug. I certainly would appreciate being informed about it, if I were him. I'd want to fix it as soon as possible."

An exhale came through the phone. "In a perfect world, that would be true. However, the people at BalanceTrakR may be aware of the problem but unwilling to invest in fixing it. We just don't know enough yet. I don't want your business to get hurt by this."

Maybe he was genuinely concerned, but she thought he was overreacting. "Remember, I'm just talking to the hotel manager. I doubt he'll call up BalanceTrakR to complain."

"Let me deal with it." The tone of command vibrated through the phone.

Now she was beginning to feel patronized. "Your partner believes I'm capable of handling it myself."

A brief silence. "Leland is very focused on solving the problem," Derek said with what she could tell was a carefully worded answer. "He doesn't always worry about the fallout."

"Seriously, I'll be fine."

"It's not a good idea," Derek persisted. "I can get out there on Tuesday."

"Yes, but I can do it tomorrow." Although she was tempted to agree with his plan so she could see him again. But that was not a good idea either, since she kept picturing him in Mr. Beaumaris's skintight riding breeches.

She thought she heard a huff of frustration coming through the phone. "Text me as soon as you're done," he said with a snap.

"I will," she snapped back.

"I'm sorry." His tone was rueful. "Leland shouldn't have bothered you on a Saturday night. I hope he didn't interrupt your plans."

"Well, he did," Alice said with a half smile as she remembered her intention to finish *Arabella* in one sitting. "But I don't mind." After all, it had gotten her a bonus phone call from Derek.

A pause. "I trust your plans can be returned to."

She thought about her book lying on the couch where she'd dropped it facedown before racing off to change her clothes for Leland's call. "Yup, not a problem."

"In that case, good night, my clever bookkeeper." He disconnected before she could respond.

My clever bookkeeper. She propped her head on her hands and slipped into a delicious dream where Derek called her other, more intimate things with "my" in front of them, generally while both of them were wearing very little clothing.

Chapter 5

The next morning, Alice pulled on taupe trousers and a pale peach blouse before slipping her feet into medium-heeled brown pumps. Only she knew that she wore peach silk-and-lace lingerie underneath, although she found herself wishing Derek knew too.

She banished the thought with some difficulty before she checked the mirror. With her hair tucked back in a neat ponytail, she projected exactly the image she wanted to: a single-practice bookkeeper just trying to track down some software she didn't buy the first time around but now wanted to look into. At least that was her cover story.

She had called the hotel to make sure the manager, Gary Woertz, was on duty, so she mentally ran through the questions Leland had posed as she drove the fifteen minutes to the Lipton Hotel.

She asked for the manager at the front desk. The clerk went from smiling to nervous so Alice reassured the young woman that she wasn't there to complain about anything. Quite the contrary, in fact. The young—and evidently inexperienced—clerk was so relieved that she didn't even ask for Alice's name but just pointed her down a corridor to the manager's office.

The door was open, so Alice knocked on the jamb before taking a step inside. The startled manager jumped up from his desk. "May I help you?"

Woertz had grown his pale blond hair out a couple of inches and spiked it with some sort of gel, but he wore the same too-large green blazer with a gold plastic name tag pinned to the pocket.

Alice didn't want to get the reception clerk in trouble so she said, "My apologies, Mr. Woertz. My name is Alice Thurber. I was hoping you could help me with some information about the accounting software, BalanceTrakR. You hosted a presentation about it here a few months ago. I attended but didn't make the decision to buy it then." She wasn't sure if he would remember she'd been there but decided not to take the chance.

Woertz's surprise melted into that artificial smile Alice hadn't warmed up to the first time she'd met him. "Please, have a seat." He gestured to the chair in front of his desk as he sat back down. "If you'll give me a second, I'll find the file." Alice settled into the burnt-orange chair that looked like a castoff from a past renovation of the hotel rooms.

Woertz made a show of riffling through the files in his desk drawer before sliding one out and flipping it open on his desk with a flourish. "Here we are. Mr. Barsky was very happy with the sales generated by the event."

"A couple of people who bought the software have been singing its praises to me, so I thought I would see if you have any contact information for Mr. Barsky. Is he the president or is he just in sales?"

"I'm not sure. You can probably find that information on their website."

In fact, it wasn't on the website, so Alice had no qualms about saying, "I looked there but Mr. Barsky isn't listed. Did he set up the presentation or was it some corporate thing? I want to get in touch with him to ask a few more questions."

Woertz rummaged around in the folder. "Mr. Barsky made all the arrangements. Oh, here's his card." He scanned the business card and shook his head. "It doesn't say what his position is."

"Could you share his phone number so I can contact him?"

Woertz turned the card over so she couldn't read it and gave her his professionally hospitable smile. "I hesitate to share this information without Mr. Barsky's permission. We're very concerned with confidentiality." He flipped through the file, pulling out the same brochure Alice already had. "Let me give you the contact number from the sales literature."

"Thank you but I found that number on the website," she said. "I just thought it would be nice if Mr. Barsky got credit for the sale since I saw his presentation here at your lovely hotel." She swept a falsely admiring glance around the bland office, the walls of which were hung with framed posters featuring inspirational clichés.

Woertz hesitated before he picked up the business card and fiddled with it. "I guess Mr. Barsky would want the commission." He widened his smile as he put the card on the desk and slid it to Alice's side. "I'd appreciate it if you could mention the hotel when you call."

"And you," Alice said, giving him a smile just as inauthentic. "After all, you organized that fantastic reception."

Alice reached for the card, but Woertz put his hand on it, saying, "Please copy the number down. I need the card back for my records."

"Of course. Sorry." She pulled out her phone and took a picture of the card. The only other information on the card was Barsky's name with a middle initial of *G* and the BalanceTrakR logo. Not informative, but at least she had the phone number—which was not the same as the 800 number listed on the website. "I don't suppose you use the software yourself, do you? I'd be interested in your opinion of it."

Woertz palmed Barsky's card as he gave her a smile of superior condescension. "I have no knowledge of the software. When you're a multinational company like the Lipton Hotel chain, you need more than a stand-alone desktop accounting system to track the money." He closed the file and folded his hands on top of it. "Corporate encourages us to run events that will benefit our community, so when Mr. Barsky asked to make his presentation, I thought it would be a positive thing."

"It was indeed," Alice agreed. "As I mentioned, several local businesspeople bought the software and are happy with it. I just hoped to get another perspective on it."

An odd look crossed Woertz's face, making his smile flicker. "You're not by any chance an auditor, are you?"

Alice laughed in a way that she hoped projected flattered amusement. "Me, an auditor? No, I'm just a bookkeeper who works in Cofferwood." She took her own business card out of her purse and handed it to him.

Woertz's smile returned full force when he scanned her card. Alice decided this was a good time to exit and stood up. "You've been very helpful. Thank you for your time."

The manager leaped to his feet and walked beside her to his door. "It's been my privilege to be of service."

Alice beat a speedy retreat to her car and headed for home, feeling very pleased with herself for getting Barsky's number. This corporate espionage stuff was a kick.

She was in the midst of changing out of her business outfit—to save it from clinging cat hairs—when her phone pinged with a text notification. She pulled on a T-shirt before she picked it up.

Text me when you're done with the manager, Derek had written.

She hadn't told him when she planned to meet with Woertz, so his timing was uncanny.

Just finished. Got a phone number for Barsky, she responded.

Her phone rang. "Everything went fine," she said before Derek could speak. "The worst that happened was that the guy thought I was an auditor. I was kind of flattered."

His deep chuckle seemed to vibrate through every cell in her body. "You enjoy striking terror into the hearts of hotel managers?"

"It's a novel sensation because I'm about as terrifying as a kitten." She padded toward her office on bare feet.

"You underestimate yourself. I'd be very afraid to have you audit my finances. You're quite . . . thorough."

Gratification tingled through her. The mighty Derek Killion at least pretended to think she was good at her job. "As long as you aren't using imaginary numbers, your audit would be fine." A little math humor to cover her reaction to his words.

He laughed, a delicious rumble of amusement. "I try to keep my imagination and my accounting separate." He paused. "Until recently, I've succeeded."

His tone was odd, almost surprised, and she wondered if it was possible that Natalie was right. Maybe Derek did have an occasional nonprofessional thought about her. He did seem to flirt with her every now and then. Awareness flickered along her veins.

"Tell me about your meeting with the manager," he said, his tone changing to business. The shift was like a glass of cold water in her face, which maybe was a good thing.

"Woertz—that's the manager—knew nothing about the software. He was just taking Myron Barsky's money for the meeting. He says that the hotel chain's head office encourages that."

"Sure. They buy cheap wine and beer and then quadruple the price they charge the company making the presentation."

"He didn't know what position Barsky holds with BalanceTrakR. The only thing on Barsky's business card was his direct phone number, which I talked Woertz into letting me copy." She expected a pat on the back for that.

Instead Derek snapped at her. "Do not call Barsky yourself. Leland and I will handle that."

"I had no intention of calling him," she said with a snap of her own. She wasn't an idiot.

"Good." He didn't apologize this time. "I would prefer that you not be involved in this any further."

"You do remember that I'm the one who found this problem, and that my clients are the ones with the discrepancies, right?"

"But there's no need for the people at BalanceTrakR to know that."

"It's just a small software glitch. Seriously, I'd be devastated if I knew that my software system was shortchanging my clients, even for tiny amounts of money. I'd want to straighten it out right away."

"Your faith in your fellow accountants is admirable but naive," he said. "Alice, please listen to me. I've experienced some ugly confrontations with people who don't like having their mistakes pointed out. I don't want you involved for your own good."

His plea seemed to come from the heart, so she simmered down. "I know you think they'll smear my reputation, but what about KRG's?"

"We have the resources to handle a little smearing."

Her insides melted and her anger evaporated in a plume of steam. When he said that he sounded just like a sexy duke.

~

Derek found Leland in the room nicknamed "Mission Control" because of the number of computer screens arrayed on desktops and walls.

Leland ignored him for a few seconds as he stared at a screen covered with letters, numbers, and symbols that Derek could not decipher. The artificial light from the monitor gave the computer wizard's tousled hair a bluish tint. The other man hit a few keys before swiveling his chair around to face his partner. "I know," Leland said. "You're pissed that your bookkeeper went off on her own little fact-finding mission because of something I said, so you came to warn me off doing it again."

"You said that the program came from Eastern Europe or Russia," Derek pointed out as he crossed his arms and glared down at Leland. "You know the kind of people who write that code. Nasty, unscrupulous people who wouldn't hesitate to destroy Alice's reputation if she got in the way of their profits."

"She was questioning an employee at a second-rate hotel chain in suburban New Jersey. He's not involved with the Russians. And sit down, for God's sake. Your intimidation tactics won't work on me."

"You don't know that he isn't involved," Derek said, continuing to stand.

Leland tilted his chair back. "I'd say that the odds are against it," he said, his drawl as thick as molasses. He used his accent when he wanted to defuse a confrontation but Derek was on to his tricks.

"You don't play odds when you're dealing with criminals."

"They're not necessarily criminals. They're just not big on quality control."

Derek grabbed a rolling chair and sat. "You'll be getting an email from Alice about the interview with the manager. That's the end of her involvement in this investigation."

Leland raised his eyebrows. "Is Alice okay with being cut out? She was the one who found the problem, after all."

"Yeah, she reminded me of that." Derek rubbed his forehead.

"Hey, Killion, I've got this," Leland said, the lean angles of his face softening. "Your plate is overflowing right now. KRG needs your mind on Argon. After all, those numbers are just slightly larger than BalanceTrakR's issue."

But the size of the numbers didn't matter to Derek. That was just a matter of some extra commas. Strangely enough, the BalanceTrakR problem was more of a challenge.

Leland continued, holding up his hand to ward off Derek's objections. "I promise to keep your bookkeeper out of it."

"As you pointed out, it may not be so easy to do that," Derek said. Although Leland's southern drawl often disarmed people in a way Derek couldn't imitate. Maybe his partner would succeed in keeping Alice away from trouble where Derek met with resistance. He frowned, not liking the thought of Leland manipulating Alice, even for her own good.

But Leland was right about Argon. Derek owed his full attention to their new client and he wasn't giving it to them. His team had gathered and analyzed the data he'd asked for. Now he needed to synthesize the solutions and present them to Argon. He knew the drill. He'd done it many times before. And maybe that was the issue.

Alice's problem might be small, but it was a novel challenge. It took him down into the trenches like the old days.

And then there was Alice herself. He rubbed his forehead again. He'd never had a problem focusing on what was important before. What the hell was wrong with him?

When he'd been engaged to Courtney, he'd been able to keep his mind on his job. That had been her biggest complaint about their relationship.

"Why are you so concerned about Alice?" Leland asked in an unnerving echo of Derek's thoughts. "You don't have the same qualms about our own consultants."

"They're trained and experienced, and they have KRG at their backs. Alice is a single-practice bookkeeper who doesn't understand how ruthless business can be."

"You've said that she's very intelligent."

"Of course she is," Derek said, irritated by his own inability to separate personal from professional. "But she also believes that if we inform BalanceTrakR about their software glitch, they will thank us profusely and fix it immediately."

"Naive, indeed." Leland steepled his fingers. He was the only person Derek knew who didn't look affected when he did that. "Now I see why you worry about her."

What worried Derek even more was that he wanted to keep Alice's crazy beliefs intact. Because when he viewed the world through her eyes, it looked like a better place.

Chapter 6

Alice pulled out her credit card to pay for her Monday lunch of take-out at the Sushi Shack. Sylvester and Audley would be thrilled by the sashimi she'd included for them. When she added a small tip and hand-wrote the total on the bill, she frowned down at the slip of paper.

This was the one paper trail she hadn't checked—the actual credit card receipts from her clients. She hadn't considered it before because one of the nifty features of BalanceTrakR was that it had an automated integration with the major credit card companies. It didn't seem possible that there would be any problem with that interface, especially such a small, sporadic one.

Maybe she needed to take a closer look.

The only client she could be sure would still have the paper receipts was Natalie's Mane Attraction because it was the most recent to have the problem. Alice had asked Natalie to retain every bit of hard copy for the month, just in case.

She winced when she thought of how many little pieces of paper she'd have to organize and compare with the automated system to see if there was some flaw.

The beauty salon was closed on Monday, so Alice dialed Natalie's cell phone. "Hey, I need to get all your charge slips from last month. If I bring you some sushi, will you meet me at the salon?"

"I don't need sushi if you tell me that the reason you're still obsessing over last month's numbers is because of the gorgeous Derek Killion," Natalie said.

"Maybe a little," Alice said. "But I have a new theory that I want to explore."

"So you're still working with him?"

"And his partner. I even went on an investigative mission to the hotel. I think I would make an excellent spy."

Natalie laughed. "I'll be there in fifteen minutes. And I changed my mind about the sushi. I'd like a dragon roll and some edamame, please."

When Alice arrived at the Mane Attraction, Natalie was leaning against the reception desk, looking almost like a teenager in her day-off attire of slim jeans, pink T-shirt, ballet flats, and minimal makeup. She gestured to a bulging envelope lying beside her hip. "Here are the receipts but you don't get to grab them and run. Sit down and eat lunch with me," the salon owner said. "I want to hear about your espionage."

They settled in the staff break room, a tiny space crammed with a round white Formica table and four pink plastic chairs. It was odd not to hear the buzz of hair dryers and hum of voices sharing salon gossip.

Alice described her foray into undercover work and sighed. "But Derek is ticked about it. He's afraid someone from BalanceTrakR will get upset and do something nasty, like destroying my business reputation. I personally believe they'll be glad to know they have a bug, so they can fix it."

Natalie shook her head. "You are such a cockeyed optimist sometimes. They're just as likely to want to cover it up so they don't have a lot of unhappy customers demanding their money back." She smiled. "I like that Derek is worried about you. That shows he cares."

"In a professional way."

Natalie pointed one of her chopsticks at Alice. "Stop it!"

"Stop what? Being honest?" Luckily, Natalie didn't know how often Derek starred in Alice's dreams. It was funny how having her dream hero be a real, live human being made her fantasies so much more vivid. Just thinking about Derek dressed in gleaming riding boots made her pulse pick up.

"You shut men down before they can even think about starting something with you," Natalie fumed. "You don't give them or yourself a chance."

Alice pointed her chopstick right back at Natalie. "People like Derek Killion don't date people like me. He's rich, successful, and gorgeous. I'm sure equally rich, successful, gorgeous women are falling over themselves to get his attention."

"Actually, according to my internet research, he's a workaholic who has very little social life outside of business. So maybe you've found the best way to his heart. Through accounting." Natalie's smile was teasing, but her smile faded as she said, "Besides, you can't judge every beautiful human being by your mother. Just because she's a self-centered bi— broad doesn't mean Derek is the same way."

"You can call her a bitch," Alice said. "I've thought worse about her at times."

Natalie had heard Gabrielle's putdown of her daughter a couple of weeks before. The hairdresser had been blowing Alice's hair dry when her mother stopped behind the chair to watch, saying, "Your hair has such a beautiful texture, sweetheart, but the color is kind of dull. You should let Natalie put some blonde streaks in it, like mine."

Alice always hoped she had gotten beyond being hurt by her mother's pinpricks but they still drew blood. Natalie thought Gabrielle did it deliberately but Alice knew the truth was worse. Her mother was trying to help her unbeautiful daughter make the best of what she had.

"Back to Derek Killion," Natalie said. "When are you going to see him again?"

"Maybe never." That depressed Alice more than she wanted to admit. "There's really no reason to. We can do everything via email and the phone."

"Find a reason to. Go visit him at his office."

"Why are you so determined to throw me together with Derek? You've never even met the man."

"Because I see the look on your face when his name comes up."

Alice glanced toward the small mirror hanging on the wall. "I have a look?"

"Your eyes get this sort of unfocused inwardness and the corners of your mouth curl up in a soft little smile. Oh, and you touch your hair. That's a sure sign that you're attracted to him."

"All I've been touching is the sushi with my chopsticks," Alice said, hoping she didn't look as gooey on the outside as she felt on the inside when Derek's name came up.

"Not the first time I mentioned him."

Alice made a mental note to be more aware of what she did with her hands. "For all we know, he's married or at least engaged. He's too big a catch not to be." Wow, she sounded like the matchmaking mamas in her Georgette Heyer novels.

"Nope, he's not. I checked online." Natalie was a super sleuth when it came to tracking celebrities' marital status. She said it was all in the service of beauty-salon gossip. Of course, Derek didn't qualify as famous but Alice's friend clearly had her trusted internet sources. Natalie hesitated before she added, "He was engaged once but they split up over a year ago."

"I knew it! No one that good-looking and that successful could stay single forever." Alice's triumph was pushed aside by her curiosity, even though she knew it would be torture to find out what beautiful woman Derek had fallen in love with. "Who was she? Why did the engagement end?"

Natalie swiped a few times on her phone, handing it to Alice. "She's a lawyer at a big Manhattan firm."

"So she's really smart," Alice said, examining the photo that accompanied the announcement of Derek and Courtney Miller's engagement.

His ex-fiancée was stylish and elegant but not knockout gorgeous, which surprised Alice. It also made her like Derek better. Despite his stunning looks, he didn't require the same from the woman he intended to marry.

"You're extremely smart too," Natalie said with a reprimand in her tone.

Alice skimmed Courtney's bio while her tiny bit of hope shriveled. "But I didn't go to Yale undergrad and Harvard Law. I'm not headed for partner at a prestigious New York City law firm." Nor did she wear designer suits and high-heeled pumps like the tall, slim woman in the photo.

"Notice that he's not engaged to her anymore," Natalie pointed out.

"Did your research uncover the reason?"

"Only that they had mutually agreed to call off the wedding."

"No speculation as to why? You're usually good at finding the dirt." She wanted to know if Derek was still nursing a broken heart.

Natalie smiled. "Neither one of them is famous—or infamous—enough to stir up that kind of gossip. The only negative I could find was that comment about Derek being a workaholic. Since you're the same way, that makes you compatible."

"Except Courtney was on partner track so she must have been pretty dedicated to her job too." And a woman with all those accomplishments couldn't hold on to Derek.

"Honey, there are all kinds of reasons that people split up, even after they get married. Maybe Courtney turned into a royal bitch once she had the ring on her finger."

Alice knew that Natalie spoke from hard experience. The salon owner had spent twelve years in an abusive marriage. Before the wedding, Natalie's then-fiancé had showered her with charm and compliments. But after they were married her ex had turned controlling, manipulative, and emotionally abusive. Natalie once said it would have been better if he'd been physically abusive because she would have left the moment he hit her. Instead she stayed until thoughts of committing suicide woke her up to the fact that her husband was about to destroy her.

It was hard to believe. Natalie seemed so secure in herself, as though she knew exactly who she was and what she wanted. But Alice understood that her friend's serenity was hard won.

Somehow Natalie seemed to know what Alice was thinking. "No, I don't think Derek turned into a jerk after he got engaged," she said. "Because you wouldn't be attracted to him if he were that kind of person."

"You don't think I'm blinded by his incredible good looks?"

"We've already established that his looks are more likely to drive you away, so there must be something else there that you're jonesing for."

Alice had been telling herself that it was pure lust—a crazy opportunity to play out a fantasy—so Natalie's words sent a tiny shock wave through her. Other than their mutual love of numbers, what else would make her dream of Derek?

"Besides, you need to get out more," Natalie said, "so you don't turn into a crazy cat lady."

Alice threw an edamame pod at her friend and stopped worrying about Derek.

An hour later, Alice emptied the envelope onto her desk. Twenty-six rubber-banded bundles of credit card slips tumbled across the wood surface, causing Audley to waken from his slumber beside her computer and begin batting the bundles onto the floor.

"Hey, buddy, don't make my job harder than it already is," Alice said, picking up the gray tabby and depositing him on the floor before retrieving the three fallen packets. She unwound the rubber band from the first one and discovered that it was wrapped in a log of all the credit card transactions with the total from that day, printed off from the BalanceTrakR software. A note at the bottom, written in Natalie's neat cursive, stated, "All present and accounted for." Followed by her initials. That meant that Natalie had checked each slip against each listed line item.

Alice trusted her friend's accuracy because, after all, it was Natalie's business. Maybe she wouldn't have to go through every single one of more than a thousand charge slips for the month.

She unwrapped the bundles and smoothed out each day's tally sheet, carefully winding the rubber bands back around the supporting credit card slips and laying them out in date order. Pulling her favorite calculator over, she added up each day's total, running the numbers twice, first forward, then backward. The two totals matched.

She got up to pull the BalanceTrakR paperwork and the bank statement from the Mane Attraction pile, flipping through the pages as she strolled back to her desk. She found the total credit card charges for the month on the BalanceTrakR printout and laid it down beside her hand-calculated totals.

For a moment, she couldn't believe what she was seeing. She took off her glasses and rubbed her eyes before sitting down hard in her chair. Seating her glasses firmly on her nose, she looked again.

There was a difference of $3.37.

She rocked back in her chair. How could that be possible? The software was disagreeing with its own daily totals.

Seizing the bank statement, she added up the deposits from the credit card companies. The Mane Attraction received major credit card deposits once a week rather than daily, so it didn't take long to come up with the total.

It matched the monthly BalanceTrakR statement.

Somewhere between the credit card charges being entered into BalanceTrakR and the total being transmitted to the bank that processed the charges, $3.37 had disappeared.

Alice's brain felt like it was going to explode as she tried to figure out how that could happen. Although she was familiar with the process of credit card transactions, she realized that figuring out where the error occurred was beyond her capabilities.

She dialed Derek's cell number.

"Alice, what a pleasure." He sounded sincere. "I'm about to go into a meeting. Can I call you back in about an hour?"

"Yes, of course, but I found the discrepancy." She couldn't keep the excitement out of her voice. "It's in the credit card charges."

"The credit card charges?" His astonishment came through the phone. "But those are processed directly through the software. We checked the totals more than once."

"I know, but there must be some weird bug in BalanceTrakR. That's why I called."

"We're going to need Leland's help," Derek said, sounding a little disgruntled about it. "I'm sorry to ask you this but could you come to the KRG office in New York this evening with all your documentation? I'll send a car for you."

Alice's heart leaped, which annoyed her. "What time?"

There was a pause as though he was thinking. "The car will be there at seven if that works for you."

Since her plans for the rest of the day consisted of feeding the cats, matching a thousand charge slips to their listing on BalanceTrakR, and taking the self-defense class with Dawn, that would work for her. Any other time she would have regretted missing the self-defense class because Anthony, the fake attacker, was so cute. However, Derek was much cuter. "I'll see you this evening," she said.

"Great work," Derek said, the admiration in his voice warming her.

She sat with the phone cradled in her hand for a few seconds, as though she could hold his compliment that way. A founding partner of an international consulting firm thought she was good at her job.

A very good-looking founding partner.

"Get a grip," she muttered and dropped the phone on the desk. With a tingling sense of excitement, she picked up the first packet of charge slips and removed the rubber band. Somewhere in these little rectangles of paper lay a clue to the missing money and she couldn't wait to find it.

Two hours later, the excitement had died down. So far the paper receipts matched the transaction list. She closed her eyes and tilted her head to rest on the chair's back. The scrawled tips were especially difficult to decipher at times, and she wondered how the receptionist decided how much to key in. She'd gotten through about two-thirds of the little packets, which meant that finishing them would take another hour.

With a groan, she sat forward and opened her eyes, grabbing another bunch of receipts. She matched up the first ten. The eleventh made her blink. The handwriting was a little scrawled but perfectly clear. And it was $3.37 more than BalanceTrakR said it should be.

"Bingo!" she shouted, fists raised in the air. Audley bolted off the credenza where he'd been peacefully snoozing.

Except she still had no idea of what weird bug was living in the bowels of the software and eating a few dollars and cents from one transaction among thousands.

Thank goodness she had filled out that form on KRG's website.

Alice walked up to the reception desk in the Manhattan skyscraper's lobby, lugging the two large leather bags that contained her laptop and the Mane Attraction's paperwork. The limo driver had offered to carry them in for her, but she decided that being driven into the city in the cocoon of the big, luxurious car was enough high living for a book-keeper from New Jersey.

"I'm Alice Thurber, here to see Derek Killion at KRG," she said, handing the night guard her driver's license as requested. While the guard typed her name into the sleek computer, Alice admired the way the marble counter was highlighted by the blond wood paneling that soared up three stories behind it. Several huge ficus trees clearly enjoyed the sunlight that must pour through the sheet glass enclosing the space. KRG had chosen an impressive building for their main office.

The guard gave her back her license. "Elevator bank on the right. Floor twenty-three."

As the elevator hummed upward, Alice scanned her wavy reflection in the polished chrome door. She had probably gone overboard by wearing her new gray suit but she wanted to project professionalism at KRG's headquarters. Her black leather pumps had a low heel that her mother would have condemned as dowdy but they were comfortable to walk in. In a decision Alice considered daring, she'd chosen a pale pink silk blouse. Of course, underneath all the business attire, she had slipped on a lacy pink bra and panties but that would remain her secret.

She drew in a breath in an effort to quell the anticipation vibrating through her.

She tried to convince herself that it was about finding the answer to her problem, but the truth was more complicated. Yes, she was somewhat nervous about meeting the legendary Leland Rockwell and asking him to put his high-tech resources at her disposal for a mere $3.37.

However, the flutter in her stomach and the fizz of excitement were caused by the thought of seeing Derek again. Was he really as good-looking as she remembered him? Her dreams had probably exaggerated his attributes, especially when she imagined him in a Regency gentleman's attire of tight buckskin trousers, a fitted hunting coat, and an impeccably tied cravat.

Her doubts evaporated when the elevator doors slid open to reveal KRG's reception area, a sleekly modern room styled in shades of taupe and blue. Derek was crossing the cerulean carpet toward her in full stride, a smile lighting his face. Her breath whooshed right out of her.

"Alice," he said, his baritone warm and welcoming. "Thank you so much for coming into the city."

She stumbled out of the elevator as her gaze roved over the perfectly fitted navy-blue suit he wore. It accentuated the breadth of his shoulders, the slimness of his hips, and the length of his legs just as effectively as any Regency duke's riding clothes.

"Let me carry those," he said, lifting the two bags from her unresisting grip without any indication of their significant weight. "Curiosity has been tormenting me ever since you called. I guess I shouldn't have dismissed the idea of checking the credit card transactions."

She was lost in the silvery depths of his eyes as he opened a glass door and held it for her, his smile still keeping the dimple in evidence. Something about that single dimple throwing the perfection of his face just slightly out of symmetry made him all the more gorgeous, maybe because it made him look real, not plastic.

"Are you exhausted from checking all those credit card slips?" he asked as his smile faded to a look of concern.

She realized she hadn't managed to say a word since she first saw him. "It was tedious and my eyesight is a little blurry," she said. "But I'm psyched that I found the error."

He stopped and gestured her through a door into a conference room where a wall of windows displayed the glittering lights of midtown Manhattan. "Nice view," she said before noticing that a man stood by the conference table. "I'm sorry. I'm Alice Thurber."

"I guessed as much. I'm Leland." His voice held the soft southern accent she'd heard over the phone as he came forward with his hand outstretched. When she shook it, she took in the computer genius. Except for his sneakers, worn jeans, and maroon T-shirt, he was not what she'd expected. In fact, his clothing was at odds with his neatly trimmed brown hair, his stylish tortoiseshell glasses, and his thin, aristocratic face. He looked like a preppy trying to slum it. "Delighted to meet you."

"A pleasure," she said before sitting in the cushy leather chair Derek had pulled out for her after he had set her bags on the polished wood table. Leland slid into a seat where two laptops stood, already open. Despite his lean build, his shoulders spanned the back of the capacious chair.

"Would you like something to drink?" Derek asked. "Coffee? Tea? Something stronger after all your work?"

"Water is fine," Alice said, noticing the aroma of fresh coffee drifting through the air. She traced it to a mug sitting by Leland's laptops.

Derek picked up a bottle of designer water from a tray and set it in front of her. Then he unknotted his yellow paisley tie and yanked it out of his collar with a zing of silk against cotton. When he flicked open the top two buttons of his shirt and exposed the muscled column of his neck, a flicker of awareness ran through Alice.

"Ahh, much better," he said. "It's been a long day of back-to-back meetings."

When he settled into the chair next to hers, she could swear she felt his body warm the air around her. "Now let's see the culprit."

Alice pulled out copies of the transaction logs, bank statement, and the offending receipt and passed them to Derek and Leland. "The first one is the credit card summary from the end-of-the-month report produced by BalanceTrakR. After deducting the bank fees, it matches the bank statement, as you can see."

Derek nodded, his attention focused on the paper.

"Next is a report of all the credit card receipts for the month, which I printed out after I noticed the discrepancy. Flip to page five and take a look at the highlighted number. Now take a look at the daily log sheet. That was printed out the day the charges were made at the salon. Just by good luck, the owner, Natalie Hart, kept all the daily logs. Check out the highlighted number." She flipped to the last page of the packet. "And now, take a look at the copy of the actual credit card receipt with the customer's signature."

Derek whistled and Leland pursed his lips. For about a minute, the only sound in the room was the rustle of papers being flipped back and forth. Alice could practically feel the crackling energy being generated by two brilliant minds working out the implications of her discovery.

Then the men exchanged a long look across the table.

"What does that look mean?" Alice asked, unable to read the silent communication.

"This isn't a bug." Leland's tone was harsh, his accent almost undetectable.

Derek nodded again.

"Not a bug? But the end-of-the-month report is wrong. You can see it right here." She jabbed at the papers with her finger. There was no way this wasn't a software issue.

"He means it's deliberate," Derek said.

"Deliberate?" Alice was bewildered. "Why would anyone deliberately throw the total off by $3.37?"

"They're siphoning off the money into another account, probably offshore," Derek said, his expression grim. "They're stealing from all their clients."

Chapter 7

"Wait, you think that Myron Barsky is stealing $3.37 from the Mane Attraction?" Alice couldn't wrap her mind around their conclusion.

"And $2.59 from Sparkle, $3.85 from Work It Out, $4.12 from Nowak Plumbing Supply," Derek said. "It's cumulative."

A delicious shiver of gratification ran through her as he quoted the exact amounts of all the discrepancies. Somehow it made her feel that he was paying attention not just to her bookkeeping problem but to her, even though she knew that was slightly crazy. "But only once every four or five months?" she said. "It hardly seems worth it."

"They appear to have sold thousands of copies of this software, possibly worldwide," Leland said.

Derek sat back. "It's a clever scheme when you think about it. They target individual small businesses whose P&Ls are only important to the owners. Most of them probably handle their own books or have a family member do them, so they're not going to sweat over an occasional tiny discrepancy the way Alice did."

"In addition, they wouldn't share the fact that they had the occasional discrepancy with anyone else, so no one would see a pattern. Except Alice." Leland smiled at her with approval warming his eyes. It felt like a major pat on the back.

She was horrified by the dishonesty of it. And then she was guilt-ridden by her part in the deception. "That's why it was so inexpensive for such a sophisticated software package. The low price was the one thing that made me leery of recommending it to my clients. It seemed too good to be true." She laughed without amusement. "And it was."

"Don't beat yourself up." Derek covered her hand where it lay on the table and gave it a brief squeeze of comfort. "You did the proper due diligence."

The warmth of his skin, the controlled strength of his grip, even the realization that he was touching her sent a roil of delicious heat bubbling through her body and blew every fuse in her brain. When he released her hand and turned to Leland, she nearly wept at the loss.

Keeping her hand exactly where it lay—in case Derek might want to touch it again—she tried to focus on the conversation while she waited for her heartbeat to settle back into a normal rhythm.

Derek's words began to filter through the haze of longing. Something about having a problem. And he was frowning. "Alice might be on Barsky's radar after she questioned the hotel manager," he said.

But Alice had met the hotel manager so she was sure he wasn't an issue. "I told him I wanted to buy the software, not that I had a problem with it. That wouldn't send up any red . . ." Alice trailed off as she remembered something that *would* send up red flags. "Darn it! I posted a question about the discrepancies on a BalanceTrakR help forum the same day I applied to your SBI. Once you got involved, I forgot all about it."

Derek muttered a low curse as Alice flipped open her laptop and searched for her question. "That's weird," she said, scrolling through the site. "It's not here. I swear this is the right forum. I guess that's why I didn't receive notification of an answer."

"Someone's got to be monitoring the posts, then." Leland scowled at his screen. "That's bad news."

"We're going to have to throw the cloak of KRG firmly around your shoulders," Derek said. "And then we have to find out who these people are."

"How will cloaking me in KRG help?" Alice asked, although she loved the mental image of Derek swirling his cape around her shoulders and then sweeping her up onto his horse. "And how do you do that anyway?"

"We are a well-established firm with both clout and resources," Derek said. "If we make it known that you're working for us, your reputation will be protected."

"How are you going to let BalanceTrakR know that?" she asked.

"We are going to visit their headquarters in Texas," Derek explained.

"Because KRG is interested in investing in BalanceTrakR," Leland said, his patrician face lit with interest in creating a plausible story. "You were doing some research into the software for us."

Derek frowned and drummed his fingers on the shiny wood of the table. "We need to create a reason KRG would hire you to look into software we were interested in."

She felt the implication like a blow. Because they had far more qualified people already on staff to do that. "You didn't want BalanceTrakR to know you were interested so you went outside the firm."

"That's a given but we need a connection to you. My understanding is that you don't regularly consult for other companies."

"Oh, right." She felt a little better. "Maybe a school connection with one of your employees?" Cofferwood itself was small, but it spilled its students into a regional high school.

"That could work. Send me an email with every school you attended. Might as well add summer camps, sports, hobbies, anything with an organized group, and the dates. I'll have HR try to find a match."

Alice nodded. "What about my question on the help forum?"

"A test," Derek said decisively. "To see if anyone responded with issues."

"And the fact that it got deleted?" Alice was enjoying their construction of the fictional scenario. Myron Barsky and his criminal compatriots wouldn't know what hit them.

"Puzzling . . . and one of the questions we want to ask them about on our visit," Derek said with an arrogant smile that showed he was envisioning how he would play it at the meeting.

"It would be interesting to hear how they get around that," Alice said, wishing she could be a fly on the wall when Derek and Leland called on the software company.

"You'll hear it," Derek said. "You're coming with me."

A swirl of exhilaration and nerves shot through her. She would be traveling to Texas with Derek, whose touch she now craved. She pulled herself together. "I thought you meant Leland," she said.

"Leland isn't the person in the crosshairs," Derek said, shooting his partner a reproving glance.

Would they go just for the day or spend a night? The possibility of sleeping in a hotel room next to Derek's lit up all the wrong parts of her body.

Leland folded his laptops shut before he stood up, tucking them under his surprisingly well-muscled arms. She'd expected a computer wizard to be less fit. "I'll start digging into the guts of BalanceTrakR. You'll need to know who and what we're dealing with before you beard the lion in his den."

"When will we be going?" Alice asked, trying to keep her mind on the business side of this.

Derek turned to Leland.

"Give me a couple of days," the computer expert said. "I have a few other projects I'm in the middle of."

"We also need to get Tully up to speed," Derek said. "He'll have ideas about how to handle the legal side of this."

Alice recalled that Tully Gibson was the *G* in KRG. "He's a lawyer?" she asked.

"He's former FBI," Leland said. "He'll know what kind of proof is needed to take these people down. Once I figure out who they are." He stopped in the doorway briefly, his casual attire contrasting with the polished wood and etched glass of the expensively appointed conference room. "We may need him for other reasons as well."

A look passed between the two men that Alice couldn't quite read, but it was not a happy one.

As Leland exited, Derek pushed his chair back and swiveled to face Alice. "I'm sorry to drag you to Texas on short notice, but I want to get you protected as soon as possible. Then we can let Leland and Tully handle the rest of the problem."

Disappointment hollowed out her chest at the reminder that Derek would be jetting off to Asia sometime soon, leaving her to finish the project with his partners.

He leaned forward. "You've done an amazing job, you know. Very few people would have bothered to even try to track down the shortfall. You've uncovered a significant crime."

He was so close, close enough that his body stirred the air around her so it stroked over her skin.

She yanked her mind back into focus. He had expressed his admiration for her *work*. "It's hard to see it as significant when you look at the size of the numbers," she said, shaking her head. "All but one of my clients said they didn't care about the shortfall and to just let it go."

"But we don't know how often the software would skim once it got started. Or whether the amounts would increase."

Alice straightened as his words ripped away the sensual haze fogging her brain. "I never considered that scenario. It could hurt my clients, even cripple some of them. Myron Barsky is a horrible human being." When she thought of his limp handshake, she had a hard time imagining that he was a criminal mastermind, but maybe the man striding around the stage, touting the brilliance of his software to a rapt audience, might be capable of stealing.

"Not so insignificant, is it?"

She pulled in a deep breath and held it, trying to retain the hint of starch from his snowy-white shirt and the clean natural fragrance that was uniquely his own without the overlay of a cologne or soap.

He seemed to be searching her face for something. She wondered if he noticed her violet perfume. In a fit of nervous anticipation, she'd sprayed on more right before the limousine had picked her up.

"Alice . . ." She could swear she felt his breath on her mouth as he spoke her name and stopped. She could see the tiny lines at the corners of his eyes and the texture of his skin stretching over his cheekbones. The urge to touch him made her dizzy with its intensity.

"I . . . what?"

"You are extraordinary," he said. For a moment, he held her gaze, as though he was waiting for something. Alice froze, torn between wanting to feel the texture of his lips and fearing the humiliation of his reaction if she offered hers.

Derek leaned back in his chair.

Frustration clawed at her. Why hadn't she just leaned a little farther forward to bring their mouths within kissing distance? Or traced a finger along the line of his jaw? Then he could have made the choice as to whether to take it one step farther.

She was such a chicken.

She needed to respond to his compliment, to bring her crazed mind back to business. Because that was what he was talking about when he called her extraordinary, not about any other aspect of her. "Thank you, but I was just doing my job."

He gave her a slow smile that pulled at something low in her belly. "Is that what I meant?"

Her breath hitched. It sounded like Derek Killion might have kissed her if she'd given him the right signal. No, she had to be wrong. It would be unprofessional for both of them. She was imagining things.

His smile faded as though it had never been. "You need to get home, and I need to work on foreign exchange. We'll touch base in the morning."

She gathered up her documents, shoving them into the leather tote without regard for order.

Derek stood, unfolding his tall, suit-clad body from the chair in a way that sizzled across her nerve endings. "I'll walk you to the car."

She shook her head. She needed to recover from the near kiss. So stupid because nothing had actually happened, yet she still felt shaken to her toes. When he started to object, she held up her hand. "I appreciate your gallantry, but I can get from here to the street without your help."

However, he walked beside her to the elevator and waited until the door slid open before giving her a slight bow accompanied by what seemed like a self-mocking smile. "Good night, Alice."

When the elevator door closed, she put on her best upper-crust British accent and said, "Good night, Mr. Beaumaris."

Derek turned away and stopped, crossing his arms and staring sightlessly at the KRG logo behind the reception desk.

He'd almost kissed Alice in the conference room. She'd been so close, her violet scent floating in the air between them, the waves of her thick hair picking up glints of light, even though it was pulled into a knot on the back of her head. He'd nearly leaned in and buried his fingers in that twist of gleaming silk so he could angle her lips to meet his. He'd wanted to taste the sweetness and brilliance of her.

What was it about her that tempted him to break all the rules of professionalism he had adhered to for his entire career?

Was it Alice's mind? He found intelligent women attractive. Courtney had been academically impressive. *Magna cum laude* at Yale. *Law Review* at Harvard.

Of course, Alice wasn't just smart. She was passionate. She took the BalanceTrakR issue as personally as he did. Using numbers for evil was an affront to her on an almost moral level.

Alice also cared about her customers in a personal way. She wanted their financial affairs to be in order because each one mattered to her. Courtney hadn't given a damn about her clients; she'd viewed them as nothing more than a means to earning the prestige of being a partner.

Then there was Alice's belief that Myron Barsky would be grateful to have the error in his software pointed out to him. Derek might once have thought that, back in the early days of KRG. Now he'd seen too much shady dealing to assume people wanted to fix things because it was the right thing to do. Alice reminded him that there were people in the business world who took the high road, not because they would get caught if they didn't, but because they couldn't imagine doing their job any other way.

But that belief blinded her to the darker side of the business world. She had dived into the plans for taking down Barsky with an innocent enthusiasm that worried Derek. She didn't understand how vicious criminals could be when protecting their profits. Barsky and his ilk would think nothing of destroying her reputation. He'd seen it happen with whistle-blowers in corporations.

He frowned. He hoped the protection of KRG would be enough to shield Alice from Barsky. Which reminded him about their upcoming trip to Texas and six hours in a private jet with the temptation of Alice right beside him in the cabin. He would need to spend that time on the Argon project but he wasn't sure he could keep his focus with the scent of violets circulating through the jet's air system.

What would Alice do if he kissed her? For a moment in the conference room, he'd thought she would close that small space between them. He'd seen something in her face, an awareness that matched his own, and he'd hoped she would meet him halfway. But she'd remained still, and somehow he'd found the willpower to sit back in his chair.

Maybe the shadow cast by the fiasco of his engagement had stopped him. Or maybe it was because if he kissed Alice, he wasn't sure he would have stopped there.

He had a vision of her lying across the conference table, naked, her pale, smooth skin glowing against the zebrawood's dark grain, while he stood between her thighs and buried himself inside her. He could almost feel the sweet curve of her breasts under his palms and the wet, hot silk of her around his cock.

He groaned as he felt himself begin to harden. But the picture was so delicious that he enjoyed it a little longer before he forced himself to banish it and head for his office.

The plane ride to Texas was going to be an exercise in self-control.

Chapter 8

Alice's dreams were sweaty, ecstasy-inducing sex scenes with Derek as the leading man. Sometimes he took off his suit and sometimes he took off his Regency tailcoat, but underneath there was always a body that sent Alice's blood sizzling through her veins. She woke up with her sheets twisted around her legs and two cats blinking at her disapprovingly from the chaise longue.

"Sorry, fellows," she said, disentangling herself and getting to her feet.

She should take a cold shower to kill the sexual arousal humming through her. Instead, she threw on a sweatshirt over her pajamas and went to the kitchen for a mug of coffee and a dose of reality.

In the cold light of morning, she tried to convince herself that she'd only imagined Derek had wanted to kiss her. Somehow she had misinterpreted his admiration for her meticulous bookkeeping as something warmer and more personal.

She wanted to burrow back into her fantasyland where Derek looked at her with lust in his eyes. Where he ripped his tie out of his shirt collar like he had last night. Where he yanked open his shirt and then came down on top of her, so she could feel his skin against her bare breasts. They were bare in her dreams because he had slowly unbuttoned her blouse and unfastened her bra with those big, capable hands.

But what if she had been right about last night's meeting? If he'd kissed her, then what? She'd be in over her head with a man like Derek. He wasn't interested in something long term or emotionally meaningful. She would be merely the indulgence of a moment's impulse.

And what would be so bad about that? Wasn't her attraction to him based on his looks? She was just as shallow as she was making him out to be.

She shook her head. She couldn't fool herself, just as she hadn't fooled Natalie. He had seduced her in ways that had nothing to do with his looks. Not that he'd meant to be seductive. Most women wouldn't find it hot that he could remember every shortfall for every one of her clients, yet it had made her insides melt like snow falling into a hot spring.

Time to turn her overheated brain to a useful task.

A half an hour later, her coffee mug was empty and Alice had documented every organization and activity she'd participated in to date. As she proofread the list, embarrassment washed through her. Someone as good at discerning patterns as Derek was would easily see the extreme ups and downs of her stepfather's financial affairs.

Two summers of sleepaway camp during a boom in the market for commercial office space. The next three summers were spent at the free town rec program because Stu hadn't foreseen the downturn in that market. Alice had started ballet class and figure skating lessons but had to give them up when Stu's insurance scheme took a hit. Both of those classes had been her mother's idea to make her more graceful.

It was also her mother's idea to talk Stu into providing tennis lessons for his stepdaughter because Gabrielle thought tennis dresses were becoming to every woman. Those lessons gave Alice's mother an excuse to hang around the country club and the good-looking young pro who taught them. Alice hadn't hated that as much as she'd expected because the tennis outfits made her feel stylish and she got to go swimming in the club's pool afterward. A lot of cute boys belonged to that particular club. However, the tennis racket was collecting dust in less than six months. Stu had lost his shirt on a start-up that he'd gotten an inside tip about.

Somehow, it never occurred to Gabrielle to get a job herself. She believed that beautiful people did not need to work because sharing their beauty was all they owed the world.

Maybe it was a good thing that Alice hadn't inherited her mother's stunning good looks. She'd be starving.

Of course, Derek's success as an accounting expert proved that not every beautiful human being expected to skate by on his looks. Maybe Natalie was right that she needed to give him more credit.

Alice shook off her reverie and hit "Send."

As she stuck a pod of toffee nut in the coffee maker, she caught her reflection in the shiny side of the stainless steel toaster oven. Her hair looked like a rat's nest, her pale skin demonstrated a lack of sunlight, and her pink hoodie clashed with her red plaid pajama pants.

"You sexy vixen, you!" she said to her reflection.

She stared at herself for a long moment. Before she could come to her senses, she scooped her phone off the counter to call in expert help, even though she feared she would regret it.

Her call was answered on the first ring.

Alice said, "Hello, Mother."

Gabrielle perched on a peach upholstered chair in the capacious dressing room of Linnea's Boutique, her long, capri-clad legs crossed, a kitten-heeled silver mule dangling off her toe. She gestured with the glass of white wine she held in her right hand. "My daughter needs something professional but with sex appeal. I was thinking a pencil skirt with a subtle slit, a tailored blouse that's not quite opaque, and some lacy lingerie to give her a feeling of sexual power."

As Alice squirmed at her mother's not-at-all-subtle description of what she was looking for, Linnea nodded and assessed Alice with what felt like a merciless eye.

"No need for the lingerie, Mom. I've got that covered," Alice said, already wondering what she'd let herself in for.

"New lingerie always gives a woman confidence."

"I have plenty of confidence," Alice protested, resisting the urge to tuck in her butt as Linnea walked around behind her, still assessing.

Gabrielle took a sip of her wine and ignored her daughter, as usual. When Linnea left to gather potential outfits, Alice's mother said, "Let me help you, just this once. I want you to be happy."

Happy? That wasn't really what Alice was expecting from Derek. She tried to find the putdown in her mother's words but couldn't. "I appreciate that, Mom."

"It's the man you had lunch with at the diner, isn't it?" Gabrielle said. "I hear he's better looking than Ryan Reynolds."

Alice had been deliberately vague about why she'd asked her mother for help with buying an outfit. She should have known that the suburban grapevine would carry the news about Derek to her mother. At least now she knew why her mother was being supportive. Her plain daughter had managed to attract the attention of a good-looking man.

Alice sighed and said with heavy irony, "Yes, he's quite good-looking, but I admire him for his talent with numbers."

Gabrielle's face lit up. "Then he's perfect for you."

Maybe that was true but it didn't mean that she was perfect for him.

"Who is he?" Gabrielle asked.

The need to impress her mother rose up and overwhelmed her better judgment. "Derek Killion, a founding partner of KRG Consulting. We're working on a project together."

Gabrielle whipped out her cell phone and tapped away with one thumb. Her eyes narrowed as she swiped a few times. Then she sat back, smiled, and took a sip of her wine. "KRG is a big deal in your world, isn't it?"

"Kind of, yes." Alice barely stopped herself from shrugging like the teenager her mother always reduced her to.

"How far beyond professional has the relationship gone?"

Leave it to Gabrielle to get to the crux of the matter. "Not at all."

Her mother looked disappointed.

"He almost kissed me last night," Alice said with a certainty she didn't quite feel.

Gabrielle's expression lightened. "So we need to find an outfit that will encourage him to carry through the next time."

Alice nodded, even though it sounded worse when her mother said it out loud. Alice knew her mother wasn't the best role model, but right now she needed support for doing the irresponsible thing.

Linnea returned with a gilded rolling rack hung with clothing, prompting Gabrielle to plunk down her wineglass and stride over. She examined each article of clothing with a steely eye before she sorted out the possibilities at high speed.

Alice watched in fascination. This was her mother in full professional mode.

Her mother turned and shocked Alice by smiling. "I've been waiting so long to do this."

Alice tentatively returned the smile. If all it took was a shopping trip to earn Gabrielle's approval, maybe she should try harder to share her mother's interests.

Her mother's smile evaporated as she pulled a couple of garments off the rack. "Now take off your clothes."

By the time the Lexus pulled into the driveway of her town house, Alice felt as though she'd been picked up by a tornado and whirled around for hours.

The number of bags sitting in the car's trunk was beyond anything Alice had expected when she'd asked her mother to give her some fashion advice. However, Gabrielle had insisted on treating Alice to four entirely new outfits, including shoes, handbags, and lingerie.

Alice had accepted her mother's generosity because Gabrielle had muted her usual criticism and instead focused on what was good about Alice's looks, a startling change that Alice still viewed with wariness. However, while Gabrielle debated the merits of one skirt over another, Alice had felt like a daughter rather than a disappointment.

"Thanks so—" Alice started to say.

"I'll help you with the bags," her mother said, opening her door and sliding gracefully out. As they unloaded their purchases, she added, "Don't forget that the rose lingerie goes under the white blouse. The pale gray is for the blue blouse."

"Got it." Alice knew that already.

"Make sure to wear your contact lenses, not your glasses," Gabrielle said.

Alice almost rolled her eyes since she had on her contacts at that moment. "I only wear my glasses when I'm working on the computer for long stretches of time."

"Well, your relationship with Derek started with work, so I just thought I'd mention it."

They trundled the goodies into Alice's hall and plopped them onto the floor. Gabrielle stood awkwardly, something her mother rarely did. She took a deep breath. "I hope we can do that again. I enjoyed it."

"I did too." Alice was surprised to find that was true, although she would need some time to recover. "Thank you so much for treating me to all this." She waved to the bags strewn around the small space.

"It meant a lot to me when you called to ask for my help." Alice was shocked to see that her mother's eyes were glistening with unshed tears. "I didn't think I had anything to offer you."

Guilt and shame speared through Alice. Wrapped as she was in the serene confidence of her astonishing beauty, Gabrielle had always seemed impervious to Alice's feelings about her. "I'm sorry, Mom. I felt the same way about you."

Her mother blinked several times. "I guess we haven't communicated well. That's my fault."

Alice shook her head. "I think we can share the blame. After all, I'm an adult."

Her mother tried for a smile but it wavered. "I'm so proud of you. You're so smart and talented. Really, the only thing I do better than you is makeup."

Alice dutifully chuckled to help her mother through the oddly emotional moment. She wasn't sure what was going on with Gabrielle but maybe it signaled some improvement in the future of their relationship.

"This man, this Derek Killion," her mother said. "He had better be good to you. Or I will have something to say to him."

"We're not really far enough along to worry about Derek being good to me," Alice said, afraid her mother was expecting too much from a relationship that might never even begin.

"Have lunch with me next week," Gabrielle said. "So I can find out if the outfits worked."

"Mom, I'm not going to share that kind of information with you."

Gabrielle's smile was smug. "Trust me, I'll be able to tell. Just be careful." Her mother's expression turned sober. "Men can be real shits."

Alice lay on the mat in the gym, a two-hundred-pound trainer named Anthony straddling her, while Dawn yelled, "Brace your feet and shove up with your hips. Hard! Then roll."

Alice thrust her hips up, her thigh muscles screaming with exhaustion. Miraculously, Anthony toppled off her while she frantically scrambled away in the opposite direction.

"That's what I'm talking about," Dawn said, pumping a fist.

Alice sprawled on her back, sweating and gasping for breath. "Anthony, please tell me you didn't go easy on me."

"No way," he said, springing to his feet with annoying ease and bending down to offer her a hand. "You knocked me off good."

"No, thanks," Alice said, rolling her head from side to side in refusal of his offer. "I need to lie here a little longer and savor my triumph."

"Okay, your reward is that we'll end the session five minutes early." Dawn clapped Anthony on his muscle-carved shoulder. "Appreciate your help."

Dawn sat down cross-legged on the mat, her straight, nearly black hair pulled back in a ponytail and her olive skin glowing against the turquoise tank top the gym's trainers wore as a uniform. Not that she had broken a sweat, despite demonstrating the proper way to do every one of the self-defense moves she'd been forcing Alice to practice over and over again. "So what's got you so revved up? You worried about something?"

Alice almost laughed at how pinpoint accurate Dawn's two questions were. Derek had her revved up and Myron Barsky had her worried. "How did you know?"

Dawn moved a water bottle within reach of Alice's right hand. "You've never flipped Anthony off you like that before. You put some real conviction into your moves tonight."

"Remember the shortfall in the gym's books that I told you about?" Alice flopped onto her side and braced herself up on one elbow. "This is just between you and me right now, but we're pretty sure it's deliberate theft by the software company."

"They stole—what was it?—three bucks? Why?"

"We're still working on that. And it was $3.85." Alice took a long swallow of deliciously cold water.

"'We'? Who's 'we'?"

So Natalie hadn't told Dawn about Derek. Alice launched into an abbreviated explanation of KRG, the SBI, and Myron Barsky's apparent perfidy.

When she paused, Dawn whistled and shook her head. "That's a lot of trouble for a few dollars, even if it's from a bunch of companies. But a criminal is a criminal, no matter how little he steals. You're smart to brush up on your self-protection."

"Even though it turns eighty percent of my body black and blue?" She hoped the bruises wouldn't show up any place that Derek might see.

"You'll thank me when some crazy Russian hacker has you in a choke hold and you know how to escape."

"I just can't believe such a computer geek would turn violent." She took another gulp of water as her breathing settled down to normal.

The notes of the minuet wafted up from the gym bag perched on a bench near the mat. Alice groaned at the thought of moving but forced herself off the floor to grab her cell phone. She glanced at the caller ID and nearly dropped her water bottle on the floor as she swiped to answer.

"Hi, Derek," she said, trying to keep her tone casual while her body pulsed with awareness.

"Is this Alice Thurber, forensic bookkeeper?" His deep voice held a teasing note.

"You know it is."

"I was expecting the official greeting, so I just wanted to confirm your identity." He was definitely teasing her.

"I figured we were past that, especially at this hour."

"Is it too late to call?" He sounded guilty.

"Of course not!" She checked the gym's wall clock. It was eight o'clock. "I just meant it's after normal people's business hours. But I know you guys at KRG don't keep to those."

"Good." There was a pause. "I just got the information about how we can connect you with KRG. I thought it might be useful to go over it in person, as well as other aspects of our cover story."

A thrill of exhilaration spiraled through her. She would see him in person before their trip to Texas.

"And I have a craving for one of Nick's Specialty Burgers," he continued. "Any chance we could have a late dinner in Cofferwood?"

"You mean tonight?"

"Short notice, I know—"

"No, it's fine," she interrupted. "I just wanted to be clear on when." And she couldn't believe her good luck.

"I'm leaving in five minutes. I'll text you when I have a better idea of how the traffic will affect my arrival time." Another pause. "I look forward to seeing you."

His words were the standard courteous sign-off but his tone held a low, seductive hint of something more than business and a burger. She felt it cascade through her abused body in a ripple of exhilaration.

She had been right last night. He *had* wanted to kiss her. The knowledge fanned the hot anticipation already coursing through her veins.

Tonight if he leaned toward her, she was going to meet him halfway. In fact, she might just lean toward him first.

When she disconnected, Dawn plunked down on the bench beside Alice's bag. "Okay, there was a whole lot of interesting body language going on during that call. What gives?"

Alice had forgotten about Dawn's superpower: her friend had a hyperawareness of people's posture and gestures. She could read emotion from them.

"That was Derek Killion, the consultant I told you about." Alice waited to hear what she might have revealed to Dawn just by her stance.

A smile tugged at the corners of Dawn's full lips. "You're holding out on me, girlfriend. He's not just a consultant. You like him."

"I admire him. He's brilliant and successful." And she wanted to kiss him. "Anyway, I have to go."

"Because . . ." Dawn crossed her toned arms and waited.

"Oh, fine! Because he's coming out here to discuss the BalanceTrakR case."

"At this hour?"

"He's very dedicated to his work." Alice caved. "And he likes Nick's Specialty Burger."

"Aha!" Dawn jumped to her feet. "I'm off for the night, so I'm coming with you. Not to Nick's, just to your house to get the rest of the story."

"Even better, you can help me decide what to wear." Alice thrust her sweat-dampened towel and empty water bottle into her duffel.

"That will take about thirty seconds," Dawn said. "Your wardrobe isn't exactly massive."

"Mother and I went shopping today."

Dawn had been shrugging into her hoodie but at that she stopped with one arm in and one out. "Has hell frozen over?"

"Sometimes you have to sell your soul to the devil when you need help."

"Gabrielle does know clothes," Dawn admitted, zipping her hoodie. "But I'm sure you paid for it."

"I think I disarmed her by asking for her advice. Then I played to her strength so she was happy. It went better than expected."

"Huh."

By the time Alice had showered, Dawn had the spoils of the shopping trip laid out on the cream velvet comforter. Alice was so wound up with nervous anticipation that she couldn't think straight, so she was grateful for Dawn's anchoring presence.

Dawn tossed the skirts aside. "Too business-y." She picked up the wispy rose lace bra. "But this will work. Now find your tightest pair of jeans."

After half an hour of trying on and discarding combinations of clothing, Alice stood in front of her mirror in a pair of jeans that hugged the curves of her hips and butt, the white silk blouse her mother had chosen today—which hinted at the lacy bra underneath in the subtlest way—and her new high-heeled black pumps. Dawn had arranged her hair to fall over her shoulders in carefully styled waves and touched up her makeup. Alice added small gold hoop earrings.

Dawn walked in front of her and flicked open the next button down on Alice's blouse. "My work here is done."

"But you can see the edge of my bra if I lean forward even the slightest bit. It's not professional."

"And that's the message you want to send." Dawn gave Alice's shoulders a quick squeeze as she grinned in the mirror. "Knock his pants off."

Alice choked on a laugh and called out a thank-you as her friend whisked out of the room. She started to refasten the button under debate but then let her hands drop again, so the silk fluttered back open over her cleavage.

Dawn was right. She wanted Derek to get the message loud and clear. If he chose not to take her up on it, then she would know where she stood with him.

ᴖ

Derek jogged up Alice's front steps, attributing his eagerness to the long ride spent wrestling with the Argon project. When she opened the door with her glorious hair billowing over her shoulders and her tempting curves wrapped in denim, he couldn't fool himself any longer. He wanted this woman. He imagined winding his fingers into the fall of her hair so he could tilt back her head and explore the valley just visible between her breasts. Or fill his palms with the lush roundness of her bottom while he held her tightly against his erection.

"I like the off-duty look," he said, walking into her foyer.

A slight flush climbed her cheeks. He wanted to brush his fingertips over it.

"My work hours tend to be shorter than yours," she said, grabbing a small purse and slinging it over her shoulder. "Are you hungry?"

He allowed a shade of extra meaning to color his words. "My hunger is growing by the minute."

Her blush deepened. She'd heard the innuendo, but she met his gaze straight on. "I've been ravenous since you called." Her voice had a sultry pitch.

Awareness licked along his nerve endings and arrowed into his groin. She was playing the same game. But was she just playing or was she as serious as he was? He offered his arm in a half-mocking gesture so he had an excuse to feel her touch. She gave him a startled look but tucked her hand through his bent elbow and stepped in close.

As her scent wafted past his nostrils, he closed his eyes and inhaled, pulling her essence into his lungs and feeling a stronger stirring low in his belly. She jostled against him slightly as they walked down the steps side by side, and he felt the contact flare through him like an electrical charge. He might skip Nick's Specialty Burger for something that he could consume more quickly.

He waved back the driver and held the car door for Alice himself. As she swung her legs in, he noticed the sexy heels she wore and his arousal surged. Now he regretted his decision to eat dinner first.

However, once in the car, Alice sat upright on her side of the seat, an expanse of leather between them, while she made small talk. Maybe he was wrong about her response to him. He frowned as he stared at the back of the driver's head. He wasn't usually this confused by a woman.

Not to mention that he had too much work to do to be this preoccupied with a sexual attraction. His partners were concerned about his handling of the Argon account, and he hated to admit that they might be right. The Small Business Initiative was his pet project, but it was pulling him away from the business that generated the profits. Leland and Tully could deal with Alice's issue just as capably—if not more so—as he could. It had become a computer-hacking problem, not a numbers manipulation.

Yet he didn't want to hand Alice over to his partners. He felt personally responsible for the difficulties BalanceTrakR might choose to create for her. Leland would not protect her from that as vigorously as Derek would.

And why?

Because Leland didn't want to strip her clothes off and run his hands over her naked skin.

Derek refused to let go of Alice's project because he didn't want to let go of Alice.

So he justified the time he spent with her by saying it was for BalanceTrakR. Why shouldn't he just ask her out like he did other women? In fact, it could be argued that he was crossing the line on a professional relationship.

He faced the truth. He had the disquieting feeling that Alice might turn him down if he asked her out for a social dinner, but she would never say no to a business meeting.

The parking lot at Nick's Diner was half-empty, but the blazing colors of neon gave it a festive air, as always. Alice couldn't remember anything she had said during the ride from her house because after her "ravenous" comment, she'd been debating how provocative she should be. Just her one statement had lit a blaze in Derek's face, making his gray eyes darken and his lips seem fuller and more sensual as they'd curved into a smoky, seductive smile.

She'd been correct about his interest in her, and he'd gotten her return message. Now she was getting cold feet. Was she crazy to sleep with a man who might ruin her for all other men when he left?

As Derek once again offered his arm in that old-fashioned way that made her think of her Regency duke fantasies, she decided that it would be worth the pain. Especially when she felt the solid muscle under the fine navy wool of his suit jacket.

Once they had settled in a booth identical to the one they'd sat in before and placed their order, Alice got the business part of the meeting going. "So, how did KRG decide to engage my invaluable services?"

"You went to high school with Joe Passapera, one of our consultants with a specialty in finance." Derek leaned back against the red vinyl banquette. "He was two years ahead of you."

"Good old Joe. I remember him fondly," Alice joked, although she had no recollection of having ever crossed paths with him. "I think we went to prom together."

Derek chuckled, a rich, deep sound that she wanted to bathe in. "Was he a good dancer?"

"He was fine on the fast dances but he just wanted to sway back and forth during the slow ones."

"What teenage boy doesn't? Dancing is a vertical expression of a horizontal desire." His eyes were smoky with innuendo.

She nearly asked Derek if he'd like to dance right there in the middle of the diner's black-and-white-tile floor because her desire was getting more and more horizontal. "Did Joe and I keep in touch after high school?" she asked instead.

Derek looked a little disappointed at her refusal to flirt with him. "He's going to email you his CV and a current photo so you can figure that out."

She searched her memory again before she shook her head. "I'm surprised we didn't overlap in math club, but I don't remember Joe at all." She took a deep breath. "So I guess you saw the pattern in my childhood activities."

"I didn't look at your background." She felt a slash of disappointment at his lack of interest until he continued. "That was confidential information between you and HR."

So he had respected her privacy. But she'd brought it up so she said, "It isn't a secret." She pulled out her phone and scrolled to the email with the listing of dates, schools, organizations, and activities before handing him her phone.

His fingertips brushed hers and a spark of awareness jumped between them. She could tell he felt it by the way that his attention locked on her before he turned it to the small screen. As he scanned the collection of ballet classes, tennis lessons, camps, and schools, the waitress arrived and slid their plates onto the table with practiced efficiency. The aroma of grease, beef, and fries made Alice salivate.

Derek murmured a distracted thank-you as he scanned her phone. When the waitress left, he glanced up. "You mentioned that your family's financial status, er, changed often."

"Very politely said. My stepfather has never believed in working nine to five. Even worse, he believes he's smarter than everyone else so he always had a can't-lose deal based on information from an inside source. They were generally disastrous." Like the one that had wiped out her college fund.

"But every now and then he succeeded and you got the private camp and the figure skating lessons."

"And then got yanked out of them. It was humiliating so I found the most dependable profession I could."

"And now you need the numbers to always add up."

He got it, as she'd known he would. That was what made him so dangerous. Not his physical perfection or the sexual pull between them, but the understanding.

"If they don't, it undermines my worldview." She gave him a crooked smile to make light of her statement but it was nearly true.

He ignored his burger. "I remember feeling that way once. But when you deal with corporate accounting, things get . . . creative." He looked away so she could see his profile with the slight bump in the bridge of his nose.

"Big numbers, big discrepancies?"

"Big numbers, lots of wiggle room." He turned back to her. "That's why I started the Small Business Initiative. To get back to problems where the answer is clear."

"You longed for a simpler life and instead you got fraud. That'll teach you." Alice cocked one eyebrow at him, trying to lighten the mood.

"But it *is* simpler. We know what's wrong. We just have to figure out how to stop it without damage to you or your clients."

"I'm not convinced Myron Barsky will care about me," Alice said, "but that doesn't mean I'll turn down an all-expenses-paid trip to Dallas."

He picked up his knife to slice his enormous burger in half. "If you're excited about a one-day business jaunt to Texas, I'd like to see how you'd feel about a trip to Paris."

"I would be swooning on the floor." She forked up a bite of Monte Cristo French toast.

He gave her a heavy-lidded look. "Hopefully, I would catch you before you hit the ground. Otherwise I wouldn't be much of a gentleman."

The image of Derek cradling her body against the expanse of his chest—preferably with his shirt unbuttoned so she could feel his skin against her cheek—sent a spiral of yearning through her. "I'll remember to do all my fainting in your vicinity."

"I can swoon quite effectively without hurting myself. Falling with authenticity—usually in a death scene—is one of the things they teach you in acting school." He picked up one-half of his burger.

"I'd like to see that," Alice said. "I guess you can sing too. Didn't you say that your father is a musician?"

"Dad didn't pass on the singing DNA. I was mediocre at best and I'm long out of training."

"Isn't your voice your voice?"

"Not when you don't have a natural talent. You learn all kinds of tricks to make yourself sound passable."

She'd still love to hear him sing in that rich baritone of his. "So you don't even belt out a song in the shower?"

That was a mistake because now she was imagining what his body would look like as water sluiced over the hard muscles she'd felt when she had put her hand on his forearm.

"I don't remember the lyrics so humming is the best I can do," he said, the corners of his lips turning up at some private thought before he took a bite of his burger.

The look of sensual appreciation that made his eyelids half close sent her imagination careening into speculation about his expression during sex.

"You said we needed to get our cover story straight," she said in a rush while shivers of arousal ran through her.

He swallowed, the muscles of his throat rippling in the open neck of his blue button-down shirt. "It's late and this burger is worthy of my full attention. Let's declare the meeting adjourned for tonight."

"Nick's cooking often has that effect on people." They'd barely touched on business, so why had Derek come all the way out to Cofferwood?

"Is it Nick's cooking or the company?" Derek's slow smile sent equal parts of tension and excitement fizzing through her veins.

Now was the time to lean in, if she had the guts. "I'm used to Nick's cooking so it must be you."

She held her breath. Every angle of his face sharpened and he put the burger down on his plate.

"Alice, I want to say something here, out in the open, so you can tell me to go to hell without hesitation."

Confusion froze her brain so that all she could do was stare at him.

"For the last twenty-four hours all I've thought about is how you would taste if I kissed you," he said, his look scorching with intent.

Excitement flared through her. "So I'm not crazy."

"Crazy?" He sounded perplexed.

"Last night you looked at me in a certain way but I thought I was wrong about it. I mean, why would you look at me that way?"

"There are many reasons why." Now his voice held a sexy rasp. "But I need to be sure about your feelings since we have a professional relationship."

"I don't work for you." And their time working together had a rapidly approaching finish date.

His focus was locked on her. "So you are perfectly comfortable with this?"

Should she ask what he meant by "this"? No, better not to put it in words that she might not like. She took a deep breath, wondering if maybe she was, in fact, crazy. After all, Derek had probably kissed many, many women, ones who knew more about kissing than Alice did. "'Comfortable' would be the wrong word. Not nearly strong enough. Don't you want me to be, I don't know, panting or something?" She was babbling because she was nervous. *Not afraid-nervous, excited-nervous.* Dear God, she was even babbling to herself.

His eyes lost none of their intensity but amusement glinted in them too.

"Panting might be more than I could aspire to." He pulled a large bill out of his wallet and tossed it on the table. "Shall we?" He stood and held out his hand to her.

For a split second she hesitated. Once she touched him, she wasn't going to be satisfied with just kissing.

She reached out and their palms met, the contact making her hiss in a breath as sensation poured through her body. His skin was warm and dry, his grip firm without being overwhelming. He drew her up from the banquette so that she stood only a whisper away from him. She tilted her head back and found his eyes blazing as he stared down at her mouth. A tiny whimper tore itself from the back of her throat as her insides turned liquid with pure want. Luckily, the noise of the diner muffled it enough that she didn't think Derek had heard it.

She walked beside him through the diner, reveling in the way women's heads turned as they passed, savoring an odd surge of gratification that Derek was claiming her in public. She did her best to act as though it wasn't a big deal, and that she wasn't quaking with a swirling jumble of insecurity, want, and residual surprise.

The limo waited in the parking lot, its dark paint distorting the reflections of the neon signs into odd squiggles. Derek swung the door open and helped her into the car, sliding in beside her without releasing her hand.

He sat close so their thighs and shoulders grazed. When the limo eased into motion, Derek lifted the back of her hand to his mouth and brushed his lips across her knuckles, sending sparks shimmering across her skin. Then he settled their hands on the hard muscle of his thigh before he sent her a smile that glinted even in the dimness of the car's interior. "Does this remind you of prom with Joe?" The rasp in his voice was still there.

"My real prom limo had about eight kids smashed into it," she said, hearing the breathless edge in her own voice. "So this is very different."

He began to stroke the back of her hand with his thumb, a gentle friction that ran up her arm and tightened her nipples.

One small touch and she was about to erupt. What would happen when he kissed her?

"Are you doing this on purpose?"

"What am I doing?"

"Building the tension."

"Maybe . . ." He moved closer to her, so their bodies came into solid contact from knee to shoulder.

Alice gave him a look, although she wasn't sure if he could see it. "That was not subtle."

"Just adding fuel to the fire." He shifted his grip so his thumb drew circles in the hollow of her palm. "It makes for a more satisfying explosion."

She scooted an inch away from him. "Now you're just playing a part."

"What part would that be?"

"The silver-tongued seducer."

He gave a deep chuckle. "I like 'silver-tongued.'"

"Enough!" she said on a strangled laugh, but his light banter eased some of her nerves.

When the limo floated to a halt in front of her town house, Derek had the car door open and was helping her onto the sidewalk before her nerves could clutch again.

He leaned in to say something to the driver that she didn't hear because she was imagining what it would be like to have Derek in her bedroom. Thank God she'd hurled all her rejected outfits into her closet and closed the door.

He released her hand and slid his arm around her waist to guide her up the walkway to her front door. The place where his hand rested on her hip felt as though it was permanently branded by the heat radiating through her clothes.

She managed to get the key out of her bag and into the lock without a fumble, which was miraculous with him so close behind her that she could feel the brush of his suit jacket against her back.

As soon as they were inside and the front door was closed, he turned her into him and banded his other arm around her waist.

"At the diner, you asked me why I looked at you that way." He nuzzled back her hair and kissed her neck just behind her earlobe, his lips firm and smooth against the skin. Shivers rippled through her as he whispered, "Because those gold hoops dangling from your ears drove me crazy with wanting to feel the skin right here." He kissed her there again. "And inhale your scent of violets."

"You know what perfume I wear," she murmured.

He brushed his nose against her neck, inhaling audibly. "It suits you in some ways, but tonight it needs a layer of roses. Deep . . . red . . . roses." His breath whispered over her skin with each word.

Did that mean that he expected her to be an experienced lover? Had his fiancée worn some exotic perfume that was far more sophisticated than her violets? Tendrils of self-doubt tugged at her shaky confidence.

He dragged his lips along the line of her jaw and then down to the hollow at the base of her throat, the silk of his hair tickling her chin. "I wanted to kiss you because when you talked about swooning, I imagined what your body would feel like in my arms. And I wanted to find out."

She forgot all about perfume. "I want that too. To touch you." She raised her free hand to slide it under his jacket, his heartbeat thudding against her palm.

The tip of his tongue grazed her skin. This time she gasped out loud and seized his lapel to pull herself closer against him. When her breasts made contact with the wall of his chest, she arched to increase the pleasure streaking through her.

Then his fingers curled around her bottom, pressing her against his erection, stoking a bonfire between her legs. He lifted his head to claim her mouth, his kiss deep and sensual as he kneaded her buttocks, making her whimper with longing. His fingers were so close to where she really wanted him to touch.

Sheer need made her crook her knee to run it up the outside of his thigh, the feel of solid muscle against her leg making her groan into his mouth.

He hooked his forearm under her knee to support her leg, giving her the freedom to move against that hard ridge under his trousers.

"You're killing me," he growled.

She rocked her hips against his erection again. "You feel very much alive to me."

He flexed his hips to meet hers, making them both moan. "Where's your bedroom?" he demanded as he released her leg.

"Follow me." A shameless hussy who she didn't know existed came to life inside her and put an extra sway in her hips as she climbed the stairs in front of him.

Suddenly embarrassed by her attempt at seduction, she looked over her shoulder and found his gaze locked on her butt. He caught her movement and lifted his eyes. "I'm thinking about how much I want to see those beautiful curves bare."

She nearly stumbled up the next step. "You're good at the verbal foreplay."

"Wait until we get to the nonverbal part," he said with a tight smile.

Desire unfurled in a hot rush between her thighs. She climbed the rest of the stairs faster than she believed she could in sky-high heels.

He stayed close as she turned left toward her bedroom. She caught a streak of black out of the corner of her eye. Sylvester was bolting from the unexpected stranger in his territory.

She had barely walked through the bedroom door when Derek came up behind her and took her by the shoulders, turning her toward the full-length mirror hanging on her closet door. "This is why I looked at you that way," he said, bringing his hands down to slide them under her breasts, so they were nestled in his palms. "Because I wanted to do this."

His touch was magnified by the sight of his hands against the silk of her blouse, turning the moment into an echo chamber of sensual delights. He curled his fingers up to tease the points of her nipples that were visible as they pushed against her blouse. An exquisite shock streaked from her breasts to her belly, igniting a shower of sparks deep within her.

She scrabbled for something to hang on to and reached behind her to find the strength of his thighs, gripping them to keep her knees from buckling. She let her head fall back against his chest but kept her eyes open enough to observe as he played. She'd never watched a man touch her like this, and it made her feel beyond decadent. His erection pushed against her bottom, sending an extra thrill through her.

When he released one breast and slid his hand down to rub his fingers between her legs, her nerve endings lit up all over her body. She was afraid she might come right then.

"Wait!" It came out as a gasp. "I want to touch you. But without all the clothes."

For a moment, he pulled her in tighter so she could feel just how hard his erection was. "I won't try to talk you out of that."

Then he let her go and shrugged out of his jacket, tossing it onto the floor.

Alice smiled, catching his wrists as he reached for the first button on his shirt. "Now I get to take over."

"What is that smile all about?" He lowered his hands to his sides.

"I was wishing you were wearing a neckcloth." Since he wasn't wearing any tie at all, she flicked open the first fastened button to reveal the tempting indent at the base of his neck.

"A what?"

"A neckcloth, like a Regency duke. So I could take my time unwrapping you." Because she was sure this would happen only once.

He made a low sound in the back of his throat that was something between a moan and a growl. "There's always my belt."

"I'll get to that."

She had planned to go slowly—to make the experience last longer—but she couldn't stop herself once she started, unfastening button after button until she reached his waist and yanked the shirttails out of his trousers. She'd known he would be beautiful but the thoroughly male reality of his chest made her stare for a long moment. The surface rose and fell with his slightly ragged breathing.

For a moment, a sense of inadequacy held her immobile, but his beauty overcame her insecurity. She raised her hands, spread her palms, and laid them flat against the slight furring of hair over his pecs. His hair felt soft and springy, his skin warm and satiny, the muscles underneath like water-polished stone, curved and smooth under her hands. The tiny peaks of his nipples went hard at her touch and he blew out an audible breath as she traced a fingertip around them. She nuzzled into the hollow at his throat, inhaling his clean, male scent with the hint of some woodsy soap. With a brazenness that shocked her, she licked him and savored the taste of salt.

"You have two more minutes before I turn the tables," he said, his voice tight with the effort of control.

"In that case . . ." She wasn't going to pass up such an opportunity. She shoved his shirt off his magnificent shoulders before she walked behind him and slid the cotton down his arms to drop on the floor. The indent of his spine and the flex of his deltoids begged her fingers to explore them. As she followed his backbone downward, she giggled. "You have dimples." She outlined them with her fingers.

"You find back dimples amusing?"

"They're . . . unexpected." She skimmed her palms down over his tight buttocks, feeling them clench under the fine wool.

"You have ten seconds left," he said with a rasp.

"That wasn't two minutes." She ran her hands back up along his rib cage and around his trim waist so she could lay her body full length against his back, her cheek pressed to the delicious expanse of his skin.

"You've heard of the theory of relativity. Time speeds up when a beautiful woman is touching you without you being able to touch her."

"But I haven't gotten to your belt." Since her exploration was about to end anyway, she did the most provocative thing she could think of. She let her fingers dance along the ripples of his abdomen before she palmed the erection that pushed against his trousers.

His whole body went tense and a strangled sound came from his throat. Enjoying her power, she slid her hands down the fabric-covered length of him and back up again. A shudder ran through him so she repeated the stroke.

And found herself embracing a whirling dervish when he spun around. "My turn," he said, the buttons of her blouse seeming to fall open magically under his touch. He peeled the silk away and cupped her breasts, his thumbs teasing along the lacy edge of her translucent, rose-colored bra. "So beautiful." He moved his touch to her already taut nipples. A streak of sensual lightning blazed from her breasts to her belly. "So perfect," he murmured before lifting his eyes to hers with a feral smile. "The bra is a delicious surprise, hiding beneath that plain white blouse."

So his ex-fiancée hadn't worn sexy lingerie? Or else she had been so sexy that he expected it from her. Which might imply that he hadn't thought Alice looked sexy.

Her muddled attack of insecurity vaporized when he bent to suck at one nipple through the gossamer fabric, the wet pull of his mouth dragging a long moan from her that ended with a, "Yesssssssss, more!"

Right now Derek found her plenty sexy.

Shifting to the other breast with his mouth, he massaged the damp, peaked nipple with his palm, the dual sensations setting loose a torrent of pure yearning. She sank her fingers into the glorious silk of his hair to hold his head there. Waves of delight washed over and through her as his mouth tugged at her breast.

She whimpered an objection when he pulled away, but it was just to unhook and whip away her bra before he returned. His mouth on her bared skin made her arch back to push her breasts farther into the friction of his lips and tongue. When her hips began to rock in time with his suction, he lifted his head. "There's something else I've imagined." His eyes flared with anticipation.

He turned her toward the mirror again. The eroticism of their two bare torsos on display made her gasp.

She expected him to touch her skin but instead he lifted his hands to her head. "Your hair is glorious," he said as he twined his fingers into it. "But now I want to see it over your breasts."

He gathered her hair from behind her back and draped it over her shoulders, arranging it so that her nipples, still glistening with the moisture from his mouth, showed through the long waves. When he picked up a strand and flicked the end over the sensitive, damp skin, she jerked in surprise at how such a soft touch could jolt electric arousal through her body. He wrapped an arm around her waist to hold her against his erection and flicked at the other nipple. When she'd fantasized about her dukes playing with her hair, they'd never done this, but they clearly lacked Derek's creativity.

"I need to see all of you," he said, dropping her hair and skimming down to the button of her jeans. He tugged it out and ran the zipper down before slipping his hands inside the loosened waistband and pushing her jeans and panties down over her hips to her ankles, baring her abruptly in the mirror. The sight of her naked body on display shocked her. She almost brought her hands around to cover herself but Derek was breathing words of adoration and lust into her ear, dissolving her shyness with molten sexuality.

His hand was splayed over her belly, his fingers just above the place she yearned for him to touch. Yet the imprint of his palm seemed to sink into her, stoking the fire beneath it.

"Please . . . ," she murmured.

"Yes." But he didn't move his hand lower. He bent and scooped her up in his arms, the pressure of skin to skin delicious. He walked to her bed and lowered her onto the comforter before he swiftly eased off her shoes and her jeans.

He reached into his pocket and brought out a condom, which he dropped on the bedside table. The sight of that made her internal muscles ripple with anticipation.

Then he jerked open his belt buckle and shucked off his trousers and briefs.

"Wow!" Alice said on a long breath as she took in the sculptural perfection of him. His muscles were sharply defined without bulging and she understood why his suits fit him so beautifully.

"I like that reaction." He crawled onto the bed to settle on his side. He skimmed one hand down her torso until his fingers slid between her legs, parting her folds and slipping inside without any resistance because she was so wet. "I like this reaction too," he rasped.

As he began to stroke in and out of her with two fingers, he shifted so that he could suck on her breast. A charge of pleasure zinged from her nipple to her belly to her clit to her toes and back again until she was mindless with pure want. "You. Inside me," she panted when she felt herself approaching the crest of orgasm.

Her eyes were closed so she felt rather than saw him reach for the condom and heard the rip of foil. And then his hips spread her thighs, his chest brushed her nipples, and he drove into her with one smooth, deep motion. The feeling of being filled all at once nearly set her off, but she fought it down, needing to prolong the experience. She made a sound of incoherent bliss as he began to flex his hips, his thrusts powerful but sensual.

Opening her eyes, she found the sculpted angles of his face drawn taut and his eyes lit with carnal intent. An unaccustomed sense of her own power surged through her.

Wrapping her arms around his rib cage, she angled her body so he hit just the right spot with every inward stroke. That rhythmic contact, the drag of his skin on her breasts, the tang of his arousal and hers, drove her to that moment of stillness where even time seems to stop. Everything focused on the unfolding deep within her that suddenly slammed into a nuclear blast of a climax. She arched and clenched and cried out his name, every muscle in her body reeling from the force of her orgasm.

He must have been holding on to his control because as soon as she began to come down from her release, he bowed back and shouted as she felt him pumping deep inside her. An echo of pleasure rippled through her before he rolled them so that she was splayed on top of him, his chest heaving underneath her.

"Alice," he murmured, his arms draped over her. "Alice, Alice, Alice."

"That's my name." Her skin glowed with a residual tingle while everything under it seemed fluid with relaxation.

He gave a ghost of a laugh. "It's seared on my brain and a few other body parts."

She smiled and nestled her cheek against his hard chest, feeling quite pleased with herself and him. As his breathing slowed to normal, he began to toy with her hair, smoothing it over her back, twisting his fingers into it, tugging it softly as he fiddled. She hummed with delight, thinking that the many years of keeping it long—with all the work that entailed—had finally paid off in a big way.

He skated one hand down the curve of her back and up the swell of her bottom, his fingertips just fluttering along the valley between her buttocks before he stopped, letting his hand rest there while little thrills flickered through her. She hoped they had a chance to make love again before he left. She'd like to take it more slowly so she could remember the reality of him moving in and on her more vividly. This first time, pure feeling had taken over so her brain had gone blank.

A shiver ran through her as her bare skin began to cool. He squeezed her behind and eased her down beside him before flipping one side of the comforter over them. She rolled halfway onto him, hooking her knee over his thigh and using his shoulder as a pillow.

She lay there, wondering what to say. Her body was completely comfortable with him but her mind was spinning in ways that stole words from her. Should she be light and funny? Should she be honest? The one thing she knew she shouldn't do was ask the questions she really wanted to. Was this something special for him? Or was she just one of many women to whom he gave this kind of mind-blowing delight?

Before she'd spent so much time with him, she would have answered it for herself without a second's hesitation. Anyone with Derek's looks and position had to be a player. But she was sure he'd been as surprised by the chemistry flaring between them as she was.

He'd had qualms about muddying the business side of their relationship. She'd been the one to dismiss them. His concern about the danger to her professional reputation was so genuine that he'd organized a whole trip to Texas when he had other, more important commitments.

In fact, he'd behaved like a decent human being, which had upended all her assumptions. Maybe it was the element of surprise that had shattered the barriers she usually hid behind.

Still, she didn't expect to date him. This was an aberration, an interlude to be savored and tucked away as a memory of the one time she'd forgotten to be a careful, rational bookkeeper.

Her eyelids began to grow heavy as satiation and exhaustion combined to pull her toward sleep. The last thought she had before she surrendered was that she would never regret saying yes to his kiss.

Derek felt Alice slide into sleep, her body softening against his side. That vulnerability tugged at something in his chest. He tucked in his chin so he could inhale the fragrance of her hair, the shy, innocent violets that were at odds with the unexpected passion of her response.

He pulled the comforter farther up to cover her shoulders while he wondered how the hell he'd ended up with a naked Alice snuggled in his arms. In mere days, she'd gone from a name on a form on KRG's website to a wild, sensual lover.

People often had the wrong idea about him. They assumed that he had his pick of women and that he would take full advantage of that. Maybe he had upon occasion in his younger days, but he'd learned that making love to a woman—even one who claimed to want nothing more—created expectations. He had learned the hard way that he didn't have time for that, then or now.

The BalanceTrakR case had taken so much of his time and attention away from the Argon project, yet he had refused to let go of it even before . . . this. Now the possibility of handing it over to his partners was out of the question. His arm tightened around Alice, making her stir momentarily before subsiding with a long exhale.

Uncertainty ripped at him. What did he really know about her? That she loved numbers as much as he did. That she depended on them for order and sanity. That she was dedicated to her job and her clients. That she had an unshakable integrity. That she made his body react with an intensity that almost shocked him.

Not much to base a relationship on.

The thought pulled him up short. He wasn't planning to have a relationship. Courtney had made it clear that his career wasn't compatible with relationships.

Case in point: he would be leaving for Asia in eight days. He had to cram two weeks' worth of work into the period between now and then. There could be no relationship.

By the time he returned from his trip, he expected that both he and Alice would have gotten over this flare of inconvenient attraction.

But he had several more hours to spend in Alice's bed, and he was damned if he was going to waste them. So he shoved the guilt into a distant corner of his brain and feathered his fingers over the curve of her breast, tracing the pink tip until she sighed and rocked against his thigh, the satin between her legs warm and wet.

Chapter 9

Alice stood at the bay window of her kitchen, sipping coffee and watching a squirrel outsmart her supposedly squirrel-proof bird feeder. Watching but not caring because all she could think about was last night with Derek. Her body hummed with satisfaction even though when she moved, there was an occasional twinge. They'd made love once more in the middle of the night and again when Derek started to slip out of the bed just before dawn. Each intimacy had followed a different rhythm and mood. Derek was an inventive lover, but that didn't surprise her. She figured he had a lot of experience.

What did surprise her was his consideration for her and what she could only call his tenderness. He'd almost refused to make love to her the third time, not because he didn't want to—she could feel the physical evidence of his interest pushing against her thigh—but because he was concerned for her well-being. She'd quickly disabused him of any doubts that she could handle it. In the dark, looks didn't matter so she could banish her insecurities; everything was touch and sound and scent.

She smiled as she remembered the sleepy yet urgent quality of that coupling in the wee hours of the morning. He'd twined his fingers with hers, anchoring their hands to the bed on either side of her head while he moved inside her, pushing her to climax with just the angle and flex of his hips and cock. It had been delicious and intense, her muscles clenching around him while her body wanted to arch up from the bed but was held down by his weight and grip. It forced all her focus on the explosion between her legs.

Her breathing grew shallow at the memory.

Reality intruded when Audley jumped onto the table she stood beside. "Hey, you're not allowed up here," Alice said, but she stroked his velvety fur, her mood so glorious that she didn't have it in her to discipline the cat.

When her cell phone danced across the table and sang the minuet, Audley barely twitched. Her cats had learned to take technology in stride. She grabbed the phone, torn between hoping it was Derek and fearing that he was calling to cancel the dinner date they'd set up for that evening. She knew he was under all kinds of pressure with his new project.

A glance at the screen killed the happy glow suffusing her.

"Holy—!" She stopped before the curse word passed her lips. The caller ID was "unknown" but she recognized the phone number.

It was Myron Barsky.

She stared at the ringing, vibrating phone while her mind raced. If she answered it, what would she say? She and Derek didn't have their cover story nailed down since they'd gotten distracted by other matters last night.

Better to let it go to voice mail for now.

It seemed to take forever before the phone went quiet. A notification pinged that she had a message. She waited for several seconds, as though Barsky would somehow know that she had picked up his message immediately.

"Ms. Thurber, I hear from Gary Woertz at the Lipton Hotel that you're looking to buy our BalanceTrakR software. That's good news! Please call me back and we'll get you all set up." A little bit of Texas twang tinged his voice but when she listened closely, there was another accent lurking there. Knowing what she did now, his tone seemed to hold a slightly threatening edge. But she had to be imagining that.

So Woertz had decided he wanted credit for the potential sale to Alice and called Barsky. Derek was not going to be happy. Actually, she wasn't happy either, now that she knew Barsky was a criminal.

Even that might not have worried her so much except for the fact that her question had been removed from the help forum. She hadn't used her full name, but a skilled hacker—which someone at BalanceTrakR was—could easily trace her IP address. Barsky might not know she had a problem with the software but someone at his company most likely did. A twinge of fear tightened around her lungs.

Time to call in the big guns. She hit Derek's number, and he answered as soon as it rang.

"Alice." His baritone seemed to caress her name, fanning to life all the flames quenched by Barsky's call. "There's not a problem with our dinner tonight, is there?"

A short flash of happiness burst inside her because he didn't want her to cancel dinner. But the pinch of anxiety killed it. "Myron Barsky just called me. I didn't answer, so he left a voice mail saying he'd heard I wanted to buy the software and to please call him back."

"Shit!" Derek said the word she'd bitten off. "So your hotel manager wanted to take credit for getting Barsky another sale. You were smart not to answer."

"We never got to discuss our cover story last night, so I didn't know what to say."

"I can't say I regret that."

His admission soothed the edge of unease that gripped her. "Did I say anything about regrets? It was just an explanation."

She had hoped for a chuckle but he clearly wasn't in a laughing mood. "Don't call Barsky back. I'll handle it from here on out. We'll have to expedite the trip to Texas but we should be able to do it in a long day on a chartered jet. How flexible is your schedule?"

A chartered jet? The expense boggled her mind since KRG would get no compensation for the trip. On the other hand, she'd have six hours in private with Derek. A lot could happen in six hours.

"I'm my own boss so I can go anytime, especially since I don't like getting phone calls from embezzlers."

"I like the phone call even less." His tone was somber but then the timbre changed to something hot. "Tonight we'll make sure to go over the cover story *first.*"

Which meant that they'd be doing other things afterward, things that made her knees go weak.

Derek strode into Leland's office with fear for Alice riding on his shoulder. He was getting bad vibes about this whole situation and he hated having Alice at the center of the storm. "Myron Barsky just called Alice's cell phone."

"Shit!" Leland snapped. "That's not good."

"As soon as I can set up a meeting with Barsky and whoever else is in charge of BalanceTrakR, I'm heading for Dallas." Derek dropped into a leather-and-chrome chair set in front of Leland's desk and ran a hand over his face in a gesture of worry. "I should have done it sooner, but I didn't know we were dealing with an out-and-out criminal."

"Given what I saw in the software, I should have spotted it myself." Leland's smooth voice was laced with self-reproach. "I was just as dismissive of Alice's expertise as you were at the beginning. If I'd known how capable she was, I would have taken it more seriously."

Derek held up his hand to stop the apology. "That's exactly why I started the SBI. We've lost touch with the fact that you don't have to work for a high-powered consulting firm to be excellent at your job. Plenty of talented people simply want to be their own boss, to control their own fate."

"Just like us back when," Leland said. "But somehow we ended up here." He swept his hand around the spacious corner office with the spectacular views.

"Hey, I'm proud of where we are but we should never forget where we came from. And that we nearly failed."

Derek remembered how his stomach had heaved the day he'd realized KRG didn't have enough money to meet their tiny payroll. He and his partners had already given up their own salaries to keep the consulting firm limping along. Presenting the news that they were broke to Leland and Tully had been the hardest thing he'd ever done, partly because his father was an unseen presence in the room. His father, who had wanted KRG to fail because it would have proved his point that Derek could just as well have pursued a career in acting. And maybe should go back to it.

He wasn't sure what had driven him harder to pursue the angel investor who had saved them—his partners' disappointment or his father's imminent triumph.

"Amen," Leland said, his expression distant with some private memory of his own.

Derek pulled them back to the present. "Where are you with breaking down the software? Not that I'm trying to rush you, but I figured I'd check in."

"The malware is not in the obvious places, but that doesn't surprise me. Whoever set this up is pretty sophisticated. I'll find it." Leland bared his teeth in a feral smile.

"I have no doubt about that." Derek pushed up from the chair. "I've got to check in with Tully now. He's pretty pissed at both of us for not bringing him in sooner."

"Why don't you let me go to Texas?" Leland said. "I can talk software with Barsky."

Astonishment ripped through Derek. Leland didn't do business trips if he could avoid it. "Why?"

"Because no one but you can handle Argon." Leland looked at him steadily. "Tully and I can handle BalanceTrakR."

White-hot anger blazed through Derek. "You think I can't do both?"

"This issue has become much bigger than giving some expert advice to a small business owner, and you're getting in pretty deep."

"Out of the question," Derek snapped. "I started this and I'm seeing it through."

He stalked out of the office but stopped a few steps down the hallway to take a deep breath. He needed to refocus on the Argon project. He owed it to the client and he owed it to his partners. That didn't mean that he was going to let anyone else go to Texas with Alice but he would spend the hours on the plane working. Alice would understand because she was as dedicated to her clients as he was to his. Oddly, the thought of Alice sitting next to him on the plane while he wrestled with foreign-exchange hedging dissolved most of his irritation and guilt.

He started down the hallway in a less combative state of mind.

When Derek walked in, Tully was on the phone. He held up one finger to indicate he was about to finish, so Derek settled into one of the cowhide-covered chairs that Tully had chosen for his office. The funny thing was that Tully was from Pennsylvania, but he'd adopted a cowboy persona. It suited him somehow.

That got Derek to thinking about Myron Barsky and his Texas headquarters. It had an all-American image that might make his clients feel more trusting . . . like Tully's cowboy facade.

"What's on your mind, partner?" Tully removed his wireless earpiece.

"Alice Thurber got a call from Myron Barsky a little while ago. She's smart so she didn't answer it, but we have to move up the trip to Dallas."

Tully cursed under his breath. "I don't like the combination of the phone call and the deleted question on the forum."

"I don't like that she's in their crosshairs now and we put her there."

Tully shook his head. "Your bookkeeper probably put herself on their radar the minute she posted that question on the help forum. It's a good thing that she came to us with it. At least we can protect her." He tilted his chair back and studied the ceiling. "I want to come with you and check out the players, but that would raise more red flags than it would settle."

"Agreed. Anything in particular you want me to look for?" Other than threats to Alice's well-being. Images from their night together flashed through his mind, retightening the tension in his shoulders.

"I don't want to wire you because they must be pretty tech savvy, so they might screen for that." Tully stood up to pace around the room, his footsteps eerily silent for someone wearing cowboy boots. The man moved like a cat. "See if you can get a tour of the facility. After all, you want to invest in them. Let me know what you see. Listen for foreign languages or accents. Make sure the signage looks permanent. Damn, I wish I could get their faces on camera," he muttered. "I've got a bad feeling about these guys."

Derek felt a jab of unease. "Do I need to worry about more than Alice's business reputation?"

Tully stopped pacing. "Well, we're dealing with folks who are in a position to steal a lot of money and we're planning to stop them. Add to that, Leland says the software is Eastern European or Russian." His jaw hardened. "An agent I know caught a Russian hacker case and let's just say that those assholes didn't have any hesitation about using violence to protect their interests."

"Shit!" Derek leaped out of his chair to take up pacing where Tully had left off, his stomach a knot of fear. "You've got to send a team to protect her now."

"I'll set it up the minute you leave my office," Tully said.

Derek stopped walking as he considered Alice's reaction. "I'm not going to tell her she's being watched. She doesn't understand how risky this could be."

"Maybe if you tell her to be careful where she goes, especially after dark, she'll take it more seriously."

She'd taken it seriously enough to call him rather than Barsky, but Derek wasn't sure she would believe that anyone would harm her physically. Her optimism was one of the things he valued about her. On the other extreme, Tully was trained to see danger everywhere, so maybe he was overreacting. Derek hoped . . .

"I'll give it a try, but Alice has her own views," he said.

"You seem to know her pretty well."

Derek gave his friend and partner a long, level stare.

"Just an observation," Tully said with a shrug.

"She's come to the attention of an unknown criminal organization, so I'm naturally concerned for her welfare." The truth of it kicked him in the gut. "And I don't like it when you're nervous. It doesn't happen often."

Tully grinned. "I'm only nervous because I have to leave the action to a bean counter like you."

◄──────

Alice had showered and was working on a client's books by the time Derek called back. "We're set up to go to Texas on Friday. Can you get away that soon?" he asked without preamble.

"Of course." She was a little hurt by his businesslike tone. "What time?"

"Early. We'll be flying out of Teterboro, so we should leave at six thirty a.m."

We. She liked the sound of that. "Where will we be leaving for the airport from?"

"If you don't object, your place." His voice had softened. "It's closer to Teterboro, with no tunnels or bridges to get through."

"No objections at all," she said as she gave a little wiggle of joy in her chair.

"In fact, I hope you don't mind if I stay at your place tonight too." He sounded oddly uncertain of his welcome.

"Want me to order in dinner from Nick's?"

"My turn to choose the cuisine. I'll bring something with me," Derek said. "In the meantime, be careful about where you go until I get there. Don't let any strangers in the door and don't wander down any dark alleys."

"Do I seem like the kind of person who hangs out in alleys?" But she felt a cold brush of alarm.

He didn't laugh. "No, but you don't seem like the kind of person who exposes embezzlers either. You are a woman of surprises."

He disconnected, leaving her openmouthed at his erroneous description of her. She lived her life to avoid surprises. She avoided risk like the plague.

Until now when risk had somehow found her.

Unease shivered through her as she hit another number on her phone. "Dawn, do you have some time to give me a refresher class on self-defense?"

By the time Derek arrived, Alice had taken a hot shower to ease the bruises Dawn's self-defense moves had inflicted on her, changed her clothes four times, and eaten a banana to silence the hunger grumbles emanating from her stomach. The bruises and hunger were forgotten when Derek stepped through her front door, dropped a large, insulated bag on the floor, and swept her into his arms. He lowered his head to slant his lips against hers until her bones practically melted. Fortunately, she was sandwiched between his big, hard body and the foyer wall so she didn't sink to the floor in a puddle of sheer pleasure.

He lifted his head to leave an inch of space between his mouth and hers. "God, I needed that!" he said.

"Tough day at the office?" she joked, sounding slightly breathless.

"Tough day worrying that you might get waylaid by evil hackers." His hold on her tightened. "I needed to see you in person to know that you're alive and well."

A thrill of equal parts delight and apprehension shivered through her. For the first time, it sank in that his worry about her safety was real.

"Would it make you feel better to know that I took some self-defense lessons at the gym today?"

"My resourceful Alice," he said, pulling away so she could see the concern in his eyes banished by the smile curving his delicious lips. "I should have known that you would go straight at the problem."

"I'm pretty sure that I can take on Myron Barsky now. He's just a computer nerd, after all."

The smile evaporated. "Don't even try. Leave that to me."

"Joking!" She released her grip on his shoulders to hold up her hands palm out. "I'm not a physical kind of gal."

"Now, that is not true, as I have discovered to my deep delight," he said, sliding his hand up between them to palm her breast so she moaned at the sparkle of want that danced through her.

"Okay, *that* kind of physical, yes," she gasped.

He stepped back but interlaced the fingers of one hand with hers. "We need to eat and get our cover story straight before you tempt me into bed."

"We could eat in bed."

He groaned but picked up the food carrier. "Work first. Your safety depends on it."

"You're a hard taskmaster." She led him into the kitchen, relishing the warmth of his hand around hers.

"And this is just the beginning of the tasks I have in mind," he said in a sexy growl that sent arousal shuddering through her.

She'd already set the café table in her bay window and opened a bottle of red wine to let it breathe. She'd splurged on it on the way home from her session with Dawn; she figured Derek was used to the good stuff and also that it might ease the aches created by twisting herself out of various attack holds.

He swung the insulated bag onto the counter and unzipped the top, releasing an aroma of garlic that had her salivating. "Italian!" she said. "Good choice!"

He sent her a glinting smile as he lifted out containers. "I figured if we both ate garlic, we wouldn't mind the aroma that might linger on our breath."

"I love a man with a plan." She opened a container marked "Pappardelle al Limone" and inhaled the delicious scents of lemon and warm pecorino cheese.

"They teach you that planning stuff in business school," he said, releasing another waft of Italian deliciousness as he flipped the top off another container and set it on the counter. "*This* is why I go to Trattoria Paradiso. The artichoke lasagna."

The array of dishes almost exceeded the dimensions of her table, but they wedged them all onto it after she removed the arrangement of Peruvian lilies and Fuji mums she'd also bought on her way home in an attempt to impress Derek with her domestic decorating.

Not surprisingly the scent of food drew Audley into the kitchen. He leaped onto the counter to sniff at the open bag.

"Audley! Off!" Alice admonished. She hoped Derek didn't mind cat paws near his food.

But Derek offered the back of his hand to Audley as a nonthreatening introduction. Clearly, he had been around animals before. "You're a handsome fellow," he said, giving Audley a stroke so the cat's back arched. "You've been keeping your roommate a secret," Derek said to Alice.

"Roommates," she said. "Sylvester is just too shy for even the smell of Italian food to lure him out. They don't attend business meetings because not everyone likes cats."

"Did you consider last night a business meeting?"

"You're the one who pointed out that we are working together." Alice picked up Audley and set him on the floor.

Derek pulled out a chair for her. As she sat, he lifted her hair away from her neck and brushed a kiss on the sensitive skin, saying, "I'm discovering the joys of mixing business with pleasure."

His touch shimmered over her skin. "Keep doing that and we'll never get to work," she said, letting her head fall back so she looked him in the eye, only upside down.

"God, I want to feel your breasts in my hands," he said, his gaze sliding down to where her arched back made her breasts very prominent. Her nipples tightened to hard points that pushed against her lace bra and he sucked in a breath. "But I am going to demonstrate extraordinary self-control."

"If you want credit for that, you're barking up the wrong tree," Alice said as he walked around the table to seat himself, leaving her to imagine the feel of his palms on her aching nipples. "I'm all for postponing work in favor of play."

"Focus," he said, picking up his fork. "The sooner we get through the cover story, the sooner I can make you scream with pure bliss."

"You are not helping," she said on a gasp as longing puddled between her thighs. She took a gulp of wine. "Okay, tell me about your conversation with Barsky."

"Try the artichoke lasagna." He served a helping on her plate. "Let's start with what I told Barsky on the phone about wanting to pay a visit to his headquarters with an eye to recommending his software to our less centralized clients. Maybe even taking a stake in the company to add capabilities for larger clients. I explained that you were doing the advance legwork for us in order to keep our preliminary investigation under wraps."

For the next forty-five minutes, they reviewed the details of KRG's fictitious plan to invest in BalanceTrakR, including Joe Passapera's recommendation of Alice as an independent consultant to the consultants. For some reason, she found that redundancy funny, but it might have been a way to sidestep her increasing concern about the upcoming meeting. Derek's insistence on trying to guess Barsky's every possible reaction and developing a strategy to deal with it drove home how seriously he took the threat to her. It also demonstrated how brilliant he would be at managing high-powered clients.

When he finally declared himself satisfied that they'd covered every angle, she slumped back in her chair, having barely tasted the delicious food in front of her. "I can see why your customers are happy with your work. You're very thorough."

"Says the pot to the kettle." His smile uncoiled some of her nervousness.

"My thoroughness is limited to numbers." But she let his praise soak in. "You've got the psychological aspect figured out too."

"Only because I've had to."

She took a bite of her nearly untouched artichoke lasagna. "Too bad we won't have time for sightseeing. I've never been to Dallas."

He raised an eyebrow. "I don't see why we can't arrange a side trip. I haven't spent time in Dallas for a couple of years myself. Do you mind if we get back here late?"

"You're the one who has a big project."

"I apologize in advance but I'm going to have to work on it during the flight," he said, reaching over to squeeze her hand. "Not the way I would choose to spend six hours on a private jet with you. However, I have an idea about how to show you Dallas."

She fought her disappointment at his dedication to work but she understood it too. It was counterbalanced by the gratification at his willingness to indulge her in a tour of the city.

He swallowed the last of his wine and picked up his plate. "How about saving dessert for later?"

"Depends on how you define dessert," she said, pitching her voice to a low huskiness.

They cleared the table and stowed the remaining food in record time. Then he stripped her jeans off and lifted her onto the kitchen counter to stand between her thighs and fulfill his promise of making her scream.

Chapter 10

As Alice slid into the black limo beside Derek early on Friday morning, she stifled a groan. Maybe that second self-defense lesson she'd taken from Dawn yesterday hadn't been such a great idea, since she had several extra bruises and a sore shoulder. It was funny how she didn't notice them while making love. This morning, though, she wasn't sure she'd be able to escape from even the geeky Myron Barsky.

However, her aches and pains hadn't stopped her from taking extra care, dressing in the blue silk blouse and gray pencil skirt her mother had bought her. Derek, already wearing his custom-tailored navy suit, had sat on the bed, watching her dress, his jaw tight with control. She'd taken her time and smoothed the fabrics over various parts of her body in a slow, sensual dance until he groaned and said he would wait downstairs.

Twisting back and forth in front of the mirror, she had decided to go crazy and substitute earrings that dangled a tiny gold tassel for her usual pearl studs. She had even added a delicate gold chain that sat in the V of her collar. However, since it was a business trip, she coiled her hair up in a tidy bun on the back of her head before she shrugged into a navy jacket.

Now she was going to fly on a private jet. That would be a thrill and a half. A hot shiver ran through her when she added the most important element to the equation: six hours on a private jet with Derek, even if he planned to work the whole time. Of course, she'd brought her laptop with her clients' ledgers too.

As the limo backed out of the driveway in the chilly predawn darkness, he took her hand, interlacing his fingers with hers as he rested it on his thigh. She loved the feel of his warm skin pressed against the vulnerable curves between her fingers. It felt so intimate. His thumb stroked across the back of her hand in a slow, sensual rhythm that sent glimmers of sensation dancing up her arm. She found herself mesmerized by the sight of his big, square hand enveloping hers.

"Are you okay?" he asked.

"About what? I'm in a limo on the way to ride on a private jet with a sexy man in a suit, before sightseeing in a city I've never visited before. That sounds like a good day to me."

His hold on her tightened. "If I hadn't seen the bruises from your self-defense lessons, I'd be yelling at you to take Barsky more seriously."

"You yell? I've never heard it." His concern felt like a warm blanket wrapped around her.

"Ask my partners." He lifted her hand to kiss the back of it. "I'll feel better when I've had a chance to meet all the players face-to-face to gauge what's going on."

It was almost true that she wasn't worried as long as Derek was with her. Nervous, yes, but not afraid. She didn't want to screw up the cover story, but the presence of this brilliant, capable man who cared about her safety in a personal way chased away most of her apprehension. No harm would come to her as long as he cast his protective shadow over her.

In fact, she was so relaxed—and maybe a little tired from making love three nights in a row—that she fell asleep with her head on his shoulder, only opening her eyes when the car came to a stop before a metal gate. The driver handed the guard some paperwork and the gate swung open. She gasped as she realized that they were driving right onto the tarmac where a sleek white jet caught a gleam from the just rising sun. The driver parked about twenty feet from the jet's steps and leaped out to open the door.

Alice climbed out of the car with care since she wasn't used to wearing such a slim skirt or high heels. She turned as Derek emerged behind her and forgot all about her bruises when the dawn found glints of gold in his hair and turned his skin to honey. She wanted to . . . no, she just *wanted*. It was that simple.

"I like the door-to-door service," she said, trying to quell her response. "And it's nice not to have to take my shoes off."

His laugh was rueful. "You get spoiled. It makes flying commercial even worse."

He surprised her by taking her hand as they walked toward the jet. She liked that he was willing to claim their relationship in a semipublic place.

An engine revved as another jet hurled itself skyward, the wind it stirred flattening her skirt against her thighs. She liked the way it felt to stride along beside Derek in her high heels as they boarded a private jet to face down a Russian hacker. Like she was in a James Bond movie.

He helped her up the short flight of steps, the strength of his arm reinforcing her trust in his ability to safeguard her. As she came through the plane's door, she scanned the interior with wonder. Cushy, cream-colored leather lounge chairs sat on a soft taupe carpet. Tables made of highly polished blond wood jutted between the chairs, offering work space. Toward the rear of the plane, a leather sofa loaded with cream-and-taupe velvet pillows ran along one side, facing a table decorated with a large vase of fresh flowers.

"Flowers on an airplane?"

"Don't worry, the vase is clamped to the table and they don't put much water in it." Derek's voice was so close that she jumped and pivoted to find him straightening just inside the door, amusement lighting his eyes. "But it's a nice touch, don't you think?"

"What about the pillows?" She waved toward the sofa. "Are they Velcroed to the couch?"

He chuckled. "They're corralled by bungee cords."

"Does this plane belong to KRG?" she asked with an awe she couldn't conceal.

"No, we just charter it regularly so I'm familiar with the decor. There's even a shower in the back. You just have to make it quick if you don't want to run out of hot water."

"Unbelievable!" She tried not to think of how he looked in her shower with rivulets of water tracing over his muscled body but her pulse sped up anyway.

He gestured to a chair at one of the tables. "Why don't you take this seat and I'll sit across the aisle for takeoff so we're both facing forward. Once we level off, you can explore further."

He leaned down to brush a kiss over her lips. "Although I hate being separated from you by even two feet."

"That's laying it on a little thick." But she patted his delicious butt as a ripple of happiness washed through her.

A soft cough sounded behind her so she spun around.

"Hello, I'm Kai." A slim, blond man in a navy blazer and khaki trousers stepped out of the forward doorway. "Would you like something to drink? Coffee? Tea? Mimosa? Bloody Mary?"

"Um, coffee would be great," Alice said as she settled into her lounge chair while a flush of embarrassment climbed her cheeks. Maybe she'd indulge in a Bloody Mary on the way home when she didn't have to keep her wits about her.

"Make that two coffees, please," Derek said. He slotted his briefcase into a pocket on the wall, shrugged out of his jacket, and tossed it over the back of another chair. "There's storage space on your side too."

"Oh, right." Alice pulled her attention away from the ripple of his shoulder muscles under the blue cotton before she stuffed her leather tote and purse into the compartment. "I guess the laws of gravity apply even on a private jet."

"The pilot says it should be a smooth flight, so you don't have to worry," Derek said, easing into his seat.

"Oh, I'm not worried. It's statistically much safer to fly than to drive on the Garden State Parkway." His presence was far more disturbing to her peace of mind than being thirty thousand feet in the air in a metal tube.

"Good point." Derek buckled his seat belt and stretched out his long, long legs, crossing them at the ankles so the polished gleam of his black wingtips caught her eye.

Kai arrived with their coffee and its accoutrements, allowing them to doctor their beverages before he cleared away the sugar and cream. "If you need me, just hit the call button," he said, disappearing back into the galley space and closing the door.

"I can't believe Kai saw me grab your butt," Alice said, consoling herself with a chocolate-dipped biscotti. "Now he probably thinks I'm some kind of an escort, not a business associate."

Derek let his gaze roam up and down her body, making hunger bloom inside her as swiftly as if he'd touched her. "I suspect he thinks I'm a very lucky man."

The longing coiled hot in her belly while the pilot's voice came through a speaker to tell them they'd been cleared for takeoff. Alice crossed her legs as though that could stifle her reaction and the plane started rolling toward the runway.

"How many times have you flown on a private jet?" she asked, trying to distract herself.

"I've lost count, but I remember my first time." His smile was reminiscent. "Leland, Tully, and I had just started KRG. We got a call from a prospective client out in Des Moines who had a very urgent problem and needed us there ASAP. It never occurred to us that we'd have a problem getting a flight so we guaranteed that we'd be there the next day. But when I tried to book us into Des Moines, there weren't any seats available. Some huge organization had decided to hold their annual meeting there that year, and Des Moines is not a major hub for any airline, let me tell you."

"I guess it's too far to drive from New York."

He nodded. "I was going to book us to Chicago and rent a car for the five-hour drive, but then Leland up and says no. He insists that we're going to do things right and charter a jet. It will impress the client, he says."

"How would they know? Were they meeting you at the airport?"

"Great minds think alike. I asked him the same thing. He just smiled and said not to worry about that. However, Tully and I nearly had a heart attack when we found out how much it would cost. Leland's answer was that you have to invest in yourselves and we needed to be fresh and ready to think when we got to the client site."

"I suppose you could justify it that way."

"Yes, except that the cost of the jet wiped out our cash reserves. However, it was almost worth it to hear how many times Leland managed to work our private jet into the conversation with the clients. Tully and I started counting after about the third one. The tally hit a dozen." His face held remembered laughter. "The funny thing is that our inquiry calls doubled the next week. Leland swore it was because the Des Moines client had told everyone that we'd flown in on our own jet. Success breeds success, he kept saying."

"Or the illusion of success breeds success." Alice loved the daring of it. She would never do something so insane.

"We took full advantage of the plane's bar on the way home. We figured we'd paid for it, so why not? Thank God no prospective clients called the next day." Nostalgia colored his words. "Those early days at KRG were quite a roller-coaster ride."

"The three of you went to business school together, right?"

"We met there. Leland needed a roommate for the apartment he'd rented, and I answered his post on the biz-school housing board. Tully was in my first-year learning team. At first, we were all a little afraid of him because he'd been in the FBI before he went to business school." Derek smiled. "We got over it. At any rate, after a summer of interning at large corporations, we all decided we wanted to be our own bosses, so we made plans to start KRG when we graduated."

"I can't imagine just deciding to start a whole company," Alice said, feeling a combination of awe and envy. "That's a big risk."

A shadow passed over Derek's face. "That was pointed out to us on several occasions, but we were cocky enough to think we could pull it off."

"And you did." She wondered who the naysayers had been because they clearly bothered him still.

"Trust me, we had a couple of close calls." The tightness in his jaw eased when he said, "You have your own company as well."

"Not the same. I am a single-practice bookkeeper. I don't have anyone else on my payroll to worry about." She shrugged with a wry smile. "Except my two cats."

He gave a choke of a laugh before the jet's engines rose to a roar and the plane blasted down the runway to launch itself upward on a steep vertical. Alice grabbed the arms of her chair and peered out the window as the plane seemed to pivot on its wingtip, giving her a spectacular view of New York City from a bird's perspective.

As the agile jet leveled off and headed away from the city, she turned back to Derek to find him watching her, a half smile curving his lips. "Thanks for giving me the seat with a view," she said as she realized he'd chosen their positions deliberately.

"It's nice to see someone enjoy it." He made a wry face. "I tend to open my laptop the moment I sit down on the plane."

The captain announced that they could unfasten their seat belts and move about the cabin. Derek unbuckled his and pulled his briefcase out from its storage bin before shifting to the chair that faced hers across the table. He seemed to fill her entire field of vision with his perfectly streaked hair, his perfectly pressed shirt stretched over wide shoulders, and his perfectly knotted tie that accentuated the muscles of his neck. Thank goodness the sunshine slanting through the window highlighted the slight bump in his nose so he seemed human and not a fantasy she'd dreamed up.

Flipping open his laptop, he fixed his eyes on her. "Before I dive into Argon, I want to go over our story again."

She rolled her eyes. They'd been through this numerous times, fleshing out details with each pass.

"I know you think I'm overreacting but we can't take any chances since we don't know what we're walking into." He reached across the table to enfold her hand in his.

He'd been on edge ever since Barsky had called back to say that they would be meeting with BalanceTrakR's president, Ted Murval. Derek wasn't bothered by Murval's title; he was bothered by the fact that his partners couldn't find out anything about the man himself.

"Once more with feeling," she said, giving his hand a squeeze. She couldn't be annoyed with him because his overpreparation sprang from real anxiety about her well-being.

For a half an hour, they ran through their fictional business proposal, trying to find any holes they hadn't seen before. Finally, Derek sat back and rubbed a hand over his face. "You've got me convinced."

"You're no slouch in the credibility department either. Must be that training as an actor," Alice said with a grin.

"You should see me do a death scene. I've been told that it's a special talent of mine."

"Right, because you can fall without hurting yourself." Alice sat back in her seat.

The amusement went out of his face. "I apologize but I have to focus on Argon now. Forgive me for being bad company."

"Don't worry. I brought my own work but I'm going to explore the plane first. I'll probably never fly on a private jet again after today." And just being in the same space with him made her happy.

"Feel free," he said, sweeping his hand around. "If you get hungry, press the call button for Kai."

She jerked her seat belt buckle open and started to stand but he was on his feet first, using their joined hands to help her up.

"Maybe one small kiss first," he said as he walked around the table.

"If you think you can stop after just one." She stepped into him so that her breasts met his chest and her thighs brushed against his. His grip on her hand turned to steel and he snaked his other arm around her waist to pull her even closer before his mouth lowered to hers.

An electric shock of sensation seared through her, and she grabbed handfuls of his shirt to hold herself against him. He slanted his lips against hers first as a question, then as a demand, and finally as a wild joining that neither one of them controlled.

When he lifted his head, flares of wanting lit his eyes. "That was only one kiss." His voice held a huskiness that ran along her veins like flame.

"But I wouldn't call it small." She was almost panting.

"God, I don't want to work on Argon."

"But you have to." She forced open her fists and tried to smooth out the wrinkles she'd made in the fine cotton.

He seized her wrists to pull her hands away. "That won't help me concentrate."

"Sorry. I was just trying to undo the damage to your clothes." But she reveled in the knowledge of her power over him. She stepped back, feeling oddly unmoored when he released her.

"I think I'll sit at the next table. Otherwise my focus may suffer." He ran one finger down her cheek before tucking his laptop under his arm and walking to the work station behind her.

Yearning still crackled through her as she walked down the aisle toward the back of the plane. It was hard to appreciate the flowers or pillows when she wanted to lay her body against Derek's from ankles to lips. A control panel by the sofa caught her eye. The graphics by the buttons indicated that it could extend out flat to become a bed. That was not a helpful image.

She kept going past the sofa to check out the bathroom. Although the walls curved and the ceiling was low enough that Derek might have duck his head to get his hair wet, it was as promised: a full-fledged shower. Of course, the thought of Derek in the shower brought back visions of water running down his naked body. The craving that already pulsed through her body grew stronger.

She couldn't even shut the door and splash cold water on her face because it would ruin the makeup she'd taken such trouble with.

When she strolled back up the aisle, Derek was typing furiously, but he gave her a quick smile as she passed.

Alice sat down and opened her laptop to work on Nowak Plumbing's books. But her mind kept wandering to the man seated a mere six feet behind her, his presence making the recirculated air of the plane seem heavy with pure sexual tension.

She yanked her attention back, reminding herself that she had to be on the alert for Myron Barsky's criminal fraud.

⌒

When Alice walked past him, her signature scent of violets drifted past Derek's nostrils, making him inhale. Alice's innocence about how the corporate world worked, her occasional delicious blush, and her wide-eyed enjoyment of traveling on a private jet for the first time evoked the delicate, woodsy flower. Her sharp intelligence and the steely determination that had led her to KRG's Small Business Initiative shredded all images of flower petals. Not to mention that her passion in bed veered more toward the deepest red roses.

The contradictions made her fascinating. Those, and the curve of her lips that kept tempting him to bend down and taste. Now every time she shifted in her chair, it jerked his attention away from the numbers swimming across his computer screen. He wanted to scoop her up and carry her back to the sofa so he could slowly strip off her sexy business clothes, yank the clips out of her prim, tantalizing bun, and spread her out naked on the leather to feast upon. His cock twitched into life again.

Irritated at his inability to keep his mind on his work, he hit the call button, asking Kai to bring him some more coffee. Alice asked for tea, her soft voice stroking over his skin like the brush of satin. Jesus, everything about her aroused him this morning.

He drew on every ounce of self-discipline he possessed to focus on the Argon reports, immersing himself in the shifting patterns of the numbers he loved so much. Just like Alice did. And there she was, waltzing through his thoughts again.

An urgent email from Leland pinged into his laptop, thanks to the plane's high-tech wireless network. As Derek read it, he muttered a curse under his breath.

> I found the issue. It's definitely not a bug. It's an encrypted subroutine tied to the credit card transaction system. I'll need some time to crack the encryption but in the meantime, tread carefully.

Derek stared at Leland's last admonition. He hoped like hell that this was just white-collar crime—the kind that didn't involve violence—but even then, Alice's professional reputation was vulnerable. This meeting with Barsky and his boss, Ted Murval, had damn well better shift their attention to KRG and away from her. The script he'd developed with Alice deliberately made her seem like a minor player, a mere incidental to KRG's powerful plans. Alice had joked about being insulted by that, but she'd gone along with it, acknowledging that it was the sensible strategy.

He didn't want Barsky to have any suspicion that she'd found the problem on her own and gotten KRG involved through the SBI portal. That would put her in even more danger of reprisals.

He closed the email, deciding not to share it with Alice until after the meeting. She was already tense about their subterfuge. He could see that she wasn't accustomed to lying, at least in a business setting. He wouldn't add more pressure.

Then he forced himself to dive back into the Argon project, although with a low thrum in his gut that twisted together desire and uneasiness.

Chapter 11

Derek insisted that they rehearse their script yet again during the limo ride from the executive airport to BalanceTrakR's headquarters. He threw some new questions at Alice, challenging her to think on her feet. When she stumbled once, his critique verged on harsh. He apologized, but there was an edge that made her jumpy.

"Once we get out of this car, stick to the cover story, even in the elevator. We don't know what kind of security monitoring they might have," he said as the car pulled up in front of a nondescript brick office building on a side street in what Derek said was a fringe area of downtown Dallas.

Panic clawed at Alice's chest, making it hard to draw full breaths. The whole thing had seemed like a little bit of a game until that moment.

Then Derek's hand covered hers where it lay on the seat. She turned to find him smiling at her encouragingly. "Anything you don't want to answer, just throw to me."

She nodded because her throat was still tight. But the strength of his grip and the warmth of his smile loosened the fist that seemed to squeeze her lungs.

The guard at the scuffed-up lobby desk sent them to the twelfth floor on an elevator lined with fake wood paneling. Alice spent the ride upward trying to remember Derek's coaching as they stood close enough that his sleeve brushed against hers. Having his big, powerful body beside her brought more comfort. She knew with a bone-deep certainty that he would protect her in the unthinkable event that it became necessary.

The elevator door opened onto a carpeted corridor. The BalanceTrakR logo hung on the wall directly opposite with an arrow pointing to the right. Derek gestured for her to precede him. She squared her shoulders and strode down the hallway with all the false confidence she could project. Behind her Derek murmured, "That's right. You've got this down cold."

He reached around her to open the glass door that also had the company's logo painted on it and they surged into a small reception area. An attractive blonde woman sat behind the desk.

"Alice Thurber and Derek Killion to see Mr. Murval," Alice announced with a pleasant but professional smile. She kept in mind that she represented KRG so she should project a bit of superiority.

"Of course," the receptionist said with a marked Texas accent. "Please have a seat."

"No need for that. I'll be happy to escort them to see Ted." Alice pivoted to see Myron Barsky advancing toward them with a smile that was far friendlier than hers for the receptionist. He wore almost the same outfit he'd had on at the hotel presentation, although today he had added a droopy tweed blazer over the jeans and white shirt, and his nondescript brown hair had been trimmed a little shorter.

Alice drew in a breath that had a little hitch in it. *Showtime.*

Myron held out his hand to Alice. "Ms. Thurber. I remember you from my dog and pony show in Cofferwood. You asked the sharpest questions." His Texas accent was more in evidence today than it had been in New Jersey.

"Please call me Alice," she said, finding his handshake as limp as the first time. "You convinced several of my clients to buy your package, so I'd say you answered them. I'd like you to meet Derek Killion."

For a moment, Barsky seemed less like a tech nerd and more like a businessman as he shot an assessing look at Derek, his pale blue eyes opaque. "A privilege," Myron said, shaking Derek's hand.

"If you're the man behind the software, the privilege is mine," Derek responded, coolly returning Barsky's evaluating stare.

The programmer lowered his eyes in an exaggerated show of modesty. "I can't take all the credit. I have a great team working with me." When he turned to gesture to another door, Alice caught a sly smile on Barsky's face. "Ted's waiting for us in the conference room."

Alice remembered her instructions to gauge whether the premises looked legitimate, but the undistinguished decor could have been in any office anywhere in the country. The signage was professional but it might have been installed that morning for all she could tell. When Myron turned into the second door down the hallway, she still couldn't judge because the conference room was as bland as the rest of the office with its oatmeal upholstered chairs and matching oatmeal-colored blinds.

However, the man who stood up at one end of the fake-wood-topped table was anything but bland. He wore a yellow, western-style shirt with bright green welting and a bolo tie clasped with a huge chunk of turquoise set in silver. Standing over six feet tall, he must have weighed at least three hundred pounds.

"I'm Ted Murval and I want to welcome you to the great state of Texas," he boomed, his greeting echoing off the painted walls of the small room. "We're sure glad you came to see us."

This was the man who ran an accounting software company for small businesses? Evidently, they had a different dress code for CEOs in Texas.

Myron made the introductions in that odd monotone of his. Maybe it was because he felt awkward socially. When they all sat down around the table where a bottle of off-label water stood at each place,

Alice couldn't help contrasting it with the impressive conference room at KRG.

Derek spoke first. "As you know, KRG hired Alice to evaluate BalanceTrakR for us because she's a skilled bookkeeper and because we wanted to remain at arm's length until we were sure of our interest. She brought back an excellent report after her clients had used it for a few months. I'm here to discuss partnering with you to bring this product to some of our smaller, less centralized clients. And possibly to expand its capabilities to serve some larger companies."

"Well, that's mighty flattering," Ted said, leaning back in his chair with a broad smile. He asked a few superficial questions, steering some of the conversation toward Alice. Derek projected the perfect impression of a confident-to-the-point-of-arrogance consultant. He allowed Alice to speak but then was faintly dismissive of her answers. Or changed the wording slightly while saying the same thing. She would have been offended if she hadn't been privy to his underlying goal.

After a few minutes of this, Ted said, "Myron, why don't you take the pretty little lady for a tour of our facility while Derek and I talk turkey."

Alice ignored the chauvinism of Ted's remark as alarm hollowed out her stomach. She and Derek hadn't planned to be separated when they'd developed their strategy.

An edge colored Derek's voice as he said, "I'd be interested in joining the tour as well."

"After we hammer a few things out," Ted said. "Then I'll guide you around myself."

The muscles in Derek's jaw tightened visibly. "I guess I can't turn that down."

Myron stood, pushed his black-rimmed glasses back into place on his nose, and waved her to the door with an ingratiating smile. Really, how scary could the techno-geek be? But leaving Derek's comforting presence behind made her feel vulnerable and exposed.

"We'll start with the help desk," Myron said, walking farther down the corridor. "I imagine you called in at some point to evaluate that." He leaned forward to peer into her face.

"I got excellent assistance all three times," Alice said truthfully.

Myron nodded, his smile widening. "We pride ourselves on keeping our customer support in-house." He opened a glass door and stood aside so she could enter first. Three rows of cubicles housed about thirty people. All wore headsets and stared at their computer screens, their chatter and keyboards generating a steady hum of noise, so she couldn't really distinguish separate conversations. The company logo was emblazoned across one wall but everything else was standard-issue office furniture as before. So they had boring taste in decorating. That didn't mean it wasn't a real company.

"Is this your whole support staff?" she asked.

He shook his head, making his glasses slide down his nose. "We have a couple of more rooms just like this. They say it reduces employee stress if we keep the spaces on a more human scale. Not as many voices all speaking at once."

That made sense but also meant that she couldn't get an accurate headcount. "I like that you offer support 24-7," she said. "Not everyone does."

"Did you also explore our user forums?" He turned to her, the smile still fixed on his lips. "We sometimes find that they have even better answers than we do since they're out there in the trenches."

Here was the key question she and Derek had anticipated. "Of course. I have to admit to probing a little bit to see if anyone reported significant issues. I'm sure you understand." She matched his smile with one that said she regretted nothing.

His expression didn't change. She was struck again by how hard it was to read anything behind his facade of "business nerd." "And did anyone have a problem?" he asked.

"None that I could find, although one of my questions simply disappeared. But I understand that the user forums are not under your control, so I don't fault BalanceTrakR for that."

"Good to hear." He let out a dramatic sigh of relief before he shepherded her out the door. "Now I'll take you to my favorite place because it's where the magic happens."

They passed two closed doors before he opened one to reveal a space about four times the size of the customer-support room. The same rows of cubicles filled the space, but many more of them. A Ping-Pong table where a game was in full swing stood in an open corner. The hum in this room was mostly of keys clicking, although a few conversations were in progress where two or three people were crowded into one cubicle, staring at the screen.

"Our software engineers," Myron said, his gaze skittering around the room. "They're quite competent."

It was a strangely unenthusiastic description but Alice let it pass. "I can practically feel the brain waves," she said, examining the mostly male, mostly jeans-and-T-shirt-clad techies. Many wore earbuds and seemed to be nodding along to music. A couple of cubicles had superhero action figures lined along the top edge. The Ping-Pong players slammed the ball at each other viciously. It looked exactly the way you'd expect a roomful of computer geeks to look.

Which bothered her, so she did something she knew Derek would not approve of. She said, "I'd love to talk with the developers who created the bank and credit card integration. That's the most brilliant part of the system."

That brought Myron's attention back to her. He pushed up his glasses. "Gosh, I wish I could let you do that." But his tone held no regret at all. "The coders would love to hear that. But it's a security thing."

"No worries." She waved her hand airily. Maybe it really was a security issue but her suspicions were not allayed.

"Speaking of security, let me show you that division of our company," Myron said, escorting her back out into the corridor. "Honestly, the people who work there kind of give me the creeps but you'll see how seriously they take their jobs. Which is important when you're dealing with other people's money."

This time he knocked on the door before opening it slowly and peering in as though he expected to be reprimanded for intruding. He ushered her into the room but stayed near the doorway, speaking in a hushed tone. "Some of these guys are hackers turned watchdogs. Some are ex-FBI. The guy at the desk is John Peters, the head honcho."

The room broadcast an entirely different vibe from the software engineers. The light seemed dimmer, possibly because nearly everyone wore black. There was no Ping-Pong table, and no people gathered in clusters at a single work station. Everyone stared intently at the computers in front of them. John Peters looked up from the multiple screens arrayed on his desk, his focus resting on Alice for a long moment before he stood and walked through the maze of cubicles to where she stood.

"Um, John, this is Alice Thurber," Myron said, shoving his glasses up with a quick, anxious gesture. He was smiling in a weird way that Alice ascribed to nerves. "She's, er, with KRG Consulting. Just visiting us."

John Peters made Alice nervous too. He wasn't as tall as BalanceTrakR's CEO but he had a neck and shoulders like a professional wrestler's. When he shook her hand, his grip was hard and uncomfortable and his expression was blank. "Nice to meet you," he said without any trace of a Texas accent and without any indication that he meant a word of his greeting.

He must have been one of the former FBI agents because his hair was buzzed short and he wore a dark suit and tie, just like they did on television, although his shirt was also dark and she kind of thought the FBI wore white shirts.

"Sorry to interrupt your work," Alice said, flexing her squashed fingers behind her back. "I'm just taking a quick tour of your facility."

"We are very careful to make sure no one finds or exploits any vulnerabilities in our system." He continued to watch her with that unreadable face. "We monitor all possible vectors constantly so that no malware or ransomware can corrupt the software."

"I can see that," Alice said, although she was out of her depth with cybersecurity. "Your vigilance is admirable."

Peters's gaze shifted to Myron, who was still smiling. The security chief and Myron simply stared at each other for a long moment.

"Thanks, John," Myron finally said, edging toward the door. "Appreciate it."

John started back toward his desk.

"Scary dude." Myron shuddered visibly as they reached the brightly lit corridor.

"Is he one of the former FBI agents?"

"I think he was, like, CIA or something really intense." Myron rubbed his palms on the sides of his jeans as though his hands were sweaty. "At least, that's the rumor. No one except HR really knows." He seemed to shake off his tense mood. "I think you've seen the most important parts of BalanceTrakR. Is there anything else I can tell you about?"

"I'm sure your boss is discussing this with Derek right now, but I'm curious as to how many copies of the software you've sold to date."

Myron gave her another unapologetic smile. "I'd have to check with Ted before I could share that information with you."

Clearly, Myron wasn't a completely clueless techno-geek. He was aware of what the boundaries of information sharing were and he wasn't worried about offending her by protecting company secrets. It reminded her of how he'd been transformed from nerd to, well, charismatic nerd during his presentation at the hotel.

"So I guess you're not going to buy another copy of the software," he said, heading toward the conference room again.

"Sorry to take away the prospective commission but hopefully, you'll get a lot more sales from partnering with KRG."

When they walked into the conference room, Derek was fuming, and Ted was leaning forward, stabbing at the conference table with his index finger as he made an emphatic point.

As soon as he saw Alice, Derek stood. "Thank you for your time, Ted, Myron." He nodded to them in turn. "I don't think we're going to be able to make a deal here."

"Sorry to make you travel all the way to Texas for nothing," Ted said, but he looked more pleased than remorseful. "I don't think Myron here understood what you were after."

Myron flinched. "I regret that, sir."

Ted waved his apology away. "Above your pay grade, Myron. No harm, no foul." He reached across the table to shake hands with Derek. "At least let Myron take you to lunch since you missed out on the tour."

"That's a generous offer," Derek said, making an obvious effort to be cordial. "However, we're going to head back to New York." Alice could almost hear him add the word "empty-handed," even though he didn't say it aloud. If she didn't know better, she'd think he was royally miffed about not making a deal with BalanceTrakR.

"Nice to meet you, Alice," Ted said in what was clearly a dismissal.

Myron ushered them out to the reception area, also shaking hands with Derek. "I wish we could do business together. I know KRG has great influence with its clients." He turned to Alice and she could swear that she saw disdain flicker across his face. "Thank you for recommending us so strongly." He gave her hand a slightly damp squeeze. "You have my number. Feel free to call with any questions you or your clients might have in the future."

As the elevator doors closed, Alice said, "Well, that was—"

Derek banded his fingers around her wrist, so she turned to see his warning frown. But she hadn't forgotten to be discreet.

"I guess your meeting with Ted didn't go so well," she said to reassure Derek.

"His terms were entirely one-sided. And nonnegotiable," Derek said, letting his irritation show.

"You'd think they'd want the kind of backing KRG could give them. Although it's a larger operation than I expected."

"Ted's got an ego. He thinks they can reach all the clients they want without us."

Derek still held her wrist. She wasn't sure if he'd forgotten until he brushed his fingertips right over her pulse point, sending a flare of delight dancing up her arm. Was that some kind of signal about their fake conversation? If so, she couldn't think clearly enough to interpret it.

So she just nodded and remained silent until the elevator disgorged them in the lobby. Derek released her wrist, making her wish the descent had been longer. She resisted the impulse to lay the fingers of her other hand where his had been.

As they walked toward the door, she couldn't help comparing the shabbiness of the building with the polished elegance of KRG's headquarters. And she was very grateful to be leaving it behind.

Chapter 12

As soon as the limo pulled away from the curb, Alice slumped in her seat. "Phew, I'm glad that's over."

"I'm sorry you had to go through that. I wanted to strangle Ted when he sent you off alone with Barsky," Derek said, giving her shoulder a brief, comforting squeeze. "How rough was it?"

The pressure of his hand made her insides melt like warm marshmallows. "Rough?" She pulled her scattered thoughts back together. "Oh, not really. My attempt at espionage didn't work, though."

"Espionage? You weren't supposed to be spying here." His brows drew down with disapproval.

"Well, I figured I'd ask a few questions since that seemed normal within the context of our visit but I didn't get a thing out of Myron. For a computer nerd, he's pretty clued in about confidentiality."

"What kind of questions?"

"Nothing that would raise any red flags." Although Myron's reactions had seemed slightly off-kilter. But she couldn't put her finger on why so she didn't mention it. "I asked to meet the coders who developed the bank and credit card integration to give them my compliments. Myron shot that down. I expressed some surprise about the number of help desk staff and was told there were more in other rooms. I wondered how many copies of the software they'd sold. I didn't really expect him to tell me that."

Derek looked increasingly unhappy with each question she repeated. "The idea was to get you out of their crosshairs," he snapped. "Why couldn't you just smile and nod?"

She smirked at his grumpiness. "Because I didn't think that would be in character as a consultant to consultants."

"Or maybe it's just not in character for *you*," he muttered.

"How was your meeting with Ted?"

He gave her a narrow-eyed look but let it go. "Strange. He seemed interested in my proposal at the beginning but by the time you returned he was throwing up obstacles in every direction. The terms he offered were downright insulting to my intelligence and he appeared to be quite pleased with that. If I had really wanted to partner with BalanceTrakR, I would have been seriously angry."

"Well, you did a great job of looking ticked off when Myron and I got back. I guess your drama major pays off in situations like that."

He huffed out a laugh. "I never thought of it that way."

"Really? You don't call on your acting chops when dealing with difficult clients?" She couldn't believe that.

"Not consciously. You know the acting career was more my father's idea than mine."

"Yeah, I still can't believe he told you that starting your own firm was too risky when he should have been cheering you on."

He hesitated for a moment before shaking his head. "Maybe I ought to thank him. The prospect of hearing him say 'I told you so' made me doubly desperate to succeed."

Alice nodded. She still needed to prove to her mother that she wasn't a failure in life.

"But that's the past," Derek said, closing the subject. "Let's deal with our current problem."

She ventured to mention her crazy idea about BalanceTrakR. "This is going to sound strange but I felt like BalanceTrakR's headquarters were sort of a stage set."

"What makes you say that?"

"The room for the coders was so clichéd. It had a Ping-Pong table and action figures on the cubicles. I mean, do software companies still have Ping-Pong tables for their developers? It almost seemed like a throwback to something that someone had seen in a movie."

Derek frowned. "What else?"

"The security staff! You know those hacker movies where the guy wears a black hoodie and sits hunched over his laptop in a dark room, searching for a back door into the CIA's supersecret system or a city's traffic-light control center? That's exactly what it looked like. The only person who looked real was the head guy, and he was genuinely terrifying." She felt the frisson of fear all over again as she remembered his blank eyes.

"Did you talk to him?"

"Just hello-how-are-you kind of stuff."

He said something under his breath that she couldn't quite make out. "No casual questions asked?"

"Not a one. I wasn't going to mess with him."

"I'm glad you have some sense of self-preservation."

She swiveled on the seat to look straight into his eyes. "Do you really think Myron Barsky is a threat?" He'd seemed more awkward than anything else.

"Maybe not Myron, but it sounds like you met someone who could be." The angles of his face were taut with disquiet. "I felt something was off with Ted Murval. You felt something was not right with the facility. That worries me."

"Well, since they're doing something illegal, it would make sense that they wanted to throw us off the scent, right?" She settled back against the seat. "And now they believe they have, so there's no reason to be concerned."

"If it was all a setup, they went to a lot of trouble and expense to trick us. That means the stakes are high." He rubbed his hand over his face. "But that's for Leland and Tully to worry about now. You're off the case."

Regret curled through her. "I guess my clients won't get their money back for BalanceTrakR. I feel badly about that."

"You can't blame yourself for dishonest behavior."

"It's funny but the worst I thought of Myron at his original presentation was that he promised a lot and I wasn't sure the software could deliver it all. It never occurred to me that he would *steal* from his users." She grimaced. "I guess I'm naive."

"You have faith in people doing the right thing. I hope you never lose that because it's a rare trait . . . except in this situation." He wrapped his hand around hers. "You need to understand that those who steal are often willing to do worse to protect themselves."

"You keep saying that, but I can't picture Myron even punching anyone in the nose. Although John Peters . . ." She shivered a bit at the memory of his implacable face.

Derek's grip tightened. "There's already a security team watching your house. Tully arranged it after Barsky called you."

First, she felt comforted, knowing that she was protected from the scary security chief. Then another implication sank in. "Even when you were there with me?"

That meant that Derek didn't mind his partner knowing he was spending the night with her. She wasn't sure what that signified.

He rubbed his thumb over her fingers and gave her a hot look. "I didn't know I'd be there at the time Tully set it up. Since we were somewhat . . . distracted anyway, I thought it was a good idea to continue with the surveillance."

"Distracted? Is that what you call it?" She edged closer so their thighs were touching.

He used his free hand to tilt her chin toward him. "When you are around, I have a hard time concentrating." Then he kissed her in a way that made her want to climb onto his lap. Instead she grabbed handfuls of his suit jacket and pulled herself in close until he raised his head.

"I see nothing wrong with your ability to focus," she said as frustration taunted her.

He husked out a laugh. "On you, it's razor sharp."

At that moment, the limo came to a stop and her door magically opened. "Welcome to Three-Sixty," a young valet said. "The best views in all of Dallas."

⌁

Derek was still fighting his apprehension about their visit to BalanceTrakR as he walked around the limo to join Alice on the sidewalk. When Ted had sent Alice off with Myron, Derek had been concerned but relieved. That meant he would be the one who asked all the hard questions so they'd focus on him. But then Alice had ignored the goal of the trip and poked at Myron with her questions. Even though she had a point about it seeming more realistic that way, she'd risked making herself a target again.

She didn't seem to grasp how serious the fraud was, but then that was part of her charm. Her perspective on the world was rosier than his. Which was hazardous when dealing with criminals, even white-collar ones. There was a real threat here. He could feel it in his gut.

He trusted her observations and instincts so her theory about the offices being a stage set heightened his sense of hovering menace. Such an elaborate setup indicated serious money being involved. That meant serious danger.

His disquiet evaporated when he saw Alice gazing up at the soaring concrete-and-aluminum tower in front of her. Her head was tilted back so the line of her throat was elongated in a way that made him imagine bending to slide his lips down the length of it and lower. He pulled himself up short as his groin tightened.

He'd nearly told the limo driver to just keep driving so he could make love to Alice in the back seat. But he'd promised her a tour of Dallas and he planned to deliver.

As he came up beside her, she shifted to look at him, her eyes sparkling with delight. "It's like something out of the Jetsons," she said with a sweeping gesture upward to the geodesic dome on top.

"It was probably built in about the same era," he said, holding the door for her to enter. "This way," he said, leading her to the elevator that bypassed the observation deck and went straight to the restaurant at the very top of the tower. He held out his phone so the guard could check the reservation confirmation that allowed them access.

"We've got a fast pass?" Alice asked as they waited for the elevator doors to open.

"Something like that." He wanted to keep it a surprise for as long as possible, just to see the expression on her face.

Another couple came onto the elevator with them but stayed close to the wall by the doors, looking nervous as they cast anxious glances at the curving glass that made up the outside wall of the car.

Alice strode right over to the glass. "This is great," she said as the elevator whooshed upward. She was so close to the glass that Derek half expected her to flatten her nose against it. He stood beside her but he wasn't looking at the Dallas skyline. He was inhaling her scent of violets and watching her face as she scanned the view, the sunlight turning the brown of her eyes to sherry and painting her cheeks with a golden glow.

"Wow, look at that cloverleaf! That's a real can of worms. Cool bridge too." She kept up a running commentary as they rose, only turning away when the elevator coasted to a full stop. Her voice waltzed through him, igniting places he needed to keep under control in public.

A recording came through a speaker. "Please step briskly off the elevator as you exit."

She looked puzzled as they stood behind the other couple waiting for the doors to open. When she stepped off into the curved hallway, she turned to him, her eyes wide with excitement. "It revolves, doesn't it?"

He couldn't help smiling as he nodded. Her wonder infected him, even though he'd eaten in more than one revolving restaurant and barely noticed the view because he was busy discussing business.

She sniffed the air. "It's a restaurant too."

"KRG has several efficiency experts on staff, so I've learned a few tricks from them. We're eating and sightseeing at the same time." He put his hand on the small of her back to steer her toward the maître d's station, savoring the curve of her against his palm.

As the host led them past the glass-enclosed wine cellar, she peered at it in a calculating way. "Wow! That's a lot of inventory to carry on the books."

"I love the way your mind works," he said.

She gave him a wry look. "Accountant brain, right?"

"I've been accused of eating, breathing, and sleeping my work, so I would hardly complain about that." He hated to think about his ex-fiancée when he was with Alice.

"You kind of have to, given your position," she said, settling into the chair the host held for her. "You don't build a company like KRG by kicking back and relaxing." Alice's words shunted Courtney aside, making his ex seem clueless.

He, Leland, and Tully had built it with blood, sweat, and tears, but also with laughter, exhilaration, and satisfaction. His father would never understand that.

"Oh my goodness, I wonder what river that is." She was looking out the window that their table stood next to.

Feeling pleased with himself for anticipating her questions about the view, he slid his phone out of his jacket pocket, swiped across the screen a couple of times, and held it out to her. "There's an app for that.

It syncs with our table location and tells you the main points of interest. Tap on one and it gives you extra information."

She took the phone from him, the tips of her fingers, with their short, unvarnished nails, barely brushing his, but even that made his skin tingle.

"You are the best tour guide ever," she said, holding his phone as though it were fragile china and touching the screen gently. He felt as though she were touching him, not his phone, and a burst of arousal hit in him the groin.

"The Trinity River," she read. "At seven hundred ten miles, the longest river whose watershed lies entirely within the state of Texas." She flashed a self-mocking smile at him. "I promise not to bore you with any more fun facts."

"I could use some educating about Texas. When I come here, I fly in, have a few meetings, and fly out again. Broaden my horizons." He meant it too. Alice's interest in her surroundings reminded him that there was more to life than meetings.

Their server, a young woman dressed entirely in black, asked what they'd like to drink. Alice put down his phone and asked for water.

"Is this a business lunch?" she asked after a moment's hesitation.

"Only in the eyes of our accounting department."

"Wine would be nice. You choose it." She threw a glance at the racks of wine they'd walked past. "All those bottles are intimidating."

"In that case, let's decide what we're eating first. Please give us a minute," he said to the server.

Alice picked up the stiff folder that held the menu and flipped it open. As she scanned it, she fiddled with the small gold tassel that dangled from her earlobe, setting his imagination alight with the urge to lick the softness of the skin right behind her ear.

She lowered the folder and grinned at him. "Well, it's not as extensive a menu as Nick's, but I think I can find something to eat on it."

She drew in a breath that sent a glint of sun along the delicate chain around her neck, drawing his eye to the *V* of her blouse. She had it buttoned up entirely too far, so that he could see not even a hint of the valley between her breasts, but he easily pictured unfastening those top two buttons to reveal that and the lace of her bra that showed faintly through the fabric. Then he imagined sucking on her nipples through her bra.

"Derek?" She spoke sharply and he realized that she'd said something while he was lost in his reverie.

"Sorry, I was trying to remember what I had eaten the last time I was here."

"Oh, of course." But he noticed a tinge of pink on her cheeks and he wondered what his expression had given away.

"The peppercorn-soaked buffalo tenderloin," he said, choosing a dish at random. It seemed very Texan.

"I'm not really much of a red-meat eater. I was thinking about the Texas quail. I've never had that before."

"Well, it beats rattlesnake."

"They don't really have that on the menu." She looked startled and scanned the folder again before twinkling at him. "I hear it tastes like chicken."

"I've never had the wish to find out." He enjoyed the fact that she was open about her unfamiliarity with haute cuisine. He was self-taught about food and wine. His Pennsylvania upbringing didn't run to high-end restaurants, but he'd had to learn fast, since he was the one responsible for wining and dining KRG's clients right from the start. It felt good to relax with someone who didn't try to one-up him. "Could I interest you in sharing the appetizer sampler of crab cakes, short ribs, and lobster tacos?"

Her face lit up. "I love samplers."

He lifted his hand to bring the server back to their table, ordering the food, a light dry white wine for Alice, and a hearty red for himself.

"That's too much wine," she said as the server walked away. "You'll be wasting most of the bottle. At least, of mine."

"The staff will enjoy it," he said, entertained by her thriftiness on his behalf. Although not that many years ago, he would have been more careful with KRG's money. In their early days, those outrageously expensive business dinners were a serious drain on their capital. Back then, he'd been the one to insist that the image was important, even while Leland and Tully grumbled that he was the only one who got to enjoy the food and wine.

"Seriously?" Her expression was skeptical.

"They won't let it go to waste, I assure you."

"That makes me feel better." She glanced out the window again. "Oh, there's that cool bridge." She picked up his phone again, cradling it in one hand as she swiped to the app. A vision of her hand cradling his cock seared through his brain before he could stop it and he shifted in his chair.

He should be drinking ice water, not wine.

"It's the Margaret Hunt Hill Bridge, designed by Santiago Calatrava," Alice read. "No wonder it's so fantastic looking."

He tried to focus on the bridge instead of on the twists of her bun that he could see when she turned her head. But his fingers twitched with the urge to find the pins holding all that hair so primly in place and release it into waves cascading over her preferably bare shoulders.

This had to be some kind of reaction to the meeting with Ted Murval, something about confronting a criminal and coming out unscathed. But Alice had done the same thing, and she appeared quite enthralled with Dallas rather than him.

"I've seen a couple of Calatrava bridges in Europe," he said. "My favorite of his structures is the art museum in Milwaukee with the wings that furl and unfurl every day. It's quite a sight."

That brought her attention back to him. She looked thoughtful as she laid his phone down. "I need to travel more."

"Sometimes I wish I traveled less," he said.

"I guess business travel can be tiring, but I wouldn't mind trying it for a while."

"Why don't you? Come work for KRG." Now where had that come from? Not that he wouldn't be happy to hire her, but it would make things complicated. *Might* make things complicated . . . if he continued to see her. "I'll get you an assignment in Milwaukee where you can also visit the bronze Fonz."

She laughed. "So tempting." She paused a moment but then shook her head. "I'm not cut out for that kind of life."

"What kind of life do you think it is?"

"High pressure. High risk. And my cats would miss me."

"You could handle the pressure. Look at how deftly you managed Myron today. Your cats I can't do anything about."

She straightened her silverware before meeting his eyes. "As you know, I'm not big on risk-taking."

"You say that but you flew down here to face someone you know is a criminal." He reached across the table to twine his fingers with hers because he needed to touch her. "I don't think you see yourself clearly."

"Maybe not, but there's a reason for that." She gave him a side-ways glance. "So tell me the whole story about how your father screwed you up."

"I wouldn't call you screwed up."

She gave him a stern glare. "Don't change the subject."

"I wasn't trying to." He sat back as the server brought their wine and they had to go through the ritual of tasting. Once they were done, he took a sip of his wine and started at the beginning. "When I got cast as Sky Masterson in *Guys and Dolls* in seventh grade, Dad lit up like a Christmas tree. I think I got the part because I was the only boy who was taller than Amber Croce, who played Sarah Brown. But I had enough of my father's DNA to enjoy being on stage, so I kept trying out and I kept getting cast as the male lead."

"Right, you got cast for your height, not your good looks." Sarcasm tinged her tone.

He shrugged. His looks were sometimes useful, sometimes detrimental in his life. "That's also just DNA. Anyway, I thought I wanted to be an actor and applied to colleges with theater arts programs."

"And accounting programs," she added.

He took a sip of his wine. "That was a happy accident. The truth was that once I saw how the theater business worked, I realized I should go in another direction. As an actor, you had virtually no control over your career. You auditioned incessantly and hoped that some casting director liked the way you looked and didn't have to hire the producer's nephew instead." He had hated the fact that hard work meant virtually nothing. And he'd seen his father's bitterness about just missing the big time.

"When did you switch to accounting?"

He looked down into his wine. "Not until I started job hunting. I lied to my father and told him I wasn't having any luck with auditions, so I had to take a day job at a brokerage firm."

"And you loved it."

"I did." Although he had felt his father's disappointment weighing him down like a boulder. "The pace. The risk . . . but with other people's money. The numbers flashing by."

"So why did you quit to go to business school?"

"To get my father off my back."

"That's not your average motive."

"It got me out of New York so he couldn't push me to go to auditions any longer. And it gave me the motivation I needed to finally tell him that I wasn't interested in being a star."

"But you are one. Just in a different business."

He snorted as he thought of his father's reaction. "Not good enough."

"And then you had the nerve to do something just as risky as acting when you graduated from business school."

"Yeah, he quoted all the statistics about start-ups failing." He took a swallow of wine. "Ironic since numbers were my thing, not his."

Alice gave his fingers a gentle squeeze and earned his gratitude by turning the conversation toward herself. "At least my mother knew I couldn't be a model," she said. "She doesn't understand my love of numbers but she appreciates the steady income it generates."

"Why would you want to be a model?" He scowled at her self-deprecation. "It has to be even less satisfying than being an actor. It's based entirely on outward appearance and whether yours fits with the current fashion trends. I can't imagine anything worse." Revulsion shuddered through him.

"My mother would argue that it takes some talent as well," Alice said. "But you're mostly right. And my looks don't fit any fashion trend." She held up her hand as Derek opened his mouth to protest. "Believe me, I'm at peace with that."

Their appetizer sampler arrived and stopped all conversation except as it related to the delicacies arrayed artistically on the platter between them. He enjoyed watching her face as she tasted each one, her expression changing from curiosity to appreciation and sometimes even to downright ecstasy. Alice's mother clearly had no idea of how beautiful her own daughter was.

When she started to lick her fingers after sampling the short ribs, he nearly grabbed her hand to finish the job himself. Then he caught her expression and realized she was deliberately teasing him. "You will pay for that later," he said in a mock growl, his cock tightening as he considered exactly how.

"I'm counting on it."

Chapter 13

As they headed to the airport, Alice snuggled into Derek and drifted in a pleasant haze, sated with delicious food—including an extraordinary bittersweet chocolate tart—and wine. Not to mention the low hum of sexual awareness they'd been playing with all through lunch.

Derek had gone quiet after buckling his seat belt, either equally replete or already focused on his big project. It was a shame he needed to work on the plane. She'd like to have had sex on a private jet; it would add to her new image of herself as a corporate spy. She gave a quiet little snort at that.

The car turned onto the tarmac and rolled up to the jet. "It's going to be hard to go back to security lines," Alice said as Derek helped her out of the limo.

He slipped his arm around her waist to steer her toward the plane. "I guess we have something to thank Barsky for since he prompted your first ride on a private jet."

She nearly stopped on the tarmac as a thought struck her. She had a lot more than a ride on a jet to thank Barsky for. If Barsky had been an honest, hardworking software coder, she would never have met Derek, never have experienced the exquisite pleasure of his body moving over and inside hers, never have fallen in love with his brilliant mind.

Whoa! *Fallen in love* was a little extreme when she'd met him less than a week ago. Yet she felt a connection to him that had nothing—well, only a little—to do with the intense physical attraction between them. He understood her on a level that no one else ever had. Because his life was built on the same foundations.

Even his looks no longer intimidated her. Not that it was possible to ignore them because his beauty was sometimes blinding. But his attitude was so different from her mother's that she could see past his DNA-blessed exterior to the man within.

However, she needed to remember that he was still out of her league in the long term. If even a woman as brilliant and accomplished as his former fiancée couldn't hold on to him, plain old bookkeeper Alice had no chance.

She glanced up at him as he strode along beside her, the sunlight turning the streaks in his hair to molten gold and outlining that tiny bump on his nose. He seemed in a hurry to get to the plane and back to work.

She leaned into him to savor the contact before he returned to being a high-powered consultant. As she did, he glanced down at her. His eyes blazed with the same intention they had held after that kiss in the limo. An answering flame seared through her.

Maybe he wasn't in a hurry to get to *work*.

He helped her up the steps and followed her into the interior of the jet that seemed suddenly smaller. Kai greeted them with sparkling water, which allowed Alice to steady herself as she slipped into her seat and buckled her seat belt. After all, Derek wasn't going to sweep her into his arms with the flight attendant looking on.

She frowned. In fact, what about Kai? For the most part, he'd made himself scarce on the flight down because Derek had indicated they wanted to discuss business. But how could they be sure that he wouldn't decide to pop out to check on them at an embarrassing moment? She shrugged inwardly, figuring that even if he did, she would never see him again.

The jet's engines revved and she tugged her seat belt tighter as they began to roll forward.

"Alice?"

She turned to see Derek holding out his hand across the aisle. She smiled and laid her palm against his. He immediately began to stroke his thumb over the bumps of her knuckles. She looked a question at him and he leaned sideways to raise her hand to his lips, brushing them against the back of it first, then angling their entwined hands so he could press his mouth to her palm. When he flicked the tip of his tongue against her skin, his touch shot straight into her core.

"Don't you have to work?" she said after swallowing a gasp.

"I'm long overdue for a vacation. I've decided to take it now."

Arousal surged through her, mixed with a feeling both sweet and guilty. He was blowing off his big project for her . . . at least for now.

A few more minutes and the plane vaulted into the sky, making her breath come faster as she anticipated the moment they could unbuckle their seat belts.

As the plane leveled off, the momentum pushing her back into the soft leather of her seat lessened. She heard the metallic clink of Derek's buckle opening, but she had already unlatched hers and was halfway out of her seat. She was going to do what she'd imagined in the limo earlier.

"Stay where you are," she said, coming to stand facing him with her hands pressing down on his shoulders.

He leaned back in his seat. "I like where this is going."

"One question. How likely is Kai to interrupt us?"

Derek pointed to a square button on the wall beside him that was marked "Privacy." It glowed bright red.

"I guess you've had sex on a plane before," she said.

A smile curled his lips. "It's used for delicate business discussions that shouldn't be overheard."

"Sure it is." She realized that if she wanted to straddle his lap she was going to have to hike up her slim skirt to at least midthigh. She grabbed a handful of the gray wool and started to pull when Derek brushed her hand away.

"Allow me." He slipped his hands under the hem and skimmed them slowly up her legs, bunching the skirt as he went. When he reached the top of her thighs, he kept going, his fingers brushing the lace of her panties until the skirt was bundled at her waist. He held it there with one hand while he dipped the other between her thighs, one finger gliding under her panties, over her clit, and inside her.

They both moaned at the same time. "You're so wet." He withdrew his finger and sucked it into his mouth. "And so delicious."

She glanced down to see the bulge under his trousers and wanted to feel it against her. Swinging one leg over his thighs, she knelt over him in the leather chair. Threading her hands into his thick hair, she bent to kiss him and sink down onto his lap at the same time. As she made contact in both places, her body went wild with sensation.

She rocked against his erection, savoring the pressure and friction as it fanned the need between her legs. Their tongues met in the same rhythm and she felt his fingers at the buttons of her blouse. The cool air of the cabin brushed over her skin as he yanked her blouse down her arms before he filled his hands with her breasts, kneading them through the bra's lace.

The flimsy material fell away as he flicked open the fastener. He tore his mouth from hers and lifted her by the hips so he could bring one breast to his mouth, the moisture and suction sending lightning streaking through her.

When he released her nipple, she whimpered her disapproval.

"Give me a second," he said. "I want to be inside you while I play."

"Yes!" She scooted back to stand while Derek unfastened his belt and trousers and rolled on a condom.

She waited until he was watching before she shrugged out of her blouse and bra. Then she unzipped her skirt and worked it and her panties down to her ankles, leaving on her heels as she stepped out of her clothes.

Derek watched her through heavy-lidded eyes, his hands gripping the seat's arms so tightly his knuckles were white. "You are so incredibly hot," he rasped.

She reveled in it—the power she had to arouse him—crooking one knee onto the cushion beside his thigh and then the other until she could feel the head of his cock brushing her clit. Derek kept his hands clenched on the chair arms while she positioned him between her legs and sank slowly downward, his erection filling the hollow inside her with a delicious solidity.

She felt the fabric of his trousers against her thighs as she seated him fully within her. "Ahh," she breathed, closing her eyes and letting her head fall back so she could simply feel.

The plane bounced slightly on some rough air, driving him deeper inside her. "Oh God, yes!" she cried.

Then his hands and mouth were at her breasts again, teasing and circling and sucking until she thought she would come without even moving.

The plane hit another mild patch of turbulence, making his teeth graze her nipple so that she cried out with the exquisite pain-pleasure of it.

"I'm sorry," he murmured against her skin before he licked the nipple.

"No, no, it felt fantastic." She tugged gently at his hair to draw him back again.

"I need to move." He wrapped his fingers around her hips, holding her just above his lap so that he slid partway out of her. Even that tiny motion sent a spasm through her inner muscles. But she fought off the orgasm, wanting to prolong the moment.

And then he was thrusting and withdrawing, his grip tightening to brace her against his movements. As he pushed up into her, he hit her clit, coiling the tension tighter and tighter until she couldn't stop it. All feeling spiraled into one moment of stillness before it blossomed into a fireball of climax, ripping through her so that even her toes clenched with the power of her release.

She barely remembered to keep her lips pressed together so that her scream was muffled to a mere groan that got swallowed up in the sound of the jet's engines.

As the final aftershock washed through her, Derek arched upward and groaned through gritted teeth, pumping so deep that he set off another tremor of orgasm in her belly.

They both collapsed down into the embrace of the big chair, Derek with his head lolling against the headrest, Alice with her cheek on the warm, hard muscle of his shoulder. The plane continued to bounce gently along, lulling her into a half sleep until she felt him shift and slip out of her. She shivered, partly from sensitivity and partly from the chill of recirculated air against her bare skin.

"We should go somewhere more comfortable," he said. "The sofa in back folds out into a bed."

"I noticed that on the way down," she murmured against his shoulder. She willed herself to move but her muscles ignored her.

Derek huffed out a chuckle. "I guess you need some help."

He held her against him as he maneuvered them both to their feet. Grabbing his suit jacket from the other chair where he'd tossed it, he wrapped her up in the cocoon of wool and silk before steering her down the aisle to the sofa bed. She loved the way his footfalls made the floor sink slightly and his big body seemed to stir the air around them.

When they reached the sofa, she pivoted to face him. "Although you look very sexy in that suit, I don't think it's fair that I'm naked and you're dressed." She reached for the knot of his tie.

He put his hands on her hips to steady her as the plane bobbed again and lifted his chin to give her room to work the silk loose. "I'm pretty sure it's a win-win situation."

"You are such a consultant." She tugged the tie out of his collar, enjoying the slithering sound the silk made against the cotton.

"They pay me big bucks for an analysis like that."

She unbuttoned his shirt, letting her fingers trail over the skin as she uncovered it, relishing the contraction of his abs as she touched them. Then she made short work of his trousers and briefs so that he stood in all his bare, muscular glory for her to drink in. "God, I love to look at you."

She was surprised by the fleeting look of discomfort that crossed his face before he walked behind her and stripped his jacket off her shoulders.

Then his fingers were burrowing into the twists of her bun, feeling for the pins holding it in place. He carefully removed them one by one until her hair uncoiled and cascaded down her back, the brush of it sensual on her skin. When he combed his fingers through it, she let her head fall back to revel in the delicious tingles dancing over her scalp.

She staggered slightly as the plane rocked and he seized her shoulders.

"I think we should take this horizontal before someone gets hurt." He hit the button that sent the sofa into motion, its taupe leather cushions sliding down and flattening into a double-size bed. "And down we go," he said, moving her to the sofa bed so that the backs of her knees hit the edge. He wrapped his arms around her and lowered her gently onto the leather, the slippery surface feeling cool against her skin.

He straightened and stood looking down at her so intently that she could almost feel his gaze roving over her body. Despite the fact that he was naked too she suddenly felt self-conscious and exposed. "Hey, come down here and share some body heat," she said, holding up her arms in an invitation.

"Gladly, but let me add some extra warmth." He flipped open a compartment behind the sofa and pulled out a comforter, shaking it open to cover her before he slid under it beside her.

"Now I'm sure you've had sex on this airplane before." She shamelessly draped herself over his body, her head on his shoulder, her knee bent over his thigh. "Otherwise how would you know that blanket was there?"

"Because I've slept on this plane before. Alone." He sounded irritated. "After a long, hard day of meetings."

Happiness flooded through her, and she stroked her palm soothingly over his chest. "Just checking."

He shook her shoulder so that she lifted her head to look at him. His expression was serious. "I can't change the way I look. But it doesn't define the way I behave."

"You're right. I'm making assumptions that I shouldn't. I'm sorry."

He kissed her and settled her against him more tightly.

Even as she relaxed in his arms, she couldn't shake off her conviction that this wouldn't last. After all, his engagement hadn't.

Chapter 14

The late-afternoon sun slanted through the windows to paint squares of light on the carpet in Alice's office. Sylvester was curled in one square, his black fur gleaming, while Audley occupied an adjacent square, the gray of his coat shimmering like velvet. Alice rolled her chair away from her desk carefully to avoid squashing anyone's tail. Jumping up, she paced around the space that usually gave her peace and comfort. But today something was missing and she knew exactly what it was.

Derek. She conjured up his broad, cotton-clad shoulders, his waving brown hair with its glinting highlights, the bump in his otherwise straight nose, and the quirk of his firm, sculpted lips. Now she knew what each one of those attributes felt like under her questing fingers or against her lips.

She felt like she had a hangover, a Derek hangover. Drinking him in for three days and now going cold turkey.

Coming to a halt in front of the window that overlooked her little patio, she crossed her arms and recalled their parting this morning, a smile curling her lips. He'd wakened her as dawn was just brushing pink across the sky and made love to her like a man who needed to imprint it on his memory. Then he'd gone to his office, saying he planned to spend all day and half the night there.

She understood. He'd been neglecting the Argon project for her problems. Now he had to put in some serious work to be ready for his trip next week. She felt guilty about her role in adding to the pressure, but she couldn't regret any of their time together.

At least she knew the end date: his departure for Asia. It was a clear, convenient way for him to break off their little affair. It helped somewhat that she would be able to brace herself for it ahead of time.

She needed a drink and friends to distract her. Grabbing her cell phone, she hit Natalie's private number. It went to voice mail, of course, because Natalie was working, so Alice left a message. Then she tried Dawn with the same results.

While she was debating whether to go to the gym to work off her dismals, her phone rang in her hand, the caller ID coming up as KRG. Her heart seemed to stop and then begin skipping around in her rib cage. But when she looked at the number itself, she realized it wasn't Derek's.

Disappointment dumped its sour taste down her throat, so that she swallowed hard before she answered.

"Alice, this is Tully Gibson from KRG." His speech had the slow cadence of the West. "Derek gave me a briefing on your trip to Texas yesterday."

She assumed that he had skipped over a few parts of the expedition.

"I wanted to ask you some questions since you were the one who saw the facilities."

He proceeded to take her through each room and person she'd met, probing for details and her impressions. He asked her to repeat her conversation with Myron as accurately as she could remember it. He was encouraging, courteous, and relentless.

When his inquisition was done, he said, "I wish more folks were as sharp-eyed and thorough-thinking as you. Makes things easier for me."

His praise dispelled some of her melancholy.

"If you don't mind, I'm going to send you a computer rendering of Myron Barsky that Derek started on with our facial-recognition software. You've spent more time with him, so I hope you wouldn't mind telling us how to refine it. I want to see if we can ID him that way since his name isn't giving us any hits."

"I'd be happy to." It would take her mind off Derek's absence. "What about Ted Murval? Did you find out anything about him?"

She thought he might have hesitated a split second. "We're working on that."

"I could give John Peters a try on the software too," she offered.

"The security guy? Yeah, if you have the time, that would be helpful." His tone changed. "Now I don't want to worry you, but Derek and I both believe you should continue to have a security presence for the next week or so. You won't be aware of them, but I want you to program the number I'm about to text you into your phone in case you feel unsafe."

Alarm twisted her stomach. "Really? I thought the trip was supposed to fix that."

"I'm sure it did. This is just a precaution. Did you get my text?"

Alice checked the text that had just pinged into her phone. "Yes, it's here. Why won't I be aware of the security team?"

"Because they're good at their job. We don't want anyone to know they're there."

"Wouldn't it be better if the bad guys saw that I was being protected?"

His chuckle was low and friendly. "It's better to take the bad guys by surprise."

"If you say so. Thanks for being concerned about me." The call ended with Tully saying the link to the facial-recognition software was on its way.

Alice swiveled her chair to see Sylvester and Audley still fast asleep. Their utter unconcern with software fraud calmed the flutters of anxiety constricting her throat. It was just Derek's bias making his partners overly cautious.

She nodded to convince herself of the explanation and turned back to her computer.

⸺

"How did she take being assigned a security team?" Derek asked when Tully disconnected.

"She wanted to know why the trip hadn't removed the need for one."

"But she didn't object?"

Tully shook his head and relief flowed through Derek. He could imagine Alice pooh-poohing the whole idea. He wanted her to know that she had someone to call if she needed help, especially when he was in Asia.

Tully gave him a long, speculative look. "You seem a mite more worried about Alice Thurber than I'd expect. Not seven days ago, you figured you could spend fifteen minutes on her problem and be done with it. Now you refuse to let Leland and me take over for you when you have bigger fish to fry."

"That was before we discovered her problem was the tip of the iceberg in what appears to be embezzlement on a large scale." Tully could be annoyingly perceptive. It was that damned FBI training in reading people. "She isn't familiar with how far people will go to protect their money, especially if it's acquired illegally. You and I are."

"You got that right." Tully didn't let up, though. "You know what happened the last time you mixed business with personal."

Anger shook Derek. But he wasn't pissed off at Tully for poking into his private life. He was furious that Tully would suggest Alice was anything like Courtney. "This is totally different," Derek said through clenched teeth.

"If you say so, partner, but you nearly worked yourself to death after she gave back the ring." Tully shook his head. "I don't want to see you go through that again."

"I won't," Derek snapped before he shifted the conversation back to the relevant topic. "You didn't tell her about Ted Murval."

Tully leaned his chair back and put his boots up on his desk, his legs crossed at the ankles. "Do you want her more worried than she already is? I'm going to make sure KRG takes all the pressure from here on out. You have to trust me on that."

Derek give Tully a hard look. "I trust *you*. I don't trust whoever the hell is behind BalanceTrakR."

⌒

"Okay, what gives?" Dawn said after the server at Winenfood took their drinks order and plunked bowls of nuts and olives on the table. "You never want to go out drinking on a Saturday night. You claim it's too noisy." Her eyes narrowed, making the sharp angles of her face stand out. "Wait, does this have anything to do with that software problem you told me about?"

Alice almost hugged her friend for giving her the easy way out. After spending an hour concentrating on refining Myron Barsky's portrait and creating John Peters's visage, she'd felt less unsettled. Which was odd, seeing as she was pointing her digital finger at two possible criminals.

But it had directed her thoughts back to business and away from Derek's hands and mouth and body. And their imminent absence.

So Alice nodded. "It's about the BalanceTrakR software." She glanced around to make sure no one was seated too close to their table before she said softly, "You know the discrepancy I found in your books, Natalie? Well, it wasn't a mistake. It was theft. The software stole that money from you."

"Are you kidding me?" Natalie looked more puzzled than upset. "Why would they bother to steal $3.37? Seems like a lot of trouble for peanuts."

Dawn held up her hand. "That's what I said but Alice thinks they're doing it to everyone who has the software, so it adds up."

"You know about this?" Natalie asked Dawn, doing that elegant eyebrow arch that Alice envied so much. "Anyway, it would take a hell of a lot of 'everyones' to make it worthwhile. How many people did they sell it to?"

"Seven in Cofferwood that I know of," Alice said. "And we're not exactly a thriving metropolis." The truth was that Natalie's point echoed her own nagging sense that she was missing something.

"It was all that free booze at the presentation," Natalie said. "It affected my fellow business owners' judgment. No offense, Alice, since I know you approved it. You couldn't have known."

"None taken," Alice said, waiting as the server delivered their drinks. But guilt still clawed at her. She picked up the copper mug that held her Moscow Mule and raised it in a toast. "Here's to friends drinking together on a noisy Saturday night."

Dawn touched the moisture-beaded neck of her Stella Artois against Alice's mug, while Natalie said, "A virtual clink from me. This Manhattan glass is too full and I don't want to spill a drop." She took a careful sip and set the glass down. "All right, let's hear your story."

"You're not going to believe this but yesterday I flew to Texas on a private jet. With Derek Killion." She told them about her strange excursion, except, of course, for the return trip. She even glossed over the whole lunch outing, making it sound as though she and Derek had discussed the BalanceTrakR situation and nothing more.

"So now I have some kind of security team following me," Alice concluded.

Dawn scanned the room. "It's got to be the guy sitting at the table in the corner alone. He's pretending to read a book but he keeps looking around."

"Nope," Natalie said with a shake of her head. "He's the electrician from Northville whose wife left him after he gambled away their kids' college funds."

Natalie knew everything about the locals, thanks to the beauty parlor gossip. She took another sip of her drink. "It's the two women at the table near the door."

"How do you know?" Alice asked.

"Because I recognize everyone else in here and not a one of them would make a good bodyguard, except Dawn."

"Me?" Dawn made a face. "I'd make a lousy bodyguard."

"I'd trust you with my life," Alice said. "You've got the moves and the muscles. And your self-defense coaching has made me less terrified. I feel like I might have some chance of escaping."

"At least you realize that it's better to escape than to try to fight," Dawn said, but she looked pleased. She took a swig of beer and studied the two women Natalie had mentioned. "I think you might be right. I'm pretty sure one of them is wearing a gun under her blazer."

"Can you see it?" Alice asked, resisting the urge to swivel around to look.

Dawn shook her head. "It's more the way the fabric wrinkles. Something's under it."

"Wow!" Alice said. "I guess I feel safer knowing that." But she wasn't sure. If her watchers were carrying guns, Tully and Derek must think there was a serious threat. "Or maybe it scares me."

"You should come stay with me for a few days," Natalie said. "Dawn, you come, as well, to be our self-defense coach. We'll have a slumber party."

"And drag you into possible danger too?" Alice shook her head emphatically. "I will *not* do that. Besides, Derek and Tully don't really think I'm a target. The whole point of the trip was to put KRG in the limelight instead, and Tully is former FBI, so he can handle problems like this."

"Well, I'm going to mention this to the police chief," Natalie said. "He can send a cruiser past your place on a regular basis. It will give them something exciting to do."

"Seriously, no," Alice said. "I trust KRG's security."

"If you weren't nervous about your safety, why did you want company this evening?" Natalie asked, eyeing Alice over the rim of her glass. "Unless it has something to do with Derek Killion on a nonprofessional basis."

Of course she would figure it out, since she had suggested that Alice jump into bed with Derek even before the expedition to Texas.

Alice swallowed the last of her drink. "Maybe." She plunked the mug down on the table. "Okay, so I, um, joined the mile-high club on the trip home." She decided not to mention their previous encounters just yet.

"Well, I'm impressed and a little surprised," Natalie said, sitting forward to eye Alice. "I'm also glad you embraced the twenty-first century. I was afraid you'd only do it in a coach-and-four."

"Okay, I've missed something," Dawn said. "You had sex with some boring old consultant who you only met a week ago? I mean, I know you like dull men, but you usually don't sleep with them that soon. Or at all, actually."

Natalie swiped at her phone and handed it to Dawn. "That's the boring old consultant."

Dawn whistled. "He looks more like a movie star."

"His father wanted him to be one," Alice said, pleased with her inside knowledge.

"Now I get it why you'd do it." Dawn handed the phone back to Natalie. "Except it's still you and you don't do stuff like that."

"Natalie told me to," Alice said with a sideways look at her friend.

"But I didn't think you would." Natalie reached across the table to pat Alice's hand. "I'm happy for you, sweetie. You needed some fun. It *was* fun, wasn't it?"

Alice felt a blush radiate over her cheeks and was grateful for the dim lighting. "Um, yes. Quite, um, fun." She sighed. "The problem is that I like him for more than just his well-muscled body."

"So date him," Dawn said. "He's obviously into you or he wouldn't have done the dirty with you."

Alice frowned. She had no idea if Derek wanted to date her. Their relationship was built entirely around the BalanceTrakR issue. "He's leaving for a business trip to Asia next week. He hasn't said anything about getting together afterward." Admitting it out loud to her friends brought on a slicing pain like a knife had just plunged into her heart. She could feel her mouth twist at the sudden agony.

"Sweetie, this was supposed to be a one-night-stand kind of thing," Natalie said, her tone gentle. "A fling to get your confidence up. You weren't supposed to fall for him."

"I know, I know. It's ridiculous to feel this way about someone I just met," Alice said, but her rational brain had gone on vacation when it came to Derek.

"I don't know why he shouldn't fall for you," Dawn said. "You're both smart. You both are crazy about numbers. He wanted to have sex with you. That seems like a pretty good beginning for a relationship."

Natalie's laugh had an edge. "Relationships have certainly been based on a lot less."

Alice couldn't bring herself to tell them that there had been more sex than just on the plane. It made her feel gullible all of a sudden. "I get it. He's out of my league."

"No, you're out of his," Natalie said. "Don't waste another thought on him, except when you're home alone and in need of some, um, relief. Remember, he doesn't have a good track record since he couldn't hang on to his fiancée."

"Maybe it was the other way around," Alice pointed out.

"I'm trying to comfort you," Natalie said.

Alice gave a strangled laugh and raised her mug. "To girlfriends! The strong women who get us through the tough times in life."

⸗

Tully barged into Derek's office like a freight train. "We've got a problem."

Tension whipped through Derek's body, banishing the fatigue and—he hated to admit it—boredom of analyzing financial reports all day. "How big a problem?"

Tully was in the office on this particular Saturday because he was monitoring Alice's security team.

"John Peters is in Cofferwood."

Derek vaulted out of his chair with a string of curses. "Are you sure?"

"About as positive as I can be without knowing the man myself." Tully held out his phone. "Check out the rendering your Alice came up with on our facial-recognition software. Then swipe right to see the man one of my team photographed casing Alice's house."

"Shit!" Derek said as he compared the two images. He couldn't argue with the identification. "What do you mean 'casing Alice's house'?"

"Just like a burglar. Strolling by and examining it from several angles."

"Is Alice there?"

"Right now she's at a bar with two friends, but my team says they're wrapping things up."

"They have to stop her from going home." Derek was out of his chair and headed for the door. "I'm going to pick her up and bring her to my place."

Tully followed him, striding down the corridor beside him. "I'd tell you to let my team bring her there but I don't think you'll listen."

"Because Alice won't listen. She can be stubborn." Derek kept seeing Alice being grabbed by the thick-necked thug in Tully's photo, his arm around her neck as he yanked back on her long, beautiful hair. Fear slammed into his chest.

"And you think you can persuade her?"

"If I can't, I'll put her in the car bodily," Derek said through gritted teeth.

"Good plan." As they reached the reception area, Tully put his hand on Derek's arm to stop him. "Don't take this on yourself, partner. Your Alice poked at the hornet's nest when she posted her question on the help forum. And as you've pointed out, she's stubborn, so she wouldn't have left it alone. It's a good thing she has KRG on her side because we can protect her."

"I sure as hell hope you're right." Derek briefly gripped Tully's shoulder. "Just tell your people to keep her safe until I get there."

On the elevator ride down to the garage, Derek second-guessed himself about taking Alice to Texas. Maybe if he'd kept her out of it, the BalanceTrakR thug wouldn't have paid any attention to her. Tully insisted that wasn't the case but Derek wondered.

When he settled into the sedan waiting for him, he faced the problem he'd been avoiding with work. His feelings about Alice. Other than his gut-clenching worry about her safety, of course.

Leaving her that morning had been so hard that he'd nearly changed his mind. He'd planned to let her sleep while he dressed quietly and left for the office. But when his alarm sounded, she'd been curled up next to him with the sweet curve of her bottom nestled against his cock. He'd gotten hard instantly, so he woke her up and took his time making love to her, hoping that maybe he would be sated enough to keep his attention on the work he desperately needed to finish. When he'd told her he wasn't returning that night, it had been a test of his own self-discipline. There had been disappointment in her eyes but she had supported his decision because she understood his commitment to his clients.

But he'd felt like crap anyway.

The truth was that he'd been blindsided by what happened between them. He'd known how attractive he found her, how much he admired the way her mind worked. What he hadn't expected was finding the other side of her, the Alice that had a hard time believing Barsky was knowingly stealing from his clients. The Alice who took the initiative to interview the hotel manager in pursuit of the truth. The understanding listener who persuaded him to spill his guts about how disappointed his father was in him no matter what pinnacle of success he reached in the consulting world.

And the sensual, passionate lover who made every molecule in his body vibrate with arousal and then release.

He had the sense that she'd shown him aspects of herself that she usually kept under wraps to maintain her persona of careful, responsible bookkeeper and to avoid the ups and downs of her childhood.

What was it about him that made her throw caution to the wind?

He led a life as careful as hers. He focused on work, making sure that he sweated every detail. Even his social life was mostly work related. He could admit now that his relationship with Courtney had been a deliberate decision rather than an emotional imperative. She had fit his image of what his spouse should be as much as he had fit hers. Except they had both been wrong.

His feelings about Alice were nothing like that. He kept fighting them every inch of the way.

Yet Alice was careful too. He'd found himself in the odd position of winning her over by demonstrating that they were kindred spirits, craving the rational, orderly predictability of debits and credits. She understood that part of him in a way few people did.

And he understood her.

But he hadn't looked beyond the resolution of the BalanceTrakR problem and his departure for Asia. He had done exactly what he always did—made his job the priority when it came to his life, just as Courtney had accused him of. Except this time it wasn't happening. He couldn't use his work to keep Alice in the background.

Yes, he wanted to make sure she was safe, but that wasn't the real reason he was bringing her back to his highly secure penthouse. He wanted to see her again, to inhale her scent again . . . to make crazy, mind-blowing love to her again.

He restrained himself from asking the driver to go faster. Tully had assured him that the man was not only well trained in evasive driving tactics but also carried a gun and knew how to use it. The driver was aware of the situation and was doing his best in the ever-present traffic in the New York metro area.

So Derek tried to relax back in his seat, tried not to remember Alice's soft breasts, tried to fight off the chilling images of John Peters's thick hands wrapped around her throat. And failed at all three.

As Alice and her friends walked toward the door of Winenfood, the two women whom Natalie had pointed out stepped in front of Alice.

"Ms. Thurber, did you enjoy the film *Vertigo*?" the woman with short brown hair asked.

Alice started as she recognized the code phrase Tully had made her memorize, so his guards could confirm their identity for Alice, if necessary. "No, it made me nervous," she answered truthfully and with the confirming code phrase.

"You need to come with us, please," the tall blonde woman said. "It's not safe for you to return to your house."

"What do you mean?" Alice spoke sharply as she thought of Sylvester and Audley. "There's not a bomb or anything, is there?"

"No, but there's a threat to you."

"Alice, is everything all right?" Natalie asked, stepping in close.

"You were right about them. They're my security team," Alice said to her friend, gesturing to her bodyguards. "They say I can't go home."

"Then you'll come to my house," Natalie said.

"No, ma'am," the brunette said. "She needs someplace with significant security."

"But where?" Alice asked.

"Mr. Killion is on his way here," the brunette answered.

A thrill ran through Alice, even as fear battered at her rib cage. "Where is he taking me?"

The blonde shook her head to indicate she didn't know. "We're just here to protect you until he arrives."

"It's okay, guys," Alice said to her hovering friends. "They're legit. I'll be safe with them."

"How do you know?" Dawn gave them a narrow-eyed glare.

"This may sound kind of ridiculous but they had a code phrase," Alice said.

Dawn's glare eased. "Okay, I'm impressed."

"Thank you," the brunette said with a sarcastic edge. "Let's get you to our car."

"What about *my* car?" Alice asked as they hustled her toward the door. She waved to Natalie and Dawn, who stood watching with matching expressions of worry.

"Give us the keys and we'll make sure it gets taken care of. I imagine you leave your garage door opener in it." Alice caught a definite note of disapproval.

"Yes, I do, because I don't get mixed up with criminal hackers in my normal life," Alice said while they strode along toward a big black SUV. "Am I allowed to know your names?"

"Sure. I'm Sara," the brunette said. "She's Pam."

"Thanks for protecting me," Alice said, thinking that those were such unassuming names for such dangerous women. She waited fifteen feet away from the car with Pam while Sara reconnoitered to make sure no one lurked on the other side or had attached a bomb to it, serious precautions that made her stomach clench with nerves.

Pam held the back-seat door open, even as she constantly scanned their surroundings. As Alice climbed in, she hoped that Pam's hyper-vigilance was just a professional habit and didn't indicate any present threat. When Sara pulled out of the parking lot, Alice asked, "Can you at least tell me why everyone thinks I'm in danger?"

The two women in the front seat exchanged a glance before Pam said, "The man you did the composite of, John Peters, was spotted near your house."

Now Alice was scared, as in throat-closing, breath-stealing, heart-squeezing scared. They'd sent their head of security all the way from Texas to her house. That was definitely not good. "Oh." She swallowed and took a deep breath. "What do you think he's doing here?"

"We're keeping an eye on him to see if we can figure that out," Pam said.

"We?" Alice asked.

"Our third team member, Ray," Pam responded.

"So what are we going to do until Derek, er, Mr. Killion gets here?"

"Keep moving."

Alice sank back against the leather seat, trying to sort through the tangle of thoughts spinning in her brain. She suddenly sat forward. "I'm not going anywhere without my cats."

She thought she heard a choke of laughter from the front seat.

"You can talk to Mr. Killion about that," Sara said, turning off the main street onto a road that led to the highway.

Alice subsided again. Despite her alarm about Peters, her heart was doing a little dance because she would see Derek again. Not only that, he was coming to personally escort her to a safer place.

She thought of what Natalie had said, that this was supposed to be a meaningless fling to help her confidence. It was the height of stupid-ity to attempt to make it into anything more, but she couldn't seem to stop. Nothing she told herself stopped the excited anticipation from alternating with the genuine dread.

Sara and Pam were not chatty, so Alice stewed in the back seat as they cruised along the parkway until a call came in on Pam's phone. Then they were discussing lines of sight and handoffs and all kinds of things Alice couldn't follow. However, she shifted forward and said, "Don't forget my cats. I'm not going to leave them in case Peters decides to blow up my house."

Whoever Pam was talking to wasn't happy when she threw the cats into the conversation, but Alice didn't care. She had been worrying about Sylvester and Audley ever since she heard about Peters lurking around her place. She'd read enough thrillers to know that villains sometimes tortured and killed their target's pets as a warning. The possibility made her stomach heave.

Pam turned around in her seat. "Okay, we're going to return to Cofferwood and set up a perimeter around the house with our team and Mr. Killion's driver, who's also trained in personal security. You and Mr. Killion go into the house, get the cats, and leave as quickly as possible."

"Right. Got it," Alice said, resisting her slightly hysterical urge to say, "Roger that."

"In and out fast," Pam repeated. "Mr. Killion says you can buy whatever you need for yourself and the cats when you get to the city, so no packing clothes or anything."

The city. So she was being taken to New York. A hotel maybe? Or did KRG have such a thing as a safe house? That was another thriller thing she wasn't sure was accurate.

Fifteen minutes later they arrived in Alice's neighborhood. Now Pam and Sara were speaking almost nonstop into the earpieces they were wearing. As they approached Alice's house, they passed another dark SUV. When they pulled into Alice's driveway, a limo glided up to the curb in front of her sidewalk.

"What's your garage-door combination?" Pam asked.

"1-1-2-3-5-8," Alice said, thinking that Derek would have recognized the Fibonacci series and gotten a kick out of it.

Pam evidently didn't or else didn't feel the need to comment as she got out of the car to punch in the code.

After they pulled into the garage, Sara twisted around to say, "Stay in the car with the doors locked until we come back. If we don't come back, get the hell out of Dodge." She handed Alice the keys, which freaked her out more than everything else that had happened so far. Sara didn't seem like the sort who would trust a rank amateur with keys if she didn't think there was a real possibility that she wouldn't return.

Alice nodded and managed to croak, "Okay." Then she climbed into the driver's seat, just in case, and sat in the locked car alone in the dark garage, wondering what she would do if John Peters suddenly appeared beside her door. "Have a heart attack and die," she muttered. "Which would be exactly what he's hoping for."

But Sara and Pam returned and escorted her into her own kitchen. Alice stopped short in the kitchen doorway, her pulse doing a slow, sensual tango.

Derek stood in her tiny foyer, the tall, muscled body she now knew every naked inch of clad in jeans and a maroon polo shirt. His arms were crossed and his face was tight with worry. When he saw her, he exploded into motion, striding over to wrap her in his powerful arms, so that her fear melted away. "Thank God you went out tonight. I can't imagine . . . if you'd been home . . ." He inhaled deeply. "It's all fine now."

"The cats," Sara prodded.

"Right," Derek said, although he was slow to release Alice. She loved the fact that he didn't complain about her concern for her pets. "Where are their carrying cases?"

"Oh . . . in the garage," Alice said. She'd been so nervous that she'd forgotten to bring them in.

"Lead the way," he said.

Alice noticed that Sara and Pam positioned themselves strategically as she and Derek moved. After they retrieved the cases, their little squad traipsed upstairs since Sylvester and Audley were not on the first floor. "Let me go alone," Alice said. "Otherwise they may hide from all the commotion."

Pam nodded. "Ray's got eyes on Peters so it's safe."

Alice checked in her office and found Audley on his favorite perch on the cat tree. She scooped him up and carried him out to where Derek already had the carrier open. Audley only put up a mild yowl of complaint at being confined. She discovered Sylvester in the laundry room, enjoying the nest of towels in the laundry basket. Since he hated going to the vet and assumed the cat carrier meant that was their destination, she wrapped him in one of the towels to avoid being scratched.

Even then, Derek had to help her wrestle the squirming kitty into his case, grabbing the cat's flailing hind legs in his big, capable hands and giving Sylvester a shove through the opening. "If you ever need a second career, you'd make a great vet tech," she joked, surprised at his willingness to get up close and personal with the hissing cat.

He surprised her even more when he said, "My mother was a soft touch, so I often got recruited to help her catch strays. I learned how to do it right purely for self-preservation."

She eyed him in his designer jeans with his perfectly styled hair and tried to picture him chasing down frightened cats and dogs. It wasn't happening.

"Don't look so skeptical," he said, picking up both cat carriers.

"I can take one," Alice offered.

He didn't bother to answer, just nodded his head toward the stairs with that arrogant tilt she'd come to enjoy because she knew it was just him being him.

When they reached the foyer, Sara said, "Wait here, please. We're going to swap the SUV out for the limo in the garage. The limo's armored."

"Good lord!" Alice muttered.

"Yes, it's serious." Derek sounded exasperated. "You don't seem to grasp that."

"I'm beginning to. Where did KRG get an armored limousine?"

"If I told you, I'd have to kill you," he said, deadpan. Then he gave her a half smile. "Tully handles security for some high-powered CEOs, so he has his sources."

"I'm pretty sure KRG is losing money on me," Alice said. "All this for free."

"The FBI is very grateful to KRG for the chance take down the BalanceTrakR conspiracy. We consider that kind of goodwill bankable."

"So why isn't the FBI here now instead of you guys?"

Derek seemed almost angry. "Do you really think I would entrust your safety to total strangers?"

She tried not to read too much into his question or into the anger hers had provoked, but a warm wave of hope rippled through her. "I, well, they're trained professionals."

"So are our people. Highly trained," Derek said. "And I feel more secure because they have to answer to me."

The warm feeling went hotter because she suddenly could see him in an embroidered waistcoat, lace foaming at his wrists and neck, his hair long and tied back with a black silk ribbon, directing his minions with ducal authority.

Pam walked back into the kitchen and beckoned to them. "Let's get this show on the road."

Sylvester's and Audley's carriers were buckled into the backward-facing seat of the limo, while Alice and Derek slid onto the forward-facing one. A male driver and Pam sat in the front seat. Evidently, Sara was going to follow them in the SUV.

"I feel like the president," Alice said as the cavalcade moved onto the street. Then she remembered the question that had gotten pushed to the back of her mind. "Where are we going?"

"To my place," Derek said. "It's on the top floor of a highly secure building, a much easier place to keep you from harm than out here. It won't be for long. Just until the FBI circle in on Barsky, Peters, and whoever else is involved in the scam."

Her breathing went shallow as her nerve endings lit up. She should show some self-respect and pretend to object but she decided it wasn't worth wasting her breath on a lie.

"It's very nice of you to take me and my cats in."

"I'm not doing it to be nice," he said. "I'm trying to keep you safe."

"It's still nice because although I'm not much trouble, my cats are kind of demanding."

Derek uttered something between a groan and a laugh. "You are more trouble than I could have anticipated in a thousand years."

That stung. "I'm sure I can find somewhere else to go if I'm that much of a problem."

"That's not what I meant."

He hooked his arm around her waist and slid her up against his side from thigh to shoulder. She snuggled into him, relishing the feel of the soft knit of his shirt against her cheek, the hard muscle of his thigh under her palm, and the scent of warm, clean man. His breath ruffled her hair as he brushed a kiss on the top of her head, and she thought she would die a happy woman if John Peters shot her right now.

He exhaled. "You've surprised me, made me feel guilty, made me feel alive, and distracted me from concentrating on a very important client."

"Okay, that's a lot to take in," Alice said, trying to remember everything that he'd said but focusing mostly on *made me feel alive*. That had to be a good thing, even if he was just referring to sex.

"Tell me about it." He kissed her temple. "I'm trying to convince myself that the only reason I came out here to get you myself was because I didn't want your death on my conscience."

"But that's not true?" She wanted him to spell it out.

"You know it's not." He shifted on the seat and his face was illuminated by a passing car's headlights as he stared down at her. "I want to strip your clothes off and make love to you. As always."

All of a sudden she needed to roll down the window to let some air into the car. "And that's bad," she said as her skin prickled with longing.

"It makes it hard to keep my mind on Argon."

"Does it make a difference that I want to strip your clothes off too?"

He let his head fall back against the seat so he was looking at the roof of the limo. "It makes it worse."

"You should feel better since you're not the only one."

"But now I have no reason not to do it." He lifted his head and nodded forward. "Except the two people sitting in the front seat."

"I thought these things had privacy screens," Alice said, scanning the clear Plexiglas window between the front and back of the limo.

"They're not going to put it up because it blocks too much of their rear view."

"How about one kiss?" she said.

His arm tightened around her waist. "That might lead to other things."

"I'm willing to risk it." She felt like one of her Regency heroines flirting in a ballroom, except here she was playing with fire.

He threaded the fingers of his free hand in her hair so he could angle her face up toward his. She twisted so that she was almost on his lap. Their lips met and her body softened. She curled into him, enveloped by his body and scent, cocooned in an armored limousine as it glided through the night.

She'd never been at bigger risk—to her heart or to her life—yet she felt safer than she ever had before.

And that was very, very dangerous.

⌒

Alice felt deliciously cozy and warm. Except someone kept shaking her.

"We're here." Derek's smooth baritone voice was right beside her ear.

She burrowed into the warm body beside her, not wanting to wake up from the perfect dream.

"Alice! We have to get out!"

Her eyelids flew open and she sat up as reality woke her. If it weren't for John Peters's shadow hanging over them, reality wouldn't be so bad, since Derek still had one arm around her waist.

"We're at my place," he said more gently. "Time to go."

"I—right." She wriggled out of his arm and pushed a stray strand of hair back from her face. It promptly fell back down but this time Derek reached out to tuck it behind her ear in a gesture that nearly made her cry. "Thanks."

He leaned in to whisper, "I look forward to seeing it loose later."

Her scalp tingled with the memory of how he'd played with it in bed. "That's a distinct possibility," she said.

He made a sound that was almost a purr, which reminded her of Sylvester and Audley, both staring at her from behind the wire gates of their carriers. "Are you guys doing okay?" she asked. "You're wondering what the heck is going on, aren't you?"

Audley meowed in response while Sylvester merely blinked.

"They're being good sports," Derek said, stretching across to unbuckle the seat belts from the carriers and place them on the floor by Alice's feet. "The concierge should have brought up kitty litter, cat food, and some cat toys already. Along with some clothes for you." He gave her a slow smile that said she wouldn't need the new clothes any-time soon. She was on board with that.

The door by Derek swung open. "All clear," the driver said. "I'll take one cat, but I need my other hand free."

Alice realized he meant that he wanted to be able to draw his gun, which made John Peters's shadow a lot bigger and darker.

Derek took Audley and their little entourage dashed from the car to the wood-paneled elevator, riding upward thirty-odd stories in tense silence. The doors opened directly into Derek's penthouse apartment, but they had to wait inside the elevator car behind Pam while the driver checked all the rooms, which took longer than Alice would have expected. When they were finally released, Alice saw a collection of cat supplies stacked neatly by a staircase that soared upward in a double-height entrance hall. The sculptural chandelier that hung in the open space would have looked at home in an art museum.

"It's two stories!" she breathed in awe, unable to wrap her mind around what the cost of such a huge apartment was. That explained why it had taken so long to make sure the place was empty of intruders.

"I think we should turn the cats loose in a confined area until they settle down," Derek said. "We'll do it in the media room so we have entertainment while Sylvester and Audley explore."

Of course, he had a media room in a place like this. Alice grabbed the litter boxes while Pam hauled a bag of kitty litter and they both followed Derek and the driver down a wide hall lit by sculptural crystal-and-chrome sconces. The silver carpet was so thick that their footsteps were completely muffled.

Derek led them into a room furnished with a massive charcoal-colored sectional sofa positioned in front of a giant flat screen hung on the wall. One wall was entirely made of windows looking out across the dark shimmer of the Hudson River to the cliffs of New Jersey. But even as she watched, a heavy curtain, propelled by some unseen electrical control, was gliding across the glass to shut out the view.

She looked around for a spot to position the litter boxes but saw only more plush silver carpeting. The idea of the cats tracking their litter over it made her cringe.

"Let me see if your concierge brought mats to put in front of the boxes," she said, setting down her load.

"I'll get the rest of the supplies," the driver said, heading for the door.

"Don't worry about the carpeting," Derek said to her. "It's rated as resistant to even hot buttered popcorn."

The mention of popcorn made Alice's stomach grumble. A smile flickered across Derek's face. "I'll get some of the food I ordered in."

After a flurry of activity, the cats' area was set up, including food and water. A selection of takeout had been brought in for Alice and Derek, while the driver—whose name she finally learned was Christian—and Pam retreated to the kitchen to eat.

Sylvester and Audley had been watching the commotion with some suspicion, their golden eyes large in the dimness of their carriers. Alice opened Sylvester's door first, picking up the big black cat and stroking him before sitting down with him on her lap. He stayed with her for a minute as he peered around and sniffed. His head swiveled toward the glass-and-chrome table holding the takeout and he leaped gracefully onto the floor to pad in that direction.

"Oh no, you don't," Alice said, grinning as she scooped him up and plunked him down in front of the gourmet cat food awaiting him. Sylvester took one inhale and turned up his nose before moving to inspect the litter boxes.

"He's definitely a cat," Derek said, his tone dry.

"You may have to guard our food," she said.

He rolled his shoulders in a stretch, his shirt tightening to give a tantalizing hint of the muscles underneath. "On it."

She released Audley, who immediately took off to explore the room. Both cats ended up eyeing Derek as he blocked their attempts to jump on the table with the human food.

"You can't blame them," Alice said, coming over to join him by the window. "It smells fantastic." Her stomach growled again and she smacked her hand over it as though she could quell the sound.

"You need to eat." Derek pulled out one of the heavy leather chairs for her.

She sank down into it, giving a little shiver when he brushed his lips against the side of her neck. As the sensation danced through her body, she felt his fingers tugging at the band holding her ponytail. "May I?" he asked.

"Yes, yes, absolutely." Her voice was breathy with anticipation.

He eased the band down her hair, taking his time so she never felt a tug or snarl as her hair loosened. When the band slid off, she tilted her head back and shook her hair free, her eyes meeting Derek's in an invitation. He took it, bending to slant his mouth over hers while his fingers tangled in her hair. He stroked one hand lightly down the taut line of her throat and skimmed it over her breast, making her arch up from the chair to feel more.

"No," he said, dropping his hands and lifting his head. "Food, first."

"Because we'll need our strength for later," she teased, even though her body was tight with frustration.

"Something like that." He seated himself across from her and picked up a plastic container. "Try this chestnut pasta with wild boar ragù. It's one of my favorites."

"Are all of these your special choices?" she asked as she accepted a serving of the pasta.

He surveyed the array of takeout. "I suppose so. It's easier just to order the usual."

She made him tell her what each dish was because she loved this glimpse into his everyday life.

"It all smells delicious, so I'm going to sample," she said, helping herself to a taste from each container.

"I remember from lunch that you like samplers." He smiled. "Tell me which you like the best. I'll keep it in mind for the next order."

The next order. She wondered when—or if—there would be another order. "Don't you think that Tully and the FBI will be able to catch John Peters tonight?"

He put down his fork. "I think you should know that Tully tracked down Ted Murval, except that's not his real name. He's an amateur actor called Jake Masters."

"Oh my gosh, so it *was* a stage set." The formerly delicious wild boar suddenly didn't sit so well.

"Your instincts were right on target." He gave her a level look. "Which means that someone spent a lot of money to fool us."

"And that means that a lot more money is at stake or they wouldn't have bothered." She shook her head. "I don't get it. Even if they sold several thousand copies of BalanceTrakR, at the rate they were embezzling, it wasn't going to accumulate anything significant for years."

He nodded. "There has to be more to it."

"That's what I keep thinking. What if the tiny withdrawals were some kind of a test run?"

"Just to make sure they could get to the funds? That could be it. Then at some point, they grab the whole transfer, rather than just a small part of it."

"They'd have to do every client on the same day, though, because people would definitely notice that and complain."

"So there's some sort of timeline, a ticking clock." He took a swallow of wine. "That concerns me."

"Because?"

"If John Peters is here, they still think you're a threat."

"I guess it's too much to hope that he's a really convincing actor, like Jake Masters." Alice decided she needed a gulp of wine too as Derek's words sank in. "Barsky probably is a real computer hacker. I would guess that he's the brains of the operation."

"Tully's got his FBI contacts working on identifying both of them." His stern expression was banished by a slow smile. "For tonight, however, we are quite safe. This building has excellent security, and our dynamic duo of Pam and Christian will provide backup. So we can relax . . . and enjoy ourselves."

She forgot all about the hunger in her stomach as another appetite flared to life, fed by his words and the flame smoldering in his eyes. "I think I'm done with dinner," she said, deciding it was her turn to tease him from behind his chair.

"You've barely eaten anything," he said.

"The food will still be here later." She stood up.

"Not if we leave the containers open on the table," he said, snapping a plastic lid over the dish in front of him. "Sylvester and Audley will have a feast."

She laughed and helped him cover the food at high speed. When she walked around the table, his face lit with anticipation. She came up to the back of his chair and rested her hands on his shoulders, just savoring the curve of muscle under the cotton shirt. Slowly, she slid her hands down over his biceps and back up to his shoulders before she twined her fingers into his hair to tilt his head sideways. Leaning down, she kissed the tendon flexing in his neck before parting her lips to flick his skin with her tongue. He sucked in a breath but didn't move, so she ran her tongue along his jawline, feeling the slight roughness of his late-night beard.

He reached up and seized one of her wrists, pulling it down to his mouth where he licked her palm before grazing his teeth over the base of her thumb. That gave her an idea. She twisted her hand out of his grasp, uncovered a slice of chocolate cake, and dipped her finger in the daub of whipped cream on top of it, bringing it back to his lips.

A low growl came from his throat as he sucked her finger into his mouth and rolled his tongue over it.

"More?" she asked, slipping her finger free.

"I'd like to reciprocate," he said, pivoting in the chair to snake his arm around her waist and pull her onto his lap.

She felt his erection under her thighs and it sent arousal searing through her. He dragged his finger through the chocolate icing on the cake and held it to her lips. She opened her mouth and sucked the rich, dense chocolate off his finger, eliciting another growl from deep in his chest. She answered with a hum of delight as the burst of flavor from the chocolate hit her tongue, his hard cock pushed at her thighs, and his free hand found her breast. It was a delicious assault that whipped the yearning inside her into a frenzy.

She seized his wrist and pulled his finger out of her mouth. "*Now,*" she said. "I want you now."

When she freed his wrist, he shoved one arm under her legs and wound the other around her back to cradle her against his chest. In an impressive display of strength and balance, he straightened to a standing position with her in his arms. "Any preference as to where?" he asked.

She scanned the room, her gaze settling on the rolled arm of the sectional. The idea that came to her made liquid heat flow through her body. "By the arm, there." She pointed. "With me over it."

There had been a hot scene in one of her racier historical romances in the drawing room with a love seat that had rolled arms. She'd always wondered what it would feel like.

He went still and looked down at her, lust and uncertainty in his expression. "Are you sure?"

"One hundred percent."

His grip on her tightened and he was beside the sofa in three strides. Setting her feet on the floor, he wrapped her in his arms and kissed her with a dark intensity that made fire run through her veins. When he broke away from her mouth, he ripped the buttons of her blouse out of their holes before he unhooked her bra and flung both garments away. She toed off her heels while he unfastened her jeans and yanked them and her panties to her ankles for her to step out of. She was naked and he was fully dressed. He ran his hands down to seize her butt and pull her up against him, the press of fabric on her skin making her gasp with the exquisite pleasure of it. When he slid his finger into her from behind, she thought she would come but she fought it down.

"You are so damn hot," he said, working his finger in and out of her as her hips pulsed with his rhythm. "Are you ready?"

"Beyond ready."

He withdrew his finger and turned her so that she faced the thick, padded arm of the sectional. She started to bend over it, but he held her shoulders. "Let me," he said, his voice a rasp.

He banded one arm around her waist and nestled his cock between her buttocks. Then he crossed his other arm over her breasts, cupping one in his palm. Once he had her tight against him, he used his weight to slowly bend her over the arm, so that her hips were trapped between the sofa and his body, his cock sliding as their positions shifted so that it rubbed against her clit.

"Derek!" she cried, feeling a clench of orgasm that she struggled to stop. She wanted to come with him inside her. Yet she loved the feeling of his body over hers.

"Don't move." His arms slid away from her and his weight lifted, leaving her feeling exposed and vulnerable in a way that drove her arousal higher. She braced her arm on the sofa cushions and waited. She knew he was staring at her as she heard the clink of his belt buckle and the rip of the condom's foil envelope. Then his hands were anchoring her hips and he was slowing pushing into her, filling the hollow ache within. When he was inside her so far that she could feel the imprint of his zipper on the back of her thighs, he stopped.

She tried to shift her hips to make him move but her position and his grip kept her still.

"I want to savor you like this," he said, as he traced down her spine with one finger, letting it brush between her buttocks.

A shudder of longing shook her. "Yes," she said on an exhale.

Once again he bent down, so she felt his shirt against her back and his cock changing angles within her. He worked his hands between the sofa and her breasts, finding her nipples with his thumbs and circling them. An electric blaze flashed from her breasts down to where his cock stretched her, making her moan.

He stroked her nipples again and flexed his hips so that he went even deeper. For a long moment, all she felt was the spreading stillness as her orgasm gathered itself into a tiny point of anticipation between her legs. Then it exploded outward, contracting and releasing her muscles around the thickness of his cock in a mind-bending paroxysm. "Oh God, yes! Derek, yes!" She thought her body would disintegrate with the intensity of it, fly to pieces with the pleasure.

He flicked at her nipples once more, sending her to another peak of climax before her muscles melted into satiation.

Only then did he straighten and begin to move inside her, his hands tilting her hips to the angle he wanted, his thrusts growing faster and stronger. She thought she couldn't feel any more bliss but he drew out every last ounce from her stunned nerve endings before he sank deep into her and shouted her name as his grip tightened with the force of his finish.

He collapsed over her, his elbows on the cushion beside hers, his breath whistling past her ear. She could feel him soften and slip out of her, making her whimper with regret at the absence.

"Alice," he murmured. "My amazing Alice."

She smiled but couldn't form a coherent thought in response. Her climax had fried her brain cells. So she lay there with Derek acting as a blanket over her sated body. She wasn't sure she could move anyway.

With a groan, he levered himself off her. "I don't want to crush you," he said before he grasped her shoulders and eased her up onto her feet as well.

She had no chance to feel cold or exposed because he grabbed a soft, gray throw blanket from the back of the sofa and whipped it around her. He snugged it up to her neck with a touch and a smile so tender her knees went weak. "Let me collect your clothes since I tossed them all over the place."

He kissed her once gently and then again with more passion. "I have a hard time letting go of you," he said with a rueful smile.

And yet he hadn't mentioned anything about seeing her again after his trip to Asia. She couldn't figure him out.

She dropped onto the couch, her body humming with satisfaction, while he scooped up articles of her clothing. How had she had the nerve to do what she'd done? Looking back on it made her cheeks warm with a blush.

He set the pile of clothing on the sofa and sat down beside her, pulling her onto his lap.

"Isn't this what got us in trouble in the first place?" she asked, snuggling into the warmth and solidity of his shoulder.

He leaned back, bringing her with him. "Which is why it bears repeating."

She peeked up to find his head tilted back and his eyes closed while a smile curled the corners of his mouth. He looked like a man who'd just had great sex. She relaxed into him again, reveling in the knowledge that she had put that expression on his face.

For a peaceful few minutes, she drifted in a haze of contentment. Then her stomach grumbled and he stirred. "Dinner may be a little cold by now. I'll take it to the kitchen and nuke it while you get dressed."

She shook her head and scooted off his lap. "No need. I've been known to eat cold pizza."

"No wonder Myron Barsky doesn't scare you."

She laughed and slipped on her panties under the blanket. He caught her shyness and walked over to the dining table, keeping his back to her while he rearranged the takeout containers. Appreciating his tact, she scrambled into her clothes quickly, sucking in a breath as her panties touched the highly sensitized spot between her legs.

"I hate to think what my hair looks like," she said as she joined him at the table.

He reached out to comb his fingers through it. "It looks like it belongs to the sexiest woman alive."

The way he looked at her made her believe he meant it and she didn't know what to do with that. "Okay, then. Let's eat."

"And the hungriest woman alive." He held her chair and dropped a kiss on the side of her neck after she sat. Little sparks crackled over her skin just from that light brush of his lips.

As she sat across from him, swapping containers, she realized that parting from him would hurt. A lot. But she couldn't regret any of what she'd done. She had become so afraid to do anything that would jeopardize the safe little world she had built with painstaking care that she had forgotten how to let go.

Somehow Derek had shown her that more was possible. He'd lulled her with his devotion to the sanity of numbers and then seduced her into forgetting about reason and rationality. Maybe it was the fact that, in the beginning, she hadn't considered that this could be a real relationship that had released her inner wild woman. Maybe it was because she still couldn't believe this man would want her of all people so it seemed like a dream. Which freed her to act like it *was* all a dream, pretending to be someone she wasn't.

The new Alice was bold and sexy and went after what she wanted. But the new Alice didn't really fit into the old Alice's life, a life she would have to return to once Derek jetted off to Asia. How was she going to stuff herself back into the circumscribed world of her town house, her cats, and her careful little business? Not that she didn't love all those things, but Derek had shown her how much bigger her world could be.

Of course, her world could never be on the level his was with private jets and expense-account meals at elegant restaurants and custom-made suits. She'd never wanted those things before, but now that she had seen what he had accomplished, she found herself wondering how much further she could have gone if she'd tried.

Derek thought she was smart and hardworking, but was that enough to succeed like he had? He'd taken tremendous risks, something she'd been terrified of. Was it too late for her to shove past the fear and try for more?

"You're very pensive," he said, refilling her wineglass. "Are you worried about John Peters? Because you shouldn't be."

"No, I can't picture anyone climbing up forty stories of steel and glass, and we have Pam and Christian to greet them if they did."

"Then what's made you so quiet?"

"Great sex. You've worn me out." She tossed him a teasing smile.

Disappointment flitted across his face. "Let me show you to the guest room, then."

"The guest room? I was hoping to sleep with you." Yup, that was the new Alice all right.

He sat back and gave her a heavy-lidded look. "If you share a bed with me, there will not be much sleeping involved. So you'll be even more worn out in the morning."

"I'm willing to take that chance." She didn't want to waste a moment of her time with him, even under threat of evil computer hackers.

"Oh, it's not a chance. It's a statistical certainty."

"Unfair!" she said, throwing up her hand in mock protest. "You know the effect statistics have on me."

"Then let's set some parameters." He stood up and came around to her side of the table. "We'll see if we get a positive skew."

She took the hand he held out, savoring the strength of his fingers as they closed over hers and pulled her to her feet. "I'm interested in the standard deviation myself."

He used their joined hands to bring her up against him, his gaze smoky with desire. "I would never say no to a little deviance."

⁓

Derek stared out the window of his bedroom at the lights of boats moving on the Hudson River. Alice slept curled against his side, her hair spread like a satin curtain across his chest. Her breast pushed at his ribs as she breathed, reminding him of how it felt resting in his palm or pressed into his mouth. Her knee was crooked over his thigh—something she often did while she slept and which he appreciated because he could feel the silken heat between her legs. His cock stirred despite having just made love to her for the second time that night.

His unexpected Alice. She threw him off-balance at every encounter, but he came back for more. Couldn't stop himself from coming back, in fact.

Because she banished the restlessness he'd been feeling. The dissatisfaction with work that he'd started the SBI to combat. She'd intrigued him with her project, engaged his mind in a different way from the complex corporate finances he usually dealt with.

She had reminded him of the honesty of numbers. People lied. Numbers eventually told the truth, as long as you were determined to track it down. Alice was committed to that truth in a way he wanted to recapture.

Her passion for the quest had somehow transmuted itself into a different kind of passion that flared between them. He frowned into the darkness. He was nearly certain that she was as surprised by it as he was. And that she didn't normally have sex with a man she knew as little as she knew him.

She struck him as something of an innocent. When she'd suggested sex over the sofa arm, he'd nearly come at just the thought of gripping the sweet curves of her ass while he drove into her. His cock hardened even more but he wasn't going to wake her from the slumber she'd fallen into as soon as they'd both come. She was exhausted.

He couldn't sleep, not because his body wasn't satisfied, but because he wanted to savor the feel of her in his arms and in his bed. It felt very right to have her in his own territory, protected by all the security he could command. He could imagine spending many nights with her cocooned in his penthouse, eating takeout, finding sexual innuendo in mathematics, and discovering new ways to use the decorator-selected furniture he'd never paid much attention to before. In fact, he hoped Tully and the FBI took their own sweet time finding Myron Barsky because it would give him an excuse to insist that Alice stay here with him.

And that threw him off-balance all over again. He'd never had any interest in having a woman share his penthouse. Courtney had been the one to suggest that she move in with him. His first reaction had been reluctance—and he should have listened to it.

Even with Courtney in residence, he'd felt it was just the place he came to sleep, to have sex, sometimes to eat, sometimes to work. She had treated it the same way.

It was not a home until Alice walked into it and made him want to wrap himself in her while the world went on outside these walls.

He didn't want to go to Asia. He didn't even want to go to the office on Monday morning. He wanted to stay here with Alice in his arms.

And that shook the very foundation of his world.

Chapter 15

Alice came awake to the feel of someone stroking down the bare skin of her back. She opened her eyes to find Derek's face mere inches from hers, an expression of lazy arousal lighting his eyes, a shadow of overnight whiskers turning the perfection of his jawline rugged. His hand strayed lower to grip her bottom, sending a shiver of longing between her legs.

"This is a good way to wake up," she said, brushing a kiss over the firm curves of his lips.

"I'm glad you think so. I let you sleep as late as I could before I had to touch you."

"How late is it?" She felt the nudge of his erection against her thigh.

"Seven forty-five." He rolled them both so he was on top of her, his chest brushing her hardening nipples, the head of his cock nestled between her thighs.

She huffed out a laugh at his idea of late. But she would rather be doing this than sleeping.

"I don't think you should laugh at me when you're in this position," he said, flexing his hips so that his cock hit her clit.

Pleasure surged from that one touch to coil in her belly, making her arch under him. She was wet and ready. She reached out to grope for the condoms on the bedside table, somehow finding one and holding it up in front of his eyes. "Inside me now. Then we can have the foreplay."

"Unexpected Alice," he said in an odd tone before he took the condom and shifted to roll it on.

He pushed up to kneel between her legs, pulling her thighs up onto his. A curve of golden-brown hair fell onto his forehead as he looked down at her. "I'm going to do this slowly and watch myself going into you," he said.

His words vibrated through her, making her muscles clench in anticipation.

He positioned his cock and began to push into her, tilting her hips so that he could slide in deep. As he entered her, the strained tendons of his neck indicated the power of his control. She could see the glaze of lust in his eyes grow stronger the farther inside he went. That and the feel of him stretching and filling her with such exquisite slowness made her try to rock her hips, but his grip on her thighs kept her still. "You wanted foreplay," he rasped.

"Dumb idea," she said on a gasp as he seated himself deeper.

His smile held a wicked challenge. "Let's see who can last longer."

"Oh, I'm so going to win," she said, tightening her inner muscles around him.

He let out a long groan. "Very effective," he rasped. "Do it again."

She obeyed, but it began to backfire as the rhythm of grip and release wound excitement into her muscles.

"Time to fight back," he said, hooking her ankles together at the small of his back before he leaned down to play with her nipples, the change in angle driving him even deeper into her.

"Oh yes!" She dug her heels into his back so she could arch up to add to the pressure of his cock and his fingers.

This time he definitely growled before he rolled her nipples, sending a lightning streak of desire from her breasts to her belly where he was lodged. She gasped and rocked so her clit hit the nest of hair around his cock. "I like this game," she said on a pant.

"Time to run the table," he said, cupping one of her breasts while he skimmed his other hand over her abs to where they were joined.

She saw the direction he was going and knew her time was running out. Using her legs for leverage, she undulated her hips while squeezing her inner muscles as hard as she could around him. The motion and pressure sent her soaring toward her climax but she fought against it, refusing to let go until he did.

He began to move in and out, his rhythm fast and hard, his hands locked under her buttocks to keep her in the position he wanted. She gave in and let him drive her up to the zenith of perfect poise, where she drifted for an instant, savoring what was to come in the crashing release of her climax. At the moment her muscles clenched on their own for the first time, he bowed backward and thrust into her while shouting her name.

She fell into the exquisite rhythm of tightening and loosening, the bliss of it exploding deep within her as she felt him pumping too. When her body felt wrung out like a happy sponge, she unlocked her ankles and let her butt lower, the sliding out of his still semihard cock making her nerves twitch with a last wisp of delight.

"I won." She gave him a seductive smile. "It doesn't matter who came first, I definitely won."

He disposed of his condom but continued to kneel, looking down at her with a satisfied laxity in his face and stance. "It was a tie."

"I can live with that." She seized his wrist and tugged at it.

He came down beside her, the front of his long body pressed against her side and his head propped on his hand. "I could live with this," he said, his palm skimming over her shoulder and arm.

A little niggle of hope rose in her chest but she swatted it down. He was just flirting with her, post-sex. It was the gentlemanly thing to do. He didn't mean he wanted to live with her beyond this moment.

He wound a strand of her hair around his fingers and used the end to brush at her breast, making the nipple pucker. "You can do that all you want, buster, but you have used me up. For now," she said, even as delicious sensations rippled over her skin.

"I can wait." He continued his marvelous torture for a few more moments. Then he bent his neck and put his lips where her hair had been, sucking ever so gently. The warmth and pull flowed through her, making her sigh and close her eyes to focus on what his mouth was doing. Then he stopped and she whimpered her regret.

"I'd like to see you when I get back from Asia."

Her eyelids flew open to find his jaw tight and his eyebrows drawn together in a near frown. The happy tap dance her heart had started stumbled to a halt in the face of his strange expression. "I'm in," she said but without the unalloyed joy she expected to feel.

"I'll call you when I get back." His face relaxed, as though some difficult negotiation had been concluded. "We should get moving before Christian or Pam comes up to get proof of life. You can use the master bath. I'll go down to the guest room." He lowered his head for a kiss that made up for his odd mood. Mostly.

꿈

Derek stood in the shower, the water from the multiple pulsing showerheads pounding into his skin, as he berated himself for botching things with Alice. He'd seen the bewilderment on her face when he'd baldly stated his desire to see her again. But he'd considered his request an admission of weakness, so he hadn't been graceful, hadn't been able to phrase it with more finesse. He needed to find the words to fix that, so she didn't wonder why the hell he had asked her out again if he was so unhappy about it. It wasn't her fault that she made him want to shirk all his responsibilities.

The irony was that, unlike Courtney, Alice wouldn't resent his commitment to his career. He was the one who wanted to chuck it all and spend the day in bed.

He shook his head, sending water splattering over the marble tiles. He *had* to work, even though it was Sunday. Not that he paid much attention to what day of the week it was when there was a job to be finished.

He dried himself off and padded back down the hallway with a towel slung around his hips. He would get dressed and make coffee while Alice was doing whatever she did on a Sunday morning. Caffeine might blast away the fog wrapped around his brain.

He walked in to hear a hair dryer humming. She'd left the bathroom door open so he leaned against the door jamb to watch her separate a swath of hair and run the dryer down and back up it until it was dry. She was also wrapped in a towel, her skin looking creamy against the pure white terrycloth. Her soft, brown eyes were not quite focused while a smile came and went at the corners of her generous, so-tempting mouth. He hoped thoughts of him and their night together were putting that expression on her face. The idea sent a spiral of satisfaction through him.

As she lifted her arms, he was overwhelmed with the urge to kiss the exquisite curve of her bare shoulder, so he strolled up behind her.

She nearly dropped the hair dryer. "Oh! I didn't hear you come in."

He lowered his lips to the satin of her skin, now scented with his soap instead of her usual violets. There was something strangely intimate in that, as though he had marked her as his. He inhaled deeply and then blew out the breath, making her giggle.

"That tickles," she said, slanting her shoulder away.

He kissed her shoulder again before straightening up. "It's strange not to smell violets."

Her eyes widened and she smiled in a way that made his heart twist. "I wasn't allowed to bring my own toiletries with me, you know."

"We'll check in with Tully to see what progress they've made. When you're ready, look in the closet. Your new clothes should be in there."

He forced himself to leave her in the bathroom, despite his desire to unwind the towel from around her breasts and bend her over the marble-topped vanity while he slid into her from behind like he had on the sofa. Instead he focused on deciding what to wear. It was all his overheated brain could handle at the moment. Even then, it took him some debate to pull out jeans and a black polo shirt.

He was slipping on black loafers when Alice walked out of the bathroom, her hair shimmering over her shoulders in brown waves. His cock jumped. "You look delicious," he said. "Like Venus rising from the waves."

"I don't think Venus wore glasses," she said with a wry smile. "But thank you."

He pointed to the half-open closet door. "Shopping bags on the counter and clothes hanging on the right."

"You have a counter in your closet?" As she walked across the room, he enjoyed the way the towel's folds moved with the swing of her hips. She pulled the door open and stared. "This is not a closet. This is a whole room. How many suits do you own?"

He grimaced even though she couldn't see him. "Too many." He remembered when it had been a thrill to be measured for a custom-tailored suit. Now he just reordered the same style in fabrics so slightly different that you practically needed a magnifying glass to find the variations.

He heard the rustle of paper bags and tissue paper before there was a laughing exclamation. She walked out with a wisp of red lace panties stretched between her hands and a flush of embarrassment on her cheeks. "Seriously! Did you ask the concierge to buy these?"

He held up his hands in a gesture of denial. "I did not, but I plan to give the personal shopper an extra tip for reading my mind. I'd ask you to model them for me but then we'd never get out of this room."

She tossed him a smile of seduction as she held the panties in front of her hips. "I hope the outside clothes are a little more, um, workplace appropriate."

"Even if they are a nun's habit, I'll know what's underneath and that image won't leave my brain until I strip that red lace off you tonight. Maybe in the shower where they'll be clinging to your skin already and I can't be sure what's making you wet, the water or my fingers between your legs."

She gave a little gasp that sent a jolt straight to his cock. His erstwhile seduction was working just as well on him as it was on her.

"I'd better get dressed before I don't want to anymore," she said, racing back into the closet.

He sat on the bed and tried to run numbers through his head so he wouldn't picture her bending over to pull on the panties, the smooth, full curves of her bottom begging for his hands to stroke them. He groaned and scooped his cell phone off the bedside table to call Tully.

Holding the phone to his ear, he waited for the ring but got silence. Frowning, he checked the screen and saw a "No cell service" message. He turned the phone off, waited a few seconds, and turned it on again.

Alice walked out of the closet, clad in jeans, a pink blouse, and the high-heeled shoes he liked so much on her. She had twisted her hair into a complicated knot at the nape of her neck, sending a pang of disappointment through him. "What did Tully say?" she asked.

"Nothing yet. My phone is being uncooperative." The screen graphics were running through the reboot process.

She picked hers up from the table by the bed, coming close enough for him to catch that tantalizing whiff of his soap on her body. She shook her head. "Mine too. It's got no service. Is that typical in your building?"

"Hell, no. Leland supervised the installation of the communication systems so it's all state of the art."

"Maybe it's just our service provider having a blip." She shoved the phone in her pants pocket. "I want to go check on Sylvester and Audley. They may never forgive me for leaving them alone in a strange place."

"And cats know how to hold a grudge." He stood up. "I'll contact Tully via the computer in my office downstairs."

He held out his hand, not wanting to spend any more time without touching her. When she laid her fingers in his without hesitation, her small bones so fragile within his grip, quiet satisfaction washed through him.

She looked up at him with an odd, bemused expression clouding her face. "This is so amazing."

He lifted their linked hands to his lips, kissing the back of hers softly, rubbing her skin against his cheek. "I don't know what you're talking about but it sounds like a compliment."

"Oh, it is," she said. She gestured around his bedroom with her free hand. "It's just so . . . out of my league. I mean, look at the size of it. In Manhattan. And the view. And . . ." She looked back at him and shook her head. "It's beyond incredible."

"I'm glad you like it but it's not out of your league," he said, bothered by her discomfort. He wanted her to feel like she belonged here. "You are far more incredible than this view."

She gave a breathless little laugh, one that sounded unconvinced. "That was definitely a compliment." Her fingers tightened around his and she stared up at him. "I'll remember it."

He didn't like the sound of that somehow, but he wasn't going to push it. Her reaction to his bedroom was not positive. For him, his apartment was like his custom suits. Once it had given him a profound sense of accomplishment. Now it was just a place that wasn't the KRG office. As they walked down the hall to the stairs, he tried to see his home through Alice's eyes. He'd bought it fully renovated because he was too busy with work to supervise a building project. He'd hired a decorator to furnish it in a clean but comfortable style. When they reached the top of the stairs, he noted the rather spectacular chandelier that hung over the double-height entrance. The gold fixture was a cascading grid of slim, interlocking bars, chunks of crystal, and angled light bulbs. It was fascinating and beautiful. And he wouldn't have paid any attention to it without Alice.

When they reached the bottom of the steps, unease plucked at his chest. "Pam? Christian?" he called as he and Alice headed toward the hallway. The guards had planned to take shifts patrolling the apartment, even though he had thought it was overkill. The second guard was supposed to sleep in the apartment off the kitchen that would have been used by a live-in housekeeper, if he'd had one.

Relief loosened the tension when he caught a flicker of movement from the hallway. But it was short-lived.

Shock ripped through him as Myron Barsky and a man who had to be John Peters walked into the entrance foyer.

Myron smiled. "Your compatriots are no longer with us."

Chapter 16

Derek heard Alice gasp as he yanked her behind him, putting himself between her and the two men.

Barsky's hair was no longer in shaggy, nerdy curls, but slicked back and snugged in a low pony tail, and his face was bare of glasses. The man still wore jeans, but the button-down shirt was crisply pressed.

And he held a handgun as casually and comfortably as though it were a cell phone. It wasn't quite pointed at Derek and Alice but clearly it would take a tiny adjustment to bring it there. Peters, on the other hand, held his gun rock steady and it was aimed at Derek's chest.

Fear supplanted shock as he desperately tried to figure out a way to get Alice out of the situation.

"What the hell?" he snarled as Barsky's words sank in. "What do you mean, 'they're no longer with us'?" His gaze strayed to the gun.

He could hear Alice muttering something unintelligible under her breath behind him while her grip on his hand turned convulsive.

"Oh, they're not dead, if that's what you're worried about," Barsky said, still smiling. "I used them as messengers to your partners. It killed two birds with one stone. Got rid of them and convinced your colleagues I'm serious."

"To deliver what message?" He needed to know what Barsky's intentions were before he could figure out what to do about them.

"To stay away from my software until further notice or something very unpleasant will happen to their partner and his girlfriend." Barsky stepped to the side. "Ivan has made coffee so why don't you accompany me to the kitchen?"

"Ivan?"

"Alice knows him as John Peters," Barsky said, gesturing for Derek and Alice to go in front of them. "He really is an expert in security, just not the cyber kind. That's *my* area of expertise."

Derek cut his glance toward the elevator door, just to see how Barsky would react.

"Oh, there's no escape that way," the other man said with unshakable confidence. "We've got all your electronics under our control so you can't call an elevator or communicate with the outside world in any way." He nodded toward the window. "Unless you managed to put up a hand-lettered sign and a helicopter flew by and happened to see it. But I think that's unlikely. Please." He waved the gun toward the hallway this time.

Derek didn't move. "Let Alice go. My partners won't tamper with your system as long as you have me as your hostage."

"Very gallant." Barsky's smile turned to a leer. "But no. You see, when we were sweeping your penthouse for guards last night, we heard your enthusiasm for each other, so I know you are more than colleagues. She stays to keep you under control."

"Asshole," Alice muttered softly enough that Barsky couldn't hear it.

The fear that had hardened his stomach into a ball of stone eased just a little. His Alice wasn't going to faint or become hysterical. He could count on her to help with whatever plan he came up with.

~

Alice's sense of unreality faded slightly when Myron Barsky confessed to eavesdropping on her lovemaking with Derek. It was funny how embarrassment could overcome terror. Not to mention that it was so sleazy, the action diminished his fright factor, even when he had a gun in his hand.

She reminded herself not to underestimate him, though, since she had done so all along. Of course, this Myron Barsky looked very different from the nerd on stage at the Lipton Hotel. He seemed taller and his shoulders looked broader because his posture was upright rather than slumped. His voice was different too, projecting a patronizing confidence. If he hadn't held the gun so expertly, she would have wondered if he wasn't an actor like Jake Masters.

Unfortunately, there was no question that John Peters—no, Ivan—was terrifying. He was dressed in the same all-black ensemble he'd worn in Texas and neither his blank eyes nor his gun wavered by a millimeter.

She made an effort to loosen her hold on Derek's hand since she was probably cutting off his circulation. He gave her fingers a gentle squeeze before tugging her forward to his side, the one opposite Barsky and Ivan, so his big body was still between them. His protectiveness reached into her heart, but also conjured up gut-wrenching images of bullets ripping into him as he shielded her. She needed to rein in her imagination because panic wouldn't help get them out of this surreal situation.

She tried to remember the self-defense moves she'd worked so hard to learn but even Dawn said that weapons changed the whole situation.

As they walked down the hall side by side, Alice could almost feel the cold steel of the guns aimed at her back. It was not a good feeling. At least Barsky wasn't going to shoot them . . . yet. He evidently needed her and Derek for an unspecified length of time.

She began to consider why and the pieces suddenly fell together. "You're going to grab all the credit card transfers at the end of the week," she blurted out. "Not just a couple of dollars here and there."

Derek squeezed her hand again. When she glanced up at him, he frowned a warning.

"Very good, clever Ms. Thurber," Barsky said from behind them. "*Too*-clever Ms. Thurber. We're also going to clean out all their bank accounts through the credit card access. Prematurely, thanks to your interference. I'm pissed off about that." Except his tone was flat and without anger.

Which made it even scarier. Derek was right. She shouldn't make him any more pissed off by discussing it further.

"You've cost me a lot of money too when I was forced to set up that fake headquarters," he said as they entered the kitchen, a place of smooth slate floors, gleaming stainless steel appliances, and pale gray cabinets. It would have been serene if there hadn't been two guns pointed at her back.

Nerves and Alice's overactive curiosity prompted her to continue to poke at the wasp's nest. "Why did you bother with all that if you were going to do this anyway?"

"Sit," Barsky said, waving his gun toward the modern trestle table set in front of the window. "Side by side, facing me. Ivan, pour them each a coffee. No need to be uncivilized."

Derek led her over to the table where they settled on two chairs with their backs to the window. Much to her relief, he pulled her hand onto his thigh under the tabletop, keeping their fingers intertwined. His strong, comforting grip calmed her racing pulse even though she could feel the tension in the hard muscle under the denim of his jeans.

Barsky slid onto a barstool at the counter while Ivan poured two steaming mugs of coffee and plunked them down on the table. She decided not to express a preference for tea.

"I set up the whole fake HQ because I wanted to see how invested you were in the problem, maybe redirect your attention." Barsky shrugged. "It became apparent that wouldn't happen. I mean, really, it was so easy to see through your little charade. I'd already figured out that you didn't work for KRG, Ms. Thurber. You were just a small-time bookkeeper who actually knew how to add and subtract but not how to keep her mouth shut. Bad luck for both of us." He smiled that creepy fake smile again. "Fortunately, I learned something else valuable that day." Barsky stared at her chest in a way that made her feel like he could see through her clothes. It was like being coated in slime. "That you would be useful leverage with KRG."

"Enough," Derek snapped.

Alice realized she'd gotten drawn down a hazardous path, so she changed the subject, remembering that her original mission had been hijacked by Barsky's unwelcome appearance. "Are my cats all right?"

"Well, Ivan kicked them across the room a couple of times but otherwise they're fine," Barsky said before his smile vanished. "Seriously, I don't give a shit about your cats. Never even saw them."

"Can we go check on them?" She wanted to make sure Barsky's first statement wasn't true. Even more, she hoped it would give her a chance to talk to Derek without listeners. "You said there's no way we can leave or call for help, so just let us go look for them. Please."

Derek's grip on her hand went tight and she glanced sideways to see a ferocious frown on his face.

"Women and their cats," Barsky said, giving Derek a wry look of false comradeship. "Ivan, take her to see her pets. Killion, you stay here."

Derek half rose. "I'm going with her."

"Do you have a gun? No, but I do." Barsky angled his weapon so the dark metal caught the overhead light. "So you stay here. Don't worry about her safety. You're more Ivan's type than she is."

Alice shuddered as the implication of Barsky's words twisted her stomach in a nauseating way. Her gaze flew to the large black-clad man stepping away from the counter, his gun held by his thigh, but Ivan's face still held no expression. Which was even more frightening. So her plan had backfired in a big way.

Derek eased back down onto his chair and turned to Alice, saying in a low voice, "Scream if you need me. I don't care how many guns are pointed at me, I'll find a way to get there."

"So melodramatic. Nothing's going to happen to her. Yet." Barsky sounded bored.

As she left the powerful comfort of Derek's presence, Alice hoped that was true.

~

"I can't figure you out," Derek said as soon as Alice left the kitchen. He wasn't sure if their separation was a good thing or a bad one. Maybe it was good to get Barsky used to them moving around in the apartment. It might give him more chances to reach some of the built-in security features that the hacker might not have discovered. Unfortunately, Alice didn't know where any of them were.

Barsky had pulled out his cell phone and was scrolling through something with one thumb while he kept the gun in his other hand. "Then don't try," he responded with no visible interest.

Derek wanted to pull Barsky's attention away from anything electronic because he was bone-deep certain that Leland and Tully were doing everything they could to wrest away Barsky's control over the apartment and its communications. Derek had shoved his cell phone in his back pocket when Barsky had surprised him, knowing that it was his lifeline to the outside world.

When KRG had hit a certain level of financial success, Tully had called a meeting to warn his partners of the very real dangers extremely wealthy entrepreneurs could encounter. He'd also had an unnamed friend of his modify their phones in a semi-illegal way so that the phones had some secret dirty tricks. The devices could look dead while still being active. They could be tracked even when they'd been turned off and smashed. They could be used to communicate in nonverbal ways. Of course, the latter meant that Leland and Derek had been forced to learn Morse code.

"It's just not enough money for all you've done," Derek said, gesturing toward the man on the barstool. "The fake headquarters, the time and coding expertise needed to break into my apartment, holding two people hostage for however long. It makes more sense to cut and run."

Barsky looked up. "It's simple. I don't like to lose."

"But why a bunch of small businesses when you could get so much more money from hacking into one large corporation?"

The other man put down his phone, making Derek do a mental fist pump of success.

"Corporate security tends to be harder to penetrate because they can afford consultants like KRG," Barsky said in a tone of a teacher instructing a particularly stupid pupil. "Small businesses are easy targets. Stupid mom-and-pop operations with no knowledge of how vulnerable their financial information is. Put enough of them together and you can get a nice return on your investment in stealing from them."

"How many software packages did you sell?" Derek asked.

"Wouldn't you like to know?" Barsky smiled. "As soon as I rip them off for their last penny, all the client information will be wiped clean so that you can't track them down and help them in any way. Another benefit of decentralized theft."

Derek was picking up an ugly undertone in Barsky's responses. "It's not just about the money."

"It's always about the money," the other man said. "But I enjoy knowing that I will destroy a whole shitload of people's livelihoods with just a few lines of computer code. That's all I had to write, you know. Just the module that breaks into the credit card transfer system. Not that it was easy. Even your resident computer genius should be impressed . . . since I'm sure he's trying to hack it without success. However, I bought the rest of the accounting system from some talented but gullible software engineers at a fire-sale price. And it's not a bad system, all in all. Too bad I'll have destroyed its reputation forever."

"Why do you want to wreck people's lives?" Derek found himself needing to know. He couldn't understand the kind of hatred Barsky projected. Personal hatred, maybe, but not hatred for a group of people just going about their business, trying to make a living.

Barsky hesitated before he pivoted on the stool to face Derek fully, his eyes hard, his posture taut. "Because my father made me stock the shelves in his pathetic little convenience store in a run-down suburb of Dallas every day after school." The man vibrated with fury. "I'm a fucking genius but he forced me to waste my time on hauling around boxes of soup. He told me that I needed to learn the value of hard work because in America that's all it takes to succeed. Some stupid Mexican could have done it just as well. But *no one* could write perfect code like I could. My father didn't understand the brilliance of his own son." He stopped to draw in a deep breath. "The happiest day of my life was when he got shot by an addict who robbed my father's crappy convenience store of $150." Barsky smiled. "I might have told the addict that the store was an easy mark."

Derek's blood chilled at Barsky's admission. So it was personal in a warped way. As personal as Derek's own ambitions had been. "It's tough when your father doesn't appreciate you," he said in a neutral tone.

"Don't feel sorry for me. My mother used my father's life insurance money to buy me the best computer equipment available at the time. She understood my brilliance." Barsky continued to smile, his eyes gleaming with malevolence. "Pretty convincing motivation for my evil scheme, don't you think?"

"It sounds true to me."

The other man shrugged. "Believe what you want. It won't matter soon. Now shut up and let me make sure your friends at KRG aren't trying to get past my firewalls." He picked up his phone again, setting off a string of mental curses inside Derek's head.

A few seconds later, he had to suppress a shout of triumph as the phone in his back pocket vibrated with three quick taps in succession. Leland had broken through.

Alice wasn't sure if she'd made a tactical error in provoking her separation from Derek. She should have guessed that Barsky wouldn't let them go together but she was convinced that the apartment would have some kind of secret alarm or escape route. She'd wanted to give Derek a chance to get to it. Now, as she walked down the hall to the media room, the space between her shoulders felt as though it had a target painted on it.

She ventured a quick look over her shoulder to find that Ivan had lowered his gun to hang by his side. Evidently, he didn't consider her a serious threat, which was, unfortunately, an accurate assessment. The only thing she could think to do was hurl one of her cats at him but that wouldn't fly for the simple reason that she wouldn't put Sylvester or Audley in danger of being injured or killed.

Yup, she was a crazy cat lady, all right.

She stopped at the door.

"Open it," Ivan said, keeping his distance from her. She chose to consider that flattering, even if it was more likely to be an unconscious action on the part of a highly trained bodyguard or whatever he was.

She eased the door open in case one of the cats was waiting on the other side. However, no cats were in sight. Sylvester and Audley were demonstrating very good sense in hiding from their captors.

She walked into the room. "Sylvester! Audley!" Not that she expected them to come. They were cats, after all, but they might emerge from their hiding places. She called again but no kitties showed up.

She couldn't stop herself from sneaking another glance at Ivan. He must have seen from the look on her face that she was wondering if he'd really kicked the cats because he gave her a terrifying stare. She practically jogged to the other end of the sofa to get away from his menacing presence.

But his glare brought up the blood-chilling question she'd been trying to ignore since she had figured out why Myron Barsky was holding them hostage: Was he going to leave her and Derek alive to tell tales once he got his money?

They could identify him and his thug but so could a lot of other people, so she wasn't sure whether that played into the decision. Barsky was annoyed with her about costing him money but was he angry enough to shoot her? She had no experience with criminals other than the fictional ones on television, so she really couldn't gauge the situation accurately.

She just knew with gut-wrenching certainty that she didn't want to die. And she didn't want Derek to die either.

Shoving down panic, she got on her knees and peered under the sofa. Sure enough, two pairs of golden eyes looked back at her. Maybe she should leave the cats there in relative safety. But Audley wriggled out to greet her.

There was immense comfort in holding the soft, warm body of her purring cat in her arms. Strangely enough, tears prickled in her eyes, making her blink rapidly. She wasn't going to show weakness in front of Ivan.

"So, you found your cat. Let's go," he said in a flat voice.

"I just want to check their food and water, please," she said, hoping courtesy would score her some points.

He nodded from his post by the closed door, so she carried Audley to the cat-feeding station. The automatic dispensers were full, and she noticed that the cat litter had been used. That meant she could cross off one small worry from her mental list. Her cats had adjusted well enough to their new environment.

Now she could go back to worrying about how to avoid getting shot.

Chapter 17

Derek rolled his shoulders to ease the tension as he waited for Alice to return from her expedition to check on her cats. He didn't want to try to pull his phone out of his pocket when there was no reason for movement. Even more stressful was wondering if she was safe with Ivan. He didn't trust Barsky's assurances that nothing would happen to her. The big Russian had the flat eyes of a psychopath. Unfortunately, despite his willingness to talk, Barsky's were equally empty.

When Alice walked back through the kitchen door, looking nervous but unharmed, relief eased the knot in Derek's stomach. He waited until Barsky glanced in her direction before he slipped his phone out of his pocket and slid it between his thighs. Now he could answer whatever messages Leland and Tully sent him. Once the phone was in emergency mode, it looked dead to the average observer but was sensitive to tapping; hence the Morse code. They'd even developed a shorthand for "yes" and "no" to facilitate communications.

Ivan waved Alice back to the table beside him without any comment.

"Are the cats all right?" Derek asked. Barsky didn't look up from his phone and Ivan simply stared at them from his station behind the counter.

"Yes, thank goodness." She reached under the table to take his hand, twining her fingers with his in a way that made him wish he had

Superman's cape of invulnerability to wrap her in. "It was a little scary, though."

"I can imagine. Had either Sylvester or Morse eaten?" He tapped his thumb against her palm in the classic Morse code rhythm for SOS: dot-dot-dot-dash-dash-dash-dot-dot-dot.

He kept his eyes on the two men but he felt her fingers tighten around his and hoped she had not given anything away with her expression. "It's, um, hard to tell because the food dispenser is automatic, you know," she said. He could hear the slight distraction behind her words but caught no telltale startled movement out of the corner of his eye. His Alice could keep her cool.

His heart leaped when she shifted her grip to lay her thumb against the back of his hand. Her spelling was slow but she tapped out an understandable, "Yes."

That was one advantage to falling in love with a nerd. For a moment, his brain froze on the thought. He'd used the word "love." But he didn't have time to focus on that for longer than a split second. There was no point in worrying over how he felt about Alice if they both died at the hands of Myron and Ivan.

He decided that Alice needed to be in on the secret of the phone, in case something happened to him. He camouflaged his movements by rolling his head as though loosening the muscles in his neck. While he hoped his upper body was distracting Ivan, he sandwiched the phone between his palm and Alice's. Then he tapped on the back of her hand, "Feel phone."

She responded with a swifter "yes" this time.

Barsky placed his cell on the counter. "So far your so-called tech wizard hasn't broken through my firewalls," he said, standing up and tucking his gun into the back of his waistband. "I'm going to use the facilities. Believe me when I tell you that Ivan can easily handle the two of you. He won't hesitate to kill you if you're too troublesome, so I suggest that you sit still."

He sauntered out of the kitchen.

Ivan shifted his position slightly so that he was facing them full-on. Tension snaked through Derek as the big bodyguard's gaze bored into them, almost as though he could see their hands through the wooden tabletop.

"Are you planning to kill us anyway?" Alice asked. "I mean, once you get your money?"

"Maybe you shouldn't ask questions like that," Derek said, his eyes locked on Ivan as he tried to gauge his reaction.

"Well, I'd like to kiss you again before they shoot us," Alice said. He caught the slight tremor in her voice but he understood that she was trying to keep Ivan's attention above the tabletop.

Not that the bodyguard was responding, but he had stopped glaring and was leaning against the island rather than standing poised to spring or to shoot.

"At least I got to fly on a private jet once in my life." Alice continued to babble. "And to visit Dallas. Not that I saw much of it, except from that wonderful restaurant. Thank you for taking me there."

He turned slightly to catch her look of adoring gratitude. She might be laying it on a little thick. "I was happy to, darling," he said, smiling down into her eyes. He meant it, even the "darling."

Real tears glistened in her eyes. "I was thinking that I need to travel more because just that little glimpse of a new place was exciting."

"When this is all over, I'll take you anywhere you want to go," he said. "Where to first?"

He snuck a glance at Ivan, who looked bored. Bored was good.

"I know everyone says Paris," Alice said, her expression pensive. "But I want to go to London and Bath to see the places my favorite books are set."

"Your favorite books?" He wanted to know this about her.

She looked down as color rose in her cheeks. "Oh, they're just for fun. Regency romances by Georgette Heyer."

What had he expected her to say? *A Tour of the Calculus?* Only hard-core mathematicians would call it a favorite. Still, he wouldn't have guessed historical romances were her choice. Another fascinating facet of Alice. "I once played an English king. In *Henry V.* 'Once more unto the breach, dear friends' and so on. Not my finest performance since it required classical theater training I didn't have."

"Shut up," Ivan snapped.

Alice jumped, her hand jerking in Derek's. He realized that she was more frightened than she appeared. He gave her hand a reassuring squeeze around the phone just as it began to vibrate. Ivan's command of silence was well timed since Derek needed to concentrate on the Morse code coming through at high speed. "S-e-r-v-i-c-e-l-i-f-t-i-n-2-0." So they were coming up in the service elevator. Leland must have taken back control without Myron knowing it. They would have to override the security camera too, but they would think of that.

As the phone went silent again, Alice tapped on his hand, "T-o-o-f-a-s-t."

It had been almost too quick for him, even though Tully made him practice occasionally, so he repeated the message for her at a lower speed.

"Y-e-s," she answered.

Myron strolled back in just then. "You had some very good computer equipment in your home office. I feel bad that I had to destroy it. Just as a precaution. Judging by the size and location of this place, you can afford to replace it."

Derek fought down a wave of fear. That left him with just his cell phone as a conduit to Leland and Tully. He'd better take good care of it.

"They keep talking," Ivan said to his boss. "Maybe in code. We should tie them up and gag them."

Derek heard Alice's sudden inhale and her hand tightened around his like steel, even as he began to plan and discard ways to keep his phone where he could reach it.

"May I have something to eat first?" Alice asked in a small, pleading voice, earning her a hard glare from Ivan and silent kudos from Derek for quick thinking.

"Does someone as important as you eat cereal?" Myron asked, directing a snarky look at Derek. "Otherwise you're out of luck."

"Granola in the pullout to the right of the refrigerator," Derek said, keeping his tone even. "Bowls in the cabinet to the left of the sink. Spoons in the middle drawer of the island."

Myron nodded to Ivan, who yanked the ingredients out of the various storage places and plunked them down in front of Alice and Derek. "You have five minutes," he growled. "No talking."

Derek squeezed Alice's hand again and she returned the pressure before releasing her grip. Under cover of shifting in his seat as he fiddled with the bowls and utensils, he slipped the phone into the front of his jeans' waistband. Relief loosened the fist in his chest, but now he needed to find a way to keep his hands free until the cavalry arrived. He did not want Alice or himself to be used as a bargaining chip.

Alice nearly whimpered when she had to let go of Derek's hand, despite knowing that help was on the way. The strength and warmth of his touch helped her fight the panic that threatened to wrench the breath out of her lungs. The thought of being immobilized and helpless at the hands of Myron and Ivan sent her throat into spasms. She sucked in several deep breaths as she made a show of filling her bowl with granola. Her hand shook so much that a dusting of grains spilled onto the tabletop. Derek must have noticed because he picked up the jug of milk and poured it over her cereal before serving himself.

Now she just had to find a way to get the granola past the fist clamped around her throat.

Derek chewed silently beside her, lifting spoonfuls to his mouth with methodical regularity, while she could only eat tiny bites. She hoped it meant that he was planning their escape instead of paying attention to what he was eating because her brain had stopped forming coherent thoughts after her request for food. It had been all she could think of to delay the terror of being bound and gagged.

She had to stop herself from glancing at the kitchen clock every few seconds. Barsky was smart enough to become suspicious that she was expecting something. But so many bad things could happen in twenty minutes. She wanted it to be over already.

Her hand shook so that milk slopped off the spoon and back into her bowl, which gave her an idea for one more delaying tactic. Then she hoped that Derek would have come up with a way to keep them free.

She forced herself to continue eating the cereal. It figured that it would be a healthy, fibrous granola that took forever to chew and swallow. She needed to finish it before Ivan decided their allocated breakfast time was up. A surreptitious glance at her watch showed that she had to speed things up, making her nearly choke on a particularly large clot of grains. Finally, she scraped her spoon on the bottom of the bowl with a rudely loud noise. Reaching for the cereal box, she refilled her bowl.

As she had hoped, Derek courteously reached for the milk, giving her the chance to collide with his arm as though she were also grabbing for the jug. The plastic container tipped over away from them, splashing its contents onto the table and the kitchen floor.

"Oh no! I'm sorry!" Alice said, channeling all the nervous stress she was feeling into her words as she tried to sop it up with her paper napkin, knowing her efforts wouldn't be effective. "I'll clean it up, if you let me have some paper towels." She started to stand up.

"Sit, you stupid bitch!" Barsky snapped. "Ivan, get her a roll of towels."

"Just leave it, Myron," Ivan said.

"You know I can't stand sloppiness," Barsky said. "Let her clean up her mess."

Ivan shook his head but found the paper-towel holder and dumped it on the table in front of Alice before backing up to the island again. "I will be watching you carefully."

Alice nodded and slowly reached for the towels, tearing off a handful to wipe up the spill from the table and piling the soggy towels in her bowl. "May I walk around the table to clean the floor?"

Ivan raised his gun and aimed it at her. "Go ahead."

Having that small black hole staring her in the face sent a wave of gut-clenching fear through her. Pushing her chair back with a squeal that made her wince, she walked in slow motion around to the front of the table with her hands held up at her shoulders. She didn't want to get killed over a simple delaying tactic.

"I'm going to kneel down on the floor now," she said, moving with great deliberation.

"I know what you're doing," Ivan said, the gun terrifyingly steady as it tracked her. "Just finish the job."

Alice knelt beside the white puddle and mopped up the milk with more thoroughness than it warranted, swiping fresh towels over the slate floor until it was bone dry. Bracing her hand on the table, she rose slowly and walked back around the table at the same slow pace before she eased down into the chair, giving Derek a quick glance to find his expression unreadable. She'd done her best. Now he had to pick up the slack. She wished she knew where the service elevator was located so she had some idea of which way to run, if given the chance.

Warmth and comfort washed through her when Derek snuck his hand under the table to give her thigh a quick squeeze before he tapped out, "G-o-o-d."

"I want to move them to heavier chairs so we can secure them better," Ivan said to Barsky. "There are some good ones in the living room. Metal and leather."

Barsky shrugged. "Why not? Might as well all be comfortable together."

Alice hated the fact that the two men moved together like a team, their guns held in a way that showed they were terrifyingly accustomed to them. She had hoped that Barsky was the nerd he pretended to be, but he didn't look at all like one now. His flat blue eyes and efficient movements were those of a man who would kill without a second thought.

Ivan went to Derek's side of the table while Barsky took up position near—but not too near—Alice. "Up," he commanded.

Derek's hand slipped off her thigh as they both rose.

"Now you come with me," Barsky said, pointing his free hand at Alice. "You"—he pointed to Derek—"with Ivan."

Are they going to separate us? Alice's lungs refused to expand. *No, no, Ivan said the living room chairs. All in the same room.*

She cast a quick look at Derek who nodded that she should go with Barsky. For a moment, a sense of unreality numbed her. She was an accountant. People didn't hold accountants hostage at gunpoint.

Then Derek collapsed, slamming his shoulder against the table before he hit the floor with a thud.

Had Ivan hit him?

"Shit!" Barsky said. "What the hell?"

Ivan stood with the gun pointed at Derek. "He just went down. Hard."

"Derek?" Alice whimpered when he didn't move. Then she remembered what he'd said about his death scenes in acting school and relief nearly swamped her. Her brain clicked into high gear. "Help him! He . . . he has epilepsy. Seizures."

"Sure he does," Barsky said, his gun on Alice. "Stay where you are." He shifted his attention to Ivan. "Is it real?"

"Yes, it is!" Alice said, letting her fear sharpen her voice. "You have to roll him onto his side so he doesn't choke to death. Let me, please! Help him!"

"It looked real," Ivan said. "That's a stone floor, and he didn't break his fall."

Just then Derek began to convulse, arching up off the floor.

"Please!" Alice begged, admiring Derek for supporting her improvisation. "You have to put something under his head or he'll hurt himself."

Suddenly, Barsky's arm was around her neck and the gun was jammed against her temple, a hard, cold circle of pressure that she could almost feel creating a bruise. Barsky yanked her against his body, sending a shudder of revulsion through her as she tried to swallow against his grip on her throat. "A little insurance in case your boyfriend is faking it," he said, pulling her away from the table so their view of Derek and Ivan was unobstructed. "Roll him," he said to Ivan.

The bodyguard tried to shift Derek with his foot, but the seizure appeared to stiffen his muscles so that his body resisted. Ivan knelt down and snaked his left arm under Derek's shoulders, grunting with the effort of fighting the convulsion. As Ivan bent to get better leverage, Derek slammed one fist into Ivan's nose and wrenched the gun out of the bodyguard's grip. He smashed the gun sideways into Ivan's temple and rolled as the big man fell forward, coming to his feet with the gun held in both hands.

Barsky's hold on Alice's throat tightened, making her cough. "That was a very stupid move. You gained nothing, and Ivan's going to be pissed when he comes to. I can't answer for what he'll do." He jerked Alice up onto her toes. "I'm pretty pissed myself."

"Don't hurt her," Derek said, his breath coming in pants. "I'll put the gun on the table. Or the floor. Wherever you want it."

Barsky loosened his hold on Alice slightly, so her heels met the floor again. That reminded her of Dawn's lessons on how to break a choke hold. Except those scenarios hadn't included a gun. However, if she could get free before Derek put his gun down, he could shoot Barsky. Would he? That two-handed grip he displayed seemed pretty expert, but she wasn't sure he would actually use his weapon. Personally, right now she would happily shoot Barsky, in the arm at the very least, for what he'd put them through.

Her captor had his left hand around her neck, so she needed to go right.

"Place it on the floor and kick it over to me," Barsky said beside her ear. "Slowly, so you don't startle me into shooting your pretty girlfriend."

"Flattery will get you nowhere," Alice said, planting her left foot in front, the way she'd practiced. She pivoted in toward her captor with her right foot, slipping her shoulder under Barsky's forearm and ducking down. She could feel the gun muzzle drag up through her hair as she turned. Then she slammed her palms against his torso and shoved with all her might, knocking him off-balance.

"Shoot him!" she yelled as she bent low and raced away from Barsky to take cover behind the island.

A shot rang out, and Alice prayed it was from Derek's gun. She heard something hit the floor with a metallic clank.

"Shit!" Barsky snarled. "You're a fucking accountant and you shot me."

"You were hurting my girlfriend," Derek said. "Now *you* kick the gun to *me*."

Alice peered up over the countertop to see Derek stop Barsky's sliding gun with his foot before he redirected it behind the table, well out of Ivan's reach. Barsky was leaning against the island holding his left hand over his right shoulder where a bright red stain was spreading across his shirt.

"She's just a fucking bookkeeper," Barsky growled. "What the hell is it with you two?"

"Alice," Derek said. "I need you to tie up Ivan. After that, you can shoot Barsky yourself."

"Can I get a towel?" Barsky asked with a strange calm. "I'm losing a lot of blood."

Alice straightened and looked at Derek to see what he wanted her to do.

Derek's face was icy with anger. "I hope you bleed to death. Where are the restraints you were going to use on us?"

"In the black duffel bag under a table in the front entrance hall," Barsky said easily. He seemed remarkably unworried by his situation, which made Alice wonder if he knew something they didn't.

"Do you know how to use a gun?" Derek asked her.

"I got a marksman badge in summer camp," Alice said. Of course, that was quite a few years ago and mostly they had used rifles. However, she had been allowed to try out a handgun a couple of times.

"Take Barsky's then, just in case."

"Do you think someone else is coming?" she asked, nerves tightening her stomach into a knot.

"It's a precaution." Derek shifted his position so that he had the table between himself and the unconscious Ivan.

Alice scooped up the gun, which was surprisingly small. Anger and fear flooded her veins in equal measure as she hurried down the hall to find the duffel sitting under a table where she and Derek couldn't have seen it when they came down the stairs. She grabbed the handles and picked it up, surprised by how light it was. She wondered if they had taken out something other than the guns.

She jogged back down the hallway. She did not want Ivan conscious when she was trying to immobilize him. When she arrived back in the kitchen no one had moved, although Barsky's shirt had gotten significantly redder. She hoped he would pass out.

Placing her gun carefully on the table, she unzipped the bag and pulled out a handful of black braided nylon loops threaded through locking mechanisms. Disentangling one, she figured out that you shoved a hand or foot in each loop and pulled the end of the nylon braid to tighten it. Luckily, Ivan had fallen on his side, so she could simply push him over onto his front.

"Can you manage him?" Derek asked as she grabbed another restraint and knelt down beside the inert bodyguard.

"Yup, I've got this." Although she was a little worried that Ivan might be pulling Derek's fake-out trick. But he no longer had a gun, so she just had to make sure he didn't grab her in a way that she couldn't escape. She was feeling pretty pleased with herself for successfully breaking Barsky's choke hold without getting shot.

However, Derek had done a good job on Ivan. The man rolled like a rag doll, his nose still oozing blood. She wondered if he was still alive before she realized that she didn't care.

She jerked one loop tight around one of his hands before pulling his wrists together in the small of his back and pushing the other hand through. After she yanked hard on the ends of the nylon to make sure it was tight, she blew out a breath she hadn't realized she was holding and sat back on her heels to enjoy the relief of knowing Ivan was no longer a threat. Then she secured his ankles and rolled him back onto his side. "He's not going anywhere," she said, standing up. The adrenaline was beginning to drain out of her system, leaving her feeling shaky.

"You're a trooper," Derek said, but his focused stare never left Barsky. "You can give him a couple of dish towels now. They're in the second drawer nearest the sink. Stay away from him, though. Just slide them across the island. He'll have to manage on his own."

She found the towels and nearly threw them at Barsky. The hacker folded a couple of them into a pad, one-handed, and pressed it against his wound. "Now what?" he said. "Your friends can't get in and you can't get out because I've got all your electronic locks shut down. It's a stalemate."

"We wait," Derek said.

"Can I sit down before I collapse?" Barsky asked, still looking unworried.

Derek gestured toward the chair Alice had been occupying, so Barsky picked up the handful of towels, walked around the table, and sank down with a wince. Derek repositioned himself by the island, roughly where Ivan had stood guard.

Alice still held the gun, keeping it loosely aimed at Ivan's inert body, but small tremors had begun to rack her body. Now that the worst danger appeared to be over, her nerves were kicking in.

She didn't want to ask Derek where the elevator was because she didn't want to give Barsky any information, but she threw a quick glance around to see if it opened into the kitchen. Unfortunately, no obvious elevator door was visible.

"Hoping for the cavalry to ride to your rescue?" Barsky asked, tossing the blood-soaked towels on the floor and folding a fresh pad. He was beginning to look a little pale and strained. But his calm bothered Alice. He wasn't acting like a man whose plans had been thwarted.

Alice looked at Derek. "I think he brought some other equipment with him in the duffel bag. I want to go check your computer room to see if there's a laptop running. I'm afraid all those small business owners will get wiped out."

Derek cursed under his breath. "There might be another hacker in there for all we know."

"We could tie Barsky up and you could come with me," she suggested.

Derek glanced at the clock. "Or we could wait."

"You can't stop it anyway," Barsky said. "It's encrypted."

The man was so confident that he was volunteering information. That couldn't be a good sign. "Then you can give us the password," Alice said, pointing the gun at him. "Or I can just shoot the computer." She liked that idea.

Barsky laughed, an unpleasant grating sound. "You're an idiot. The program is not running on the laptop itself."

"I still might shoot it," Alice said. It would relieve some of her anger and frustration.

There was a groan before a string of Slavic muttering emanated from Ivan. She was willing to bet that it wasn't G-rated. Even though she had pulled the restraints tight herself, she wished he had stayed unconscious. Checking her grip on the gun, she aimed it at the reviving thug with as much steadiness as she could muster. Now she agreed with Derek's decision to wait for the cavalry that Barsky was so scornful of.

Barsky said something in whatever language he and Ivan spoke. Ivan grumbled a reply and tried to sit up.

"Shut up!" Derek barked. "Ivan, stay down! As you can see from your friend, I won't hesitate to shoot if necessary."

The big man subsided on the floor. Alice had the suspicion that he might even be relieved.

However, she kept her gun trained on Ivan anyway. Until Derek said, "About time you got here. We had to deal with the situation ourselves since you took so damn long." But there was a smile in his voice.

Alice glanced around to see a door at the back of the kitchen swing fully open. A large, dark-haired man dressed in black with "FBI" printed in white letters on a bulletproof vest stepped into the kitchen, a gun held at the ready. "We were trying not to get you killed."

Two more men in the same garb followed him. Behind them came Leland, only his vest was strapped on over his usual jeans and T-shirt. He also held a gun with a surprising ease that indicated he knew how to handle it.

"Oh, thank God!" Alice said as relief coursed through her body, turning her knees to jelly. She had to lean against the island to avoid collapsing on the floor. Her gun clattered onto the countertop.

Derek was at her side immediately, his arm around her waist. "Are you all right?" he asked.

"Just my adrenaline draining away all at once." She sagged into him and felt tears well in her eyes. Wrapping her arms around him for a moment, she drew comfort from the solidity of his body. But she knew they had things to do so she took a deep breath and straightened away from him. "I'm fine. We need to get Leland to Barsky's laptop to stop the transfers."

He kept his arm around her waist and turned them both. "Leland, we think Barsky's laptop is in my office. Tully, maybe we should bring Barsky with us."

The man who had come through the door first hauled Barsky to his feet none too gently, making the hacker wince. "Where's the laptop?" he demanded, doing something to Barsky's injured arm that made the man jerk in pain.

"The office," Barsky confirmed through clenched teeth.

"Move," Tully said, shoving him around the table.

"You can't stop it," Barsky boasted.

"We'll see," Leland said, joining Derek and Alice as they followed Tully.

One of the FBI agents brushed past them. "Gibson, let me clear the way first," he said. "There may be others."

Tully stepped aside with a nod. "Make it fast. We have a deadline, only we don't know what it is."

"The office is three doors down on the left," Derek called.

Now that she was anchored by Derek's arm around her waist, Alice's brain began to function again. "Will our cell phones work now? I'd like to call my clients to see if they can get their banks to lock down their accounts somehow."

Leland pulled his cell out of his pocket and swiped a few times with long, elegant fingers. "Good to go now."

The agent signaled them that the office was empty. As they walked in, Alice gasped. Three large monitors lay on the floor, smashed as though someone had stomped on them repeatedly. Other equipment was strewn around with wires and electronic guts ripped out. Even the high-end ergonomic chairs had been knocked over. A shiver of delayed terror coursed through her. Barsky was angrier than he had let on.

"What the hell happened here?" Leland asked.

Barsky started to laugh but Tully did that thing to his arm and the laughter cut off abruptly.

Derek released Alice to right one of the chairs before offering it to her. "I've got a laptop in the safe."

Leland picked up a chair and seated himself in front of the only viable computer in the room: Barsky's. The screen was blank but he typed in something and a string of unintelligible code appeared. Leland studied it for a moment, his eyes laser focused, before he began typing again.

"Can you stop it?" Alice asked.

"Maybe," Leland said. "If the encryption is the same. I broke the other subroutine."

Barsky muttered something. Tully smiled a scary grin. "You think you're good but Leland is better."

Derek put his backup laptop on the desk beside Leland and booted it up. "Alice, do you know which of your clients' banks process the credit card transfer on Sundays?"

"Yes!" She hadn't thought of that angle. She rolled her chair through the debris to Derek's side and began listing them.

"Okay, I'll start with the biggest bank," he said, pulling his cell phone from his pocket. "I have a couple of contacts there who will pick up on a Sunday morning. Maybe I can get them to hold the transfer until Leland works his magic."

Leland was typing madly while Tully stood guard over Barsky, occasionally speaking into his earpiece. Evidently, more FBI agents had arrived because new faces appeared at the door. Alice walked to a far corner and pulled out her phone, calling Natalie first.

"Are you okay?" her friend asked. "Where are you?"

"I'm at Derek's penthouse in the city and I have a heck of a story to tell you but that's not why I'm calling. I want you to do your best to reach your bank's customer service and get them to put some kind of hold on your account so nothing comes in and nothing goes out. Otherwise you could lose everything. Tell them there's malware in your accounting software that's trying to steal everything out of your account."

"Everything?" Natalie's dismay was clear. "That would wipe me out."

"I'd tell you to transfer it to another account but it's Sunday and I don't know if it would happen fast enough. Also, I don't know if the software can attack associated accounts as well. Get the bank to shut down access, if you can. Now I have to call my other clients."

She tapped the number for Sparkle, hoping the owner would pick up on a Sunday. She thought of all the other small businesses scattered across the country who had no idea that they might lose everything today. That pissed her off royally and she wanted to punch Barsky in his bleeding shoulder. She noticed that no one had offered him medical treatment yet, which she approved of. She was a little shocked at her heartlessness but the man had held a gun to her head.

She had to leave a message for Sparkle and Nowak Plumbing but she reached three other BalanceTrakR clients, as well as Dawn, who said she'd track down the gym owner pronto.

Derek was just ending a call. "Okay, they're shutting down all credit card transfers at AmBank for two hours. That's all the time they can give us."

"No worries," Leland said, running one hand through his already mussed brown hair. "I'll break this long before then."

Barsky said something in whatever language he spoke.

Tully looked down at the hacker, whom he had pushed into a chair. "You know, I think I'll just take you someplace where we won't bother these folks and see if I can persuade you to tell us how to stop this piece-of-shit software."

Tully's powerful body, clad entirely in black, projected controlled menace. One of his big hands held his gun and the other was balled into an impressive fist.

"You couldn't hurt me enough to make me tell you anything. You have to follow rules," Barsky sneered.

"See this vest." Tully pointed to his broad chest. "It's only borrowed. I don't work for the FBI anymore."

He gave Barsky a look that sent a tremor of fear through Alice but the hacker didn't flinch. He really *was* crazy.

Derek finished another call. "We have two hours from INC Bank. The next three are going to be a little tougher because I don't have the same inside track at those."

He'd gotten two major national banks to respond to him on a weekend, taking significant action just on his say-so. For the first time, Alice grasped just how elevated Derek and his partners' connections were. "Friends in high places," she muttered.

"Shall I take Barsky to your home gym for a workout?" Tully asked.

Derek shot him a glance. "I have faith in Leland. Although maybe if we can't stop the transfers soon, we'll consider it."

Alice didn't know whether he was serious but she was pretty sure Tully was and she wouldn't want to be Myron Barsky if that happened.

There was a weird silence and Alice realized that Leland had stopped typing and was frowning at the screen, the reflection of the computer monitor lighting his glasses. Was that a good thing or a bad thing?

"The transfer code's going active." He began typing furiously again.

"Can you stop it?" Derek asked.

"Doing my best."

No one spoke as Leland's fingers flew over the keyboard. Even Barsky's gaze was locked on his nemesis. As the seconds ticked away, Barsky began to smile. "Once the subroutine transfers the money to my offshore account, you'll never be able find it again."

"Yeah, I know the drill. It will get transferred out immediately to various other untraceable accounts. It's nothing original," Derek said. "That's why we have you here. For insurance."

The typing stopped. Once again all attention turned to Leland. Ever so slowly, the corners of his mouth began to turn up. "I blocked the transfers but Barsky's subroutine still thinks they're going through. Any future transfers will be blocked as well. Now I can take my time with unraveling Barsky's mess."

"That's not enough," Derek said with urgency. "Barsky said the subroutine would wipe out all the client records when it finished making the transfers."

"Got that covered too." Leland leaned back in his chair and stretched out his long legs under the desk. "I have it totally isolated now. No communication with the outside world. It's just talking to itself."

Alice slumped back in her chair as relief eased the tension in her muscles. Derek shot her a look of pure triumph.

Leland turned to Barsky. "You should have used more than one account and more than one financial institution to receive the money. You made it too easy to intercept by keeping it to a single payee."

"Why the fuck would I worry about that?" Barsky spat, his face nearly white with anger and pain. "This should have been simple. It *would* have been simple, except for these two stupid accountants being some kind of fucking ninjas."

"All right, we don't need you anymore," Tully said, jerking Barsky to his feet and speaking into his earpiece. Two agents appeared at the door. "Take him down to the ambulance."

As Barsky passed her, he gave her an ugly look. Derek stepped in front of the hacker to halt his progress. Derek's expression was even more terrifying than Barsky's when he said, "You're going to jail for a long, long time, but I want you to know that I'll be tracking you every day of your life. Remember this: I didn't hesitate to shoot this time. I won't hesitate to shoot the next time."

Barsky just snarled as Derek stepped back.

An odd sense of comfort warmed Alice, loosening more of the nerves that still held her body in a tight grip. Derek would be protecting her into the future.

When the hacker had been escorted out of the office, Tully holstered his gun and sat down in the chair Barsky had vacated. "I'm sorry he got the jump on my security team. That shouldn't have happened." He gave Alice an apologetic nod, his expression stern with self-recrimination. "Ma'am, I'm especially regretful that you had to go through the hell of being held hostage."

Alice was beginning to feel shaky again but she summoned up a smile. "We all underestimated Barsky, myself more than anyone else."

Derek strolled over to drop a hand on her shoulder with a gentle squeeze. "Luckily, Barsky underestimated *you*." He turned to Leland and Tully, his expression grim. "Barsky had her in a choke hold with a gun to her head. She made this incredible move to break his grip, shoved him off-balance, and gave me a clear shot at him. Without her courage, we'd probably be in a standoff at gunpoint right now."

"It wouldn't have helped if you hadn't had that very convincing epileptic seizure," Alice said. "That put Ivan out of commission."

"So Barsky wasn't kidding when he said you were a couple of ninjas," Leland said, even as he kept an eye on the computer screen. "I wondered about that." He swiveled to face Alice and Derek. "I owe you an apology too. I thought my electronic security system was unbeatable but Barsky got past it."

Derek waved a hand in dismissal. "None of us were expecting to deal with a psychopath who's also a computer genius."

"Well, genius might be more than he deserves," Leland said. "But he's very good."

Tully held up a finger to silence them as he listened to his earpiece. When he lowered it, he said, "Now we know how Barsky was planning to escape. A helicopter just landed on the roof of the building. We're taking the pilot into custody but the agents think he's just hired help, not part of the BalanceTrakR organization."

"He must have had a lot of clients to go to such trouble and expense," Alice said.

"It was more than the money," Derek said. "He hated his father, who was a small business owner. Dad didn't recognize his son's genius." He smiled down at Alice. "He also hated to lose to a couple of expletive-deleted accountants."

Tully stood up. "I have a lot of respect for accountants, especially you, ma'am." He tipped an imaginary hat to Alice. "Without you a whole lot of folks would have lost their livelihoods, maybe even their life savings."

"Tully's right," Leland said. "If you hadn't been so conscientious and persistent, no one would have caught this until it was too late."

Derek smiled down at her. "Alice is nothing short of amazing."

The admiration on his face and the compliments from his partners were too much for her. She could feel tears welling up in her eyes. She stood up. "I need to go check on my cats."

"Your cats?" Tully repeated.

"Of course," Derek said, putting his arm around her waist once again and steering her to the door.

Now she had to work hard to force the tears back because she didn't want Derek to see her cry.

When they got to the media room, the door was wide open. "Oh no!" she said, breaking away from Derek to dash into the room. Someone had opened the curtain so she could see clearly that neither cat was in sight. Calling their names, she dropped to her knees and peered under the couch. Both were there, their gold eyes bright in the dimness.

"Thank God!" She slumped back onto her heels, all the pent-up emotions of the last couple of hours overwhelming her. Uncontrollable tears streamed down her cheeks.

She heard the door to the room close and then Derek was beside her. He offered his hand to help her up but her knees just wouldn't support her. Instead she dropped her face into her hands and tried not to sob too loudly.

"Alice!" Strong arms wrapped around her shoulders, pulling her against Derek's chest where he knelt beside her. "Are the cats hurt?"

She burrowed into him, her tears soaking into his shirt. "N-n-n-o, they're . . . they're fine as far as I know."

"What is it? Barsky won't be able to hurt anyone ever again, I promise." His concern made her cry harder.

"I-I thought we were going to die. Those guns . . ." She shuddered at the memory of the chilling black holes staring at them.

"I would have a found a way to stop that." She felt the brush of his lips on the crown of her head.

"That made it even worse because I knew you would," she wailed. "I kept imagining your body riddled with bleeding bullet wounds." Her imagination conjured up the image again and another shiver ran through her.

"Alice, it's over." His embrace tightened in comfort while one of his hands stroked up and down her back, soothing her. "We're both alive and well. And so are Sylvester and Audley."

She tried to chuckle but it came out as more of a choked sob. "You renamed him Morse."

"It can be his new middle name."

The tears slowed as Derek's warmth and strength soaked into her, dissolving the fear and tension. "You scared the heck out of me with that fall, though. You must be bruised from hitting the table with your shoulder."

"My shoulder's fine. Part of the technique is to reduce the distance you fall by doing it in two parts. Hitting the table meant I had a shorter distance to go before meeting the floor. I used my hand to make a lot of noise on the tabletop, which makes it sound even more authentic and provides a distraction." He kissed the top of her head again. "You put the finishing touches on by claiming I was epileptic. That was quick thinking."

"I was sort of afraid it was true because you were so convincing."

"Then you returned the favor and scared the hell out of me when you broke away from Barsky." His stroking stopped and he pulled her closer. "He had a gun pointed at your head."

"I didn't want Ivan to get loose, especially since he would be majorly pissed off at you." She flinched as she thought of what the huge, awful man might have done to Derek. "My friend Dawn—who taught me the self-defense move—says a gun changes the whole situation. But I think she would approve of what I did." Dawn believed in surviving.

His hand came up to cradle her head against his chest. "I can't argue with the results, but I would have preferred a less risky solution."

"That's the irony of all this," she said. "I went into accounting to avoid risk, but a few tiny little bookkeeping discrepancies got me held hostage at gunpoint by two criminals. Which proves that you can't avoid risk in life. It's crazy to try."

"A good lesson for both of us," he said, his voice a rumble against her cheek. "This might not be the best time but I need to ask you something."

She leaned back so that she could look at him, curiosity and a touch of nerves making her breath go shallow. "Go ahead."

He brushed back a damp tendril of hair that was clinging to her tear-stained cheek. "I'd like you to come to Asia with me. You said you wanted to travel and I'm about to go on a trip so it could work out well." His expression was strangely uncertain.

"But it's a business trip," she said, stunned by the unexpected invitation. "You have to work."

"I'll arrange for a guide for you while I'm working, but I intend to take plenty of time off to sightsee with you." His face lit up. "I want to see the world the way you saw Dallas. With delight and wonder. I want to experience it through your eyes."

"Really? You didn't mind all my statistics about the Trinity River?" But a thrill of excitement ran through her.

"You have to ask me if I mind statistics?" His smile glinted.

She was trying to sort through all the implications, but the one fact that kept bouncing around in her head was that Derek wanted her company for his big trip. On top of that, he planned to take time off from his huge important project to be with her. "I . . . When do you leave?"

"Does that mean you'll go?" His eyes blazed with hope.

"I . . . maybe." She took a deep breath. "Does this mean we might have a relationship?"

"Yes, of course it does. That's why I want you to come." He slid his hands down to take hers as they knelt facing each other. "We haven't known each other for long but you understand me in ways no one else does. You remind me of what I have lost sight of in my life." He paused while he seemed to search her face. "I'm falling in love with you, Alice. I hope that I can convince you to fall in love with me."

Shock rippled through her. Derek was in love with her? Here it was: the biggest risk of all. To admit her feelings to him . . . and to herself. Because this man could break her heart into jagged pieces. But today had seared a life lesson into her soul.

She laid her palms against either side of his face, feeling the contrasting textures of his skin and hair. "I've already fallen. I'll go with you." As soon as she said the words, joy exploded through her.

He stood and pulled her up with him. Wrapping his arms around her, he kissed her with a fierce possessiveness that made her toes curl in her high-heeled pumps.

"You'll never regret it," he whispered against her lips.

This incredible man loved her and she loved him in return. No matter what happened in the future, nothing could make her regret that.

"I know," she whispered back to him.

Epilogue

Six months later

"There!" Natalie secured the pearl garland into Alice's soft upswept bun with a hairpin. "You look just like one of your Regency heroines."

"Not yet," Gabrielle said, scooping up a pearl necklace and fastening it around Alice's neck. "We have to get the accessories right too. Stand up, dear."

Alice carefully scooted to the edge of the beauty salon chair and eased to her feet. It wasn't so simple when one was wearing a costume that would look familiar to Jane Austen. She loved the long, pale lavender crepe dress that opened down the front over a white satin slip with bands of pearls draped across the opening. Her white satin slippers were striped with the same lavender. The plunging neckline was edged with pearls that made her skin seem to glow. Gabrielle had found the whole ensemble in a costume shop in Manhattan when Derek had invited Alice to a costume charity gala.

"Now the jewelry." Gabrielle clasped a pearl bracelet around each of Alice's upper arms, an authentic detail about positioning she'd found in researching period costumes. She handed Alice a pair of pearl drops for her ears. Next came the long white gloves, bunched just below the elbow, another period detail. Finally, she draped a deep purple cashmere shawl over her arm.

"Wow!" Dawn said from the salon chair next to Alice's. "You look like you just walked off the set of a *Pride and Prejudice* movie."

Alice twisted back and forth to see herself from all angles. "Natalie, that hairstyle makes my neck look like a swan's. It's gorgeous." The dress style suited her figure too, with the Empire waist that emphasized her bust in a good way and the flowing skirt that skimmed over her hips. The neckline was a little lower than she was comfortable with but Gabrielle had added some double-sided tape to keep it in place.

"You look beautiful because you *are* beautiful," Gabrielle said, her words strangely choked up.

Alice smiled at her mother. "Thanks, Mother, but I have to give credit where credit is due. This was a team effort."

Alice and her mother had slowly been establishing a better relationship since their surprisingly successful shopping trip. Of course, Gabrielle adored Derek. In her more cynical moments, Alice suspected her ability to capture the interest of such a good-looking man raised her mother's opinion of her daughter. But she mostly thought that Derek's notice had simply allowed Gabrielle to see her daughter in a different way, and she appreciated the real connection she was forging with her mother.

Gabrielle handed Alice her spangled fan and beaded purse before turning away to grab a tissue and carefully blot her eyes.

Dawn jumped off the chair. "Let's practice that curtsy one more time." When she heard about the costume ball, she had taken on the role of dancing instructor. Alice pointed out that no one was going to dance a minuet, but Dawn had insisted on teaching Alice the finer points of a waltz.

"Happy to practice dancing," Alice said. "It's a lot less stressful than breaking a choke hold."

"Hey, that came in handy when you needed it," Dawn said.

"Too true." Alice pushed the memory away before she lifted her long skirt a couple of inches, crossed her right foot behind her left, and sank down while bending her neck just a fraction.

"Perfect!" Dawn said. "Remember to keep your shoulders down and back."

"With this neckline, I pretty much have to or everyone will get an eyeful." But Alice loved how feminine and alluring she felt when the petticoat brushed against her silk stockings, tied at the knee with garters. She couldn't wait to see what Derek looked like in his Regency finery. They'd rented their costumes separately to surprise each other.

There was a knock on the salon door before Christian, now Derek's regular driver, walked in. "Whenever you're ready, I'll be waiting outside."

Derek had called earlier to say he was hung up at work, so he was sending the limo to pick her up. He would meet her at the gala.

The driver left them to a flurry of hugs. As she gave Natalie a gentle squeeze, a sense of gratitude flowed through Alice. She was not only lucky in love but also lucky to have such women in her life. She stepped back to look at the three of them, so different from each other, yet working together for Alice's sake. "Thank you all. You are the most wonderful support network ever."

"Are you kidding me? You saved my salon," Natalie said, although she too looked a little misty-eyed. "Now go have fun!"

Alice slid onto the leather car seat with Gabrielle's expert assistance so she didn't wrinkle her gown. She didn't dare rest her head on the seat back because she didn't want to muss Natalie's masterpiece of coiled braids and tresses. So she stared out the window without really taking in the scenery.

She thought back to the most recent journey she and Derek had taken. When business had required that he go to London, he'd invited Alice to join him. He had even timed it for her least busy week of the month so she could take care of her clients remotely. She had loved wandering the streets of the city while he was working, but missed being able to share the small wonders with him. However, she had described all the major sights over dinner and even later as they lay entwined in the bed of the Westminster Suite at the St. James's Hotel and Club. Derek had reserved it for the fabulous terrace that overlooked the city, including the London Eye and the Shard.

The best part of the trip, though, had been their long weekend in Bath, where she had truly felt as though she had stepped into a Georgette Heyer novel. They'd visited the Pump Room and tasted the nasty, mineral-laden spring water. Derek had been fascinated by the Roman baths that still functioned as they had centuries before.

But that wasn't what occupied her mind now. On the plane home from England, Derek had asked her to move into his penthouse in Manhattan. It was a big step. She had Sylvester and Audley to think of, of course. If she put a bird feeder on Derek's terrace, would the birds come up that high to eat and provide feline entertainment?

But more than that, she was still a little overawed by the grandeur of his life. When they were at Alice's town house, she could pretend that Derek was just her boyfriend. When she went to Manhattan with him, his wealth and power were more obvious. To every logistical problem she'd raised, he'd had a solution, of course.

Just as she was working through all the pros and cons again, the limo slid to a halt. She focused on what was outside her window and saw a narrow, unfamiliar road lined with trees, now almost bare of leaves.

"Christian, why are we stopping here?" she asked, a tiny spurt of fear jabbing at her. She was still occasionally haunted by nightmares of Myron Barsky pointing a gun at her. Then she would wake up to the sound of Derek whispering in her ear that she was safe. She would snuggle into the security of his big solid body, inhaling his warm male scent, and her world would right itself again.

The door swung open and she heard Tully's voice say, "Ma'am, if you'd be so good as to step out of the car."

Relief banished the fear. And then that was replaced by wonder. Tully was wearing a Regency coachman's outfit of a great coat with multiple capes and tall leather boots. The costume suited his big, muscular build. Behind him stood a shiny black carriage with two glossy bay horses hitched to it. Of course he would be able to drive a coach-and-pair.

"Good heavens! What's going on?" she asked.

"May I escort you to your carriage?" Tully asked, bowing and holding out his arm crooked at the elbow.

"I . . . of course. Thank you." She laid her hand on his forearm. "You're not going to tell me what this is all about, are you?"

He grinned and shook his head.

"All right, then, can you at least give me the latest update on how the investigation into Barsky is going?" It broke the historical mood, but it wasn't so easy to get information when the FBI was involved.

"Leland and the Feds have traced another hacking attack to Barsky. Even if they can't prove he's guilty of it, they've got him nailed for BalanceTrakR, thanks to you," Tully continued. "They're very grateful."

"The gratitude goes both ways. I want him kept in jail for a long, long time. Although I think I'm even happier that Ivan's in captivity. He was really scary."

"Yeah, he's done some things that I won't share with you. Those they will able to prosecute him for. Truth is, I prefer dumb thugs like Ivan to smart psychopaths like Barsky. The smart ones are harder to catch." She saw the guilt cloud his face. "And a lot more dangerous."

She held up her gloved hand. "Please don't apologize again." Tully was still beating himself up over the fact that she'd been taken hostage on his watch.

She squeezed his arm as they reached the carriage. He carefully helped her into the high vehicle, where he put a hot brick under her feet and spread a blanket over her lap before he closed the door. The October chill invaded the red velvet upholstered interior, so she wrapped her shawl around her shoulders. The carriage rocked as Tully sprang into the driver's seat and set the horses in motion.

Her heart was racing with curiosity and excitement as the carriage swayed along behind the trotting team. They continued up the tree-lined roadway before turning onto a stone-paved surface that ran alongside a grand fountain filled with water-spouting statues. They turned again to pull up in front of a stone mansion with a wide set of steps leading to a cathedral-size double door adorned with ornate metalwork.

It swung open to allow light and faint strains of music to spill out. A man dressed in the elaborate livery of a footman, with satin breeches, a coat embellished with gold braid, and a white wig, came down the steps to open the carriage door. As he offered his hand to help her down, she saw the tortoiseshell glasses and realized that it was Leland.

"You should wear a wig more often," she teased as she climbed down.

"It itches," he said with a grimace. But it suited his aristocratic bone structure.

"I guess there's no point in asking you what's going on either," she said as he escorted her up the steps.

"None whatsoever." He led her through the door and into a grand hallway with an inlaid parquet floor, a huge bronze chandelier, and not another person in sight. "However, you'll be happy to hear that BalanceTrakR is about to become a legitimate accounting service. The FBI approved KRG's takeover of the software today."

"That's wonderful news! A lot of small business owners will be thrilled." She'd had to transfer her own clients back onto their old accounting systems while KRG and the FBI worked out a way to keep BalanceTrakR up and running for the thousands of customers who'd purchased it. The software was such a good system that the clients—including Alice—wanted to keep using it. Although it was somewhat off mission, KRG had proposed to make it part of their Small Business Initiative. As Derek said, this was another way to help small entrepreneurs.

Leland led her across the beautiful wood floor, where he threw open another door, bringing them onto a landing at the top of a grand staircase. "Miss Alice Thurber," he announced in a stentorian drawl before giving her a wink, bowing low, and retreating.

She had an impression of ornate gold frames around huge paintings, gilded sconces with flickering lights, and a swirl of motion and color, but what drew her eye was the man waiting for her at the bottom of the richly carpeted steps, his hands behind his back, his face lifted to hers.

As she came slowly down the stairs, her dress trailing on the oriental carpet, her heart felt like it was going to swell right out of her chest. Derek looked magnificent in a blue cutaway coat that emphasized his broad shoulders and narrow waist. He wore tightly fitting tan pantaloons that outlined the powerful muscles in his thighs while his calves were encased in gleaming, knee-high Hessian boots with gold tassels. His cravat was snowy white, his waistcoat cream brocade. A gold watch fob dangled from his waist.

He was every one of her favorite Regency heroes brought to life. Happiness and anticipation quivered through her, making her breath quicken. She hoped she didn't spill out of her low bodice.

As she reached the last step, he bowed, the blond streaks in his hair catching flickers of light. "Miss Thurber, a pleasure to see you this evening."

"Mr. Killion, you are too kind." She remembered Dawn's instructions about her curtsy and inclined her head only slightly.

He held out his hand while his eyes traveled over her neck and shoulders, scorching a trail across her skin. "May I have this dance?"

"I believe I'm free, sir." She laid her gloved hand against his palm and felt the strength of him when his fingers closed over hers.

As he led her onto the black-and-white-marble floor, she realized that the motion she'd registered in her peripheral vision was a projection of dancers, all wearing Regency dress, twirling over the walls and paintings while the strains of a waltz filled the room.

"A waltz. How daring!" she said, getting into the spirit of the scene.

"I wish to touch more than just your gloves." His voice and his eyes told her how much more. "I want to feel the way your body moves against my hand."

"Mr. Killion, that is most improper." She tapped his shoulder reprovingly with her fan.

"Most," he agreed.

She laughed with a breathless sound, their silly banter sending desire on a slow slide through her.

He took her shawl, her fan, and her reticule and tossed them on a nearby chair. For a moment, he simply stood and looked at her, the skim of his gaze making her skin tingle everywhere.

Then he took her right hand, using it to pull her in closer to him before his right arm circled her waist so that her skirts brushed the top of his boots.

"La, Mr. Killion, you will scandalize the gossips if we dance this close together."

"Let 'em talk," he said, looking down at her with a smile of utter tenderness. "Soon I hope they'll have no right to complain."

The oxygen whooshed out of Alice's lungs. Now she knew why he had created this beautiful fantasy for her. Nerves shimmered through her, not because she didn't know what her heart wanted but because she wished to answer him in a way that was worthy of the occasion.

But he began to lead her in the graceful, elegant turns of the waltz, his arms firm so that she never stumbled. She understood why Regency mamas worried about their daughters dancing. She had to focus on the most subtle movements of his body so that she could follow him in the steps of the dance. The brush of his thigh against hers, the imprint of his warm palm against the thin material of her gown, the closeness of his lips—all fanned the arousal simmering through her. "You waltz well, Mr. Killion."

"Another skill learned from theater school, although I practiced a bit last week." His smile alone sent a melting feeling through her bones. "I hope you don't mind that I didn't wear proper ballroom attire but I liked the boots."

"I didn't even notice because I like the boots too. And the tight pantaloons." She gave him a flirtatious sideways glance.

His grip tightened so that her breasts now pressed against his jacket with every turn, sending sparks down into her belly.

"I considered being the Duke of Avon because he's one impressive fellow but the wig and the heels put me off that idea," he said. "So I opted for some combination of Mr. Beaumaris, Lord Damerel, and the Marquis of Alverstoke since I remember those being favorites of yours. Beaumaris for his wealth, Damerel for his witty banter, and the Marquis of Alverstoke for his title."

"I actually called you Mr. Beaumaris the first time I came to your office. Just as the elevator doors were closing."

"So I chose well . . . in more ways than one." Again the glow in his eyes stole her breath.

Alice couldn't decide whether she wanted to dance with Derek forever or she wanted the music to end so she could stop being so keyed up about what would happen next. But end it did, the projected dancers around them all bowing and curtsying to each other. She and Derek did the same.

When she straightened, he took both of her hands in his, his grip light but inexorable. She looked up at him to find he was taking a deep breath. "Alice, you are—and always will be—amazing to me. You amaze me with your integrity, your courage, your passion, and your love of numbers." His smile had an edge of nerves, which shocked her. She forgot to inhale as his words tumbled through her brain while she tried to remember each heart-touching one. "I fell in love with you in less than a week, something that no longer surprises me. Since then I have only come to love you more and more deeply."

When he gracefully sank to one knee, she gasped.

"Will you do me the honor of becoming my wife?" he asked, his full attention locked on her.

There was no thought of how to answer him. She nearly shrieked, "Yes! Yes! Oh my God, yes!" All her doubts evaporated as though they'd never existed. She tugged her hands free so that she could bend down to thread her gloved fingers through his hair and kiss him with all the love that surged through her.

He gave her a kiss in return before he took her wrists to pull them away from his head. "Let me stand up and kiss you properly."

When he rose, she threw herself into his embrace and wound her arms around his neck. He reciprocated by splaying one hand on her back and the other on her bottom to pull her hard against him. Their lips met in a kiss of such intensity that she could feel it in the roots of her hair, setting her scalp tingling in a delicious way. The rest of her body was on fire. She wanted to wrap herself in him.

Finally, she pulled back because she had something important to say. Looking into his beautiful face, she put every ounce of emotion into it. "I love you so much. I love everything about you." It wasn't enough. "You are more wonderful than an unqualified opinion from an auditor."

His smile was pure delight. "Now I know you truly love me. Wait!" He released his hold on her. "I have something for you, but we need to remove this." Picking up her left hand, he began to pull off the kid glove, one finger at a time. By the time he lifted her wrist to his mouth, brushing his lips over the pulse point while he looked into her eyes, she felt his touch expand in a ripple of bliss over every inch of her skin.

Reaching into the pocket of his jacket, he pulled out a tiny black velvet pouch. As he shook the pouch, spilling a ring onto his open palm, he gave her an apologetic glance. "The coat was too tight to fit the box into."

Taking her hand with a caress of his thumb to her palm, he slid the ring onto her fourth finger. "It was made in England around 1806," he said. "If you'd rather have something more contemporary, just say so."

"This is perfect." The ring was composed of one large diamond surrounded by a cluster of smaller diamonds, evoking the shape of a flower. The gold band had touches of black enamel scrolling around it. When she moved her finger, the diamonds threw off sparks of light. She smiled at him. "Absolutely perfect."

"Then we should celebrate." He clapped his hands loudly three times and commanded, "Bring champagne!"

Alice looked around as a concealed door swung open and Leland appeared, carrying a silver tray dotted with champagne flutes. Behind him Tully—minus his greatcoat—carried a silver tub filled with ice and several bottles of champagne. Then Gabrielle, Natalie, and Dawn spilled through the door.

Happiness fizzed through her with more bubbles than all the champagne. She turned to Derek, hoping that he could see the wonder she felt at such love.

He did, because his insanely beautiful face reflected every bit of what she was feeling. It wasn't rational. It wasn't probable. It wasn't anything that her careful life of numbers had promised her.

It was so much more that her world tilted and spun before it resettled with Derek at its center.

He pulled her back into his arms and lowered his head so their lips were an inch apart. "If you keep looking at me like that, our friends will have to drink all the champagne without us."

She leaned into him. "Have you ever made love in a carriage? I hear it's even better than on a jet."

His mouth came down on hers and everything faded away except love.

Acknowledgments

I spend a lot of time interacting with characters who exist only in my imagination, which might indicate that I am verging on insanity. Fortunately, I have a fantastic group of real people—publishing professionals, personal friends and family, and readers—who keep me on the positive side of that thin line. I offer heartfelt thanks to:

Maria Gomez, editor beyond compare, who believes in me and my work. She brings every aspect of my books to their finest possible level.

Jane Dystel and Miriam Goderich, literary agents extraordinaire, who support my career in every way, large and small. I got very lucky the day I signed on with them.

Colleen Lindsay, Adria Martin, Kyla Pigoni, and the entire superb Montlake author team, who get the word out about my books by all sorts of exciting, innovative means.

Andrea Hurst, brilliant developmental editor, whom I had the joy of meeting in person after many years of corresponding across the continent. Being book people, we were instant kindred spirits. Not to mention that she makes my books the best they can be.

Karen Brown and Sarah Engel, eagle-eyed copyeditor and painstaking proofreader, who save me from profound embarrassment by catching my many mistakes of continuity, grammar, typing, and spelling.

Eileen Carey, inspired cover artist, who captures the essence of my story in a single image, a very difficult task that she performs with true artistry.

Miriam Allenson, Lisa Verge Higgins, and Jennifer Wilck, my treasured critique group, who strengthen my work and my spirit, supporting me when I most need it. They are pure platinum.

The whole crew at Velvet Salon in Lyndhurst, who generously took the time to share their bookkeeping methodology with me. I changed a few things in service to the story, so please don't think that they have the same problems with their books that Alice's clients had.

Tony Jenkens, excellent cousin and expert techie, who did his best to make my computer nerd and my villainous hacker sound authentic. Any mistakes are entirely my own.

Brodie, my goofy golden retriever, whom I had to let go just after this book was finished. My sweet old boy offered furry comfort and unconditional love whenever the writing life became tough. I miss him so much.

Rebecca and Loukas, aka Dr. Darling Daughter and Super Son, my extraordinary children, who impress me, inspire me, make me laugh, and show me what love truly is.

All my fabulous readers and fans, who keep me writing by buying my books and chatting with me on social media, via email, and even with the occasional snail mail card. Without you, my characters would be chicken scratches on paper. With you, my imaginary friends spring into vibrant life. You're the best!

About the Author

Photo © 2015 Lisa Kollberg

Nancy Herkness is the award-winning author of the Second Glances, Wager of Hearts, and Whisper Horse series, published by Montlake, as well as several other contemporary romance novels. She is a two-time nominee for the Romance Writers of America's RITA Award, and has received many other honors for her work, including the Book Buyers Best Top Pick, the Bookseller's Best award, and the National Excellence in Romance Fiction award.

Nancy graduated from Princeton University, where she majored in English. In addition to her academic work in literature, she was accepted into Princeton's creative writing program, and her senior thesis was a volume of original poetry.

After graduating, Nancy had a varied career that included retail management and buying, COBOL programming, computer systems sales and marketing, and a brief stint as a receptionist at a dental office. Once her children were in school full-time, she sat down and wrote *A Bridge to Love*, her first romance novel to be published.

A native of West Virginia, Nancy now lives in suburban New Jersey.

For more information about Nancy and her books, visit www. NancyHerkness.com. You can also find her on Facebook and Pinterest.